FRESH OLD BOUNTIES

GOOD BAD MAGIC
BOOK 3

ISA MEDINA

1

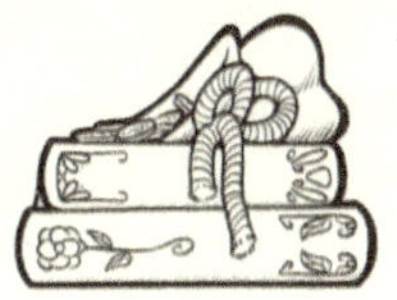

IT WAS an overcast early October morning in Olmeda, and I was posing in front of the Tea Cauldron.

Hannah, my favorite magic-unaware repeat customer, crouched in the middle of the street, taking photos. She had assured me she could fix them later on her computer to make them as bright as I wanted, but I rather thought the lack of sunshine made me and the shop look cozy and inviting and so very witchy.

Perfect branding.

A slow grin curved my lips as I mentally ran through all the fun teas and potions I'd planned for Halloween.

At a delivery truck's honking, Hannah stepped closer to the curb.

"Let's do a few more, Hope," she called. "Act casual."

My limbs immediately became stiff plastic, and I lost all control over my hands as my smile became worthy of adorning comic book covers—in the villain category.

I should've drunk one of my own soothing potions before embarking on this adventure.

"That's it," Hannah said enthusiastically. "Let me see the T-shirt logo."

Hooking my thumbs on the belt loops of my jeans, I cocked my hips like I was in some kind of western. A cowgirl with a cauldron printed on her front rather than a flannel shirt. My jaw tensed with the need to chew some gum.

"Less stiff, please."

Think of Grandma, Hope. Think of the shop. Your *shop.* *Your dream come true.*

Sure, I still had a few months left on my probation, but recent events had proven that I could conquer anything thrown into my path. Converting dark magic users with placebo potions? Not a problem. Surviving sabotaging, murderous best friends? Been there, done that. Saving the local shifter alpha through the use of *good* magic instead of dark? Child's play.

Yes, the shop was still not one hundred percent mine, but it might as well already be. Grandma might no longer be around to enjoy it, but I'd realized our dreams for her.

My smile was so bright, we didn't need a single ray of sunshine to illuminate the street.

"Perfect!"

Hannah took a few more shots, ignoring the honks from a passing car. Being a professional photographer, she had been the obvious choice when I'd decided the shop's website and social media could do with a photographic update.

She had even given me a discount.

While the secret magical side of the shop was thriving, the monetary side could use a boost. As soon as I was done taking these pictures, I was putting up Halloween decorations. With a name like the Tea Cauldron and its old brick facade and multi-pane windows, how could the shop fail to attract visitors during the season?

The door of the shop next to mine opened, and a couple of

men stepped out. The Corner Rose was an old, two-story building forming the corner of the block, with the store on the first floor and the living quarters on top. It had been closed down since its owner died trying to kidnap and murder me.

But that was history. Since then, I'd done several cleansing spells to clear the street of bad vibes, and walked Fluffy, the world's purest fluffball of a dog, around the block.

I frowned at the men as they talked in hushed whispers in front of the ex-antiques shop. Mr. Lewis had died in severe debt, and the shop had gone to the bank instead of Dru, who'd been his manager for years. Was the bank showing the property to prospective buyers? Dru had attempted to buy it from them, but they had deemed her too much of a risk for such a big loan.

One of the men, handsome and tall with dark brown skin and close-cropped hair, caught my stare and gave me a curt nod of acknowledgment.

Startled, I lifted a hand to wave at him. Should I invite him over and ask if he was interested in the shop or would that be too weird? Before I could decide, the two men got into a blue car parked by the corner and drove off into the distance.

Never to be seen again? For Dru's sake, I hoped so.

"Check these out." Hannah walked up to me and showed me some of the shots on her camera.

I forced myself to pay attention to the small screen and made sounds of agreement even though I couldn't tell the difference between the shots.

"I'll bring you the best in a couple of days, and we can discuss if you want any alterations," she added.

"Thank you so much, Hannah. You're a lifesaver."

She smiled. "I can always use the work, and these will look lovely in my portfolio."

As would the promotional cards I'd agreed to stock in the shop. My counter might not be prime real estate like Bosko's, but you never knew when a visitor would be interested in beautiful professional photographs to remember their awesome vacations in Olmeda.

Dru thought it'd pollute my cozy witchy branding if my counter became a mountain of leaflets, but then Dru didn't even wear the shop's cozy witchy uniform, so what did she know?

"Try everything once—the results might surprise you," I murmured.

Hannah's eyebrows crept up her forehead. "Your shop's new slogan?"

My mouth fell open. "Hannah, that's...perfect!"

"You came up with it, not me," she said with a laugh as I ran inside the shop.

I waved her a belated goodbye through the shop's glass door, then climbed onto the shelf behind the counter to grab the small blackboard listing the day's specials. I wiped the top clean and grabbed the white and green chalks.

"You forgot to flip the open sign," chided one of the stools on the other side of the counter. Theodora Bagley, evilness incarnate and previous witch owner of the shop, come back to haunt me—literally.

"I'm not open yet." I bit my tongue as I used my best handwriting to cram *Try everything once, it might surprise you!* where the dull *Today's Specials* had been written. Truly, how had it not occurred to me before? Such a great way to remind people that one must try to be adventurous.

"What were you doing outside?" the stool asked like a suspicious teacher after a student was gone thirty minutes on a bathroom break.

"Taking photos for the shop's website." I wiped *surprise* and rewrote it with added swirls to match the font on the shop's logo. Much better.

"Ah, I never liked taking photos of the shop. It brings bad luck, you know."

"Bad luck is a self-defeating way of thinking." Besides, by bad luck, she probably meant flying under the radar. If I were a murderous dark witch living in a murder house, I would also try to keep a low profile.

A witch's power came from their spirit and had natural limits. Herbs and certain potions and crystals could help focus that power, streamline it for a better spell, but its potency could never breach the witch's own limit.

That went out the window when you added unwilling blood into the mix. Blood taken from an unwilling source twisted the magic. It opened spells to do things well beyond what should be possible. Bonus points if the blood came from another paranormal—mages, shifters, demons, berserkers, and what have you.

Dark magic was amoral, illegal, and forbidden. It hadn't stopped Bagley from running a dark magic business from this shop while alive, though. It also hadn't stopped her from trying to dark magic herself into surviving death.

Now she was stuck in random objects in the shop, and I was stuck with her.

"Say, child," the devil's spawn said in her grandmotherly voice, "I was thinking it's rude not to mention me in that webpage of yours."

"Well, it was rude of you to murder people in the upstairs bathroom." I put down the green chalk and surveyed my writing with a critical eye. It would do. It just needed some more swirls and a couple of pumpkins to give it that extra oomph. Maybe a witch hat.

Bagley's cackle filled the shop. It was a cozy space, big enough for a couple of tables, a shelf with merchandise on one side, and enough room for people to sit at the counter and converse. An archway covered by a bead curtain led into the back, where a small kitchen, a storage room, a tiny bathroom, and the stairs going to the living quarters on the second floor completed the floor plan.

"The advance of any scholarly pursuit requires sacrifices, dear," Bagley said.

Scholarly pursuit? Hah. "The only pursuit you advanced was that of money."

It still stunned me how the old hag had kept her murderous, dark magic deeds a secret for so many years. The Witch Council had no idea, and the residents of Olmeda had considered her a beloved witch, a pillar of the community known for her delicious cookies. Hell, they'd even given her a commemorative plaque for her years of service.

If they knew the cookies had been made with unwilling blood, they probably would take it back.

"You are so rude." Bagley tutted. "Youth these days, no manners!" I could almost hear the stool scraping against the hardwood floors as the witch shook her nonexistent head. "I'll have you know that a lot of research and study went into the spell that saw me as I am now. If it hadn't been for my untimely murder, I have no doubt I'd have succeeded in gaining my own fully corporeal form after death."

"And how many people had to die for that to happen?" I shuddered at the thought. Truly, she should've been offed decades ago.

"A witch never reveals her secrets. Unless," she added slyly, "you want to help me be more comfortable? A little tit for tat? Some names in exchange for a little help?"

That was the problem with being haunted by an entity of unknown evil depths like Bagley—she'd tempt you with something you really wanted, count on the goodness of your heart, then grab your hand, take the arm, and eat your soul.

"I think I'll pass, but thank you."

I rounded the counter and grabbed the haunted stool, pulling it away from the counter.

"Child? What are you doing? No—don't sit on me," she said, all outrage. "Don't you dare!"

I plopped my butt down on the comfy top and squirmed to make sure I was seated properly.

Grandma would probably not have approved of this specific brand of revenge, but a girl had to make her own rules.

"You wretched, ungrateful excuse for a witch!" came from under me. "Have some respec—"

The front door flew open and Dru burst into the shop.

2

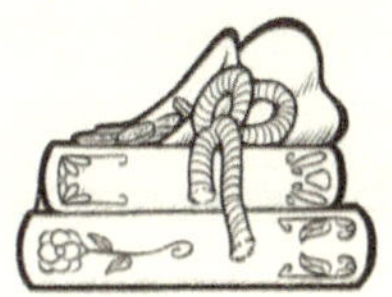

"Hope," Dru exclaimed, her eyes zeroing in on me. She was uncharacteristically disheveled, with her tight black curls flying everywhere and a distinct lack of accessorizing.

"You missed the photo shoot," I said. My lower lip stuck out in a pout all on its own. I'd wanted to get a shot with her to frame in remembrance once she found a better paying job and abandoned me.

"Whatever." She stomped up to me and gave me such an intense glare I wondered if my bank had bounced her paycheck.

"Okay?" I managed.

"I need your help."

"My help?"

She let out a frustrated noise and went around me and the corner to pour herself a coffee. She drank it in four gulps.

"What's going on?" Dru was usually so cool and collected that seeing her so agitated was like the rules of the universe had been upended.

She turned and planted her hands on the counter, a ferocious scowl furrowing her brow as she glared at the opposite wall.

"Someone's trying to buy the Corner Rose."

That explained the bad mood. "I *was* wondering. I saw two men come out of it earlier."

"You did?" she asked sharply. "Who were they? What did they look like? Did you talk to them? What did they say? Did they give you a business card?"

I instinctively retreated from the barrage of questions, almost falling off the stool. "They looked like businessmen. I didn't talk to them. They got into a car and drove off."

She slammed her hand on the counter, making me jump. "Hope!" Her eyes narrowed. "Are you *sure* they didn't talk to you?"

"Completely sure. One of them nodded at me, but that was it."

"Nodded? How? Describe it. No, wait. Show me."

I bobbed my head up and down in a jerky motion.

"Was he about this tall?" She lifted a hand above her head. "Lean, dark and handsome, cropped black hair? Like he just came out of a magazine cover?"

"Ye—"

"Argh!" She threw up her hands, then took a few deep breaths.

"And old enemy?" I guessed cautiously.

"My ex-boyfriend!"

Ooh. "Oh."

Dru's glare reached volcanic intensity. "'Oh?' He's trying to buy the Corner Rose and all you have to say is 'oh'?"

"Bad, very bad. We should kill him and bury his body in Ian's cemetery."

A harrumph of approval came from under me, and I kicked one of the stool legs.

Dru looked like she was actually considering my suggestion. Reveling in it, really, judging by the way she licked her lips.

"Was it a bad breakup?" I ventured.

And regretted it immediately as her fulminating stare attempted to bore a hole through my head.

"He broke up with me after my parents gave him *my* job at their company. My job! The one they had promised me! He went behind my back and conned them into thinking he was better for the position."

I winced. "Ouch."

"Elijah Preston is a cold, soulless bastard who deserves to rot in Hell."

"Totally."

She thumped a fist against the counter. "I will not let him buy my store."

"Of course not."

She fell silent for a few seconds, probably going through every highlight of her relationship with this Preston man. Or every way she could dispose of his corpse without getting caught.

"You wanted to work for your parents' company?" I asked, trying to distract her. And satisfy my curiosity. In the witch business, it paid to multitask. "Are they in the antique business?"

"They own a stationery store chain," she said distractedly, obviously still mulling over the best way to deal with her ex—Ian's cemetery or the shifter's forest hole for unwelcome guests. "Tabbies."

I gasped with excitement. "Your parents own Tabbies? Oh, my God. Last Halloween I got their—"

She glowered. "If you say 'witchy stickers,' I'm going to shove them down your throat."

"Horrible, horrible stuff." I shook my head in obvious disappointment. "So ugly. I burned it all up."

Dru snorted but appeared mollified.

I wanted to ask if she was trying so hard to get the Corner Rose as a way to show her parents they had made the wrong choice in hiring her ex over her, but then it was kind of obvious, wasn't it?

"Can you make some kind of potion to knock him out for a few days?" she asked casually. "A little something that'll keep him out of the way while I fix this."

"Sleeping potions don't last that long."

"I was thinking more like food poisoning," she muttered. "A week living on the bathroom floor might teach him a lesson."

I ignored that. "I take it he's still working for your parents?"

She answered with a glare.

That would be a yes, then. "So they're trying to expand Tabbies into Olmeda? Interesting." And smart, but I wasn't about to say that out loud. The Tea Cauldron and the Corner Rose were part of the old, charming part of Olmeda. While most shops in the area catered to tourists, a stationery shop with the correct merchandise angle could do quite well.

"You can't let that happen," Dru said.

I blinked in surprise. "Me?"

"Preston *can't* get the Corner Rose."

"But there's nothing I can do. It's not my building." I had written her a letter of recommendation for the bank and attempted to have the Witch Council give her a hand. Since Dru was a demon and not a witch, that hadn't worked out. Like my letter to the bank.

"You can complain to Sonia."

Her words took me aback. "Sonia?"

A wicked, slightly deranged smile split Dru's face. "It's a paranormal-owned company. They can't open a shop without the Association's permission. As a member, you can lodge a complaint."

And Sonia Aguilar, as the president of Olmeda's Paranormal Business Owners Association, held all the power.

I was awestruck by Dru's genius. "Your parents really chose the wrong person."

She straightened, her chest expanding. "Duh."

Her idea was amazing, but there was one small problem. Tapping my fingers on the counter, I mulled it over. "But you know Sonia hates me. If I complain, she might allow them to open to get back at me."

"Nah, she doesn't hate you. She's like that with everyone."

By "that" Dru meant antagonistic, detail-obsessed, and perennially unsatisfied.

"I think the idea is great, but I'm not sure I'm the correct person for it."

Dru leaned forward, daring me to look anywhere but her. "You will do this for me, Hope," she enunciated very clearly.

I appreciated that she hadn't attached an "or else," or wasn't attempting to blackmail me, unlike pretty much anyone else who had needed something from me so far in Olmeda. It was enough to make me a little teary eyed.

Waving her glare away, I blinked repeatedly.

"What's wrong with you?" she demanded.

"Nothing," I choked out. It felt so good to have a true best friend who didn't want to murder me in the literal sense. "Yes, of course I'll help."

Dru nodded sharply, satisfied, then charged around the counter and toward the door, hooking a hand on my elbow on the way. "Great. Let's go."

"Now?" I asked, allowing myself to get dragged.

"Now."

3

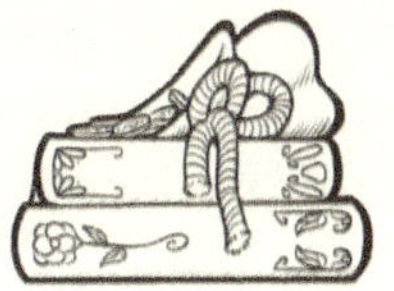

SONIA OWNED a costumes and party favors store several blocks away from the Tea Cauldron. Even with the overcast sky threatening rain, tourists filled the streets of Old Olmeda, and the sight brought another smile to my lips. So many people, so many future parched throats. I hoped talking to Sonia wouldn't take long because with both of us here, there was nobody left to woman the shop and reap the benefits.

Like most shops in this part of Olmeda, Sonia's was also open on Sunday. I peered through the display window, featuring a colorful fairy and a flashy pirate mannequin, hoping she wasn't around and feeling immediately guilty at the thought. Dru deserved my best foot forward.

"Fear is like a waterfall, mighty but crossable," I murmured.

"She doesn't hate you," Dru repeated impatiently. Grabbing my elbow again, she pushed the door open and dragged me inside.

The shop was small and colorful, full to the rafters with racks of costumes and an assortment of masks, wigs, garlands, and anything one would ever need to have a good time. My gaze snagged on a man's *sexy firefighter* ensemble, and I wondered how it'd look on Ian. Very good, I decided, my belly filling with instant butterflies. Most excellently, in fact. Perhaps I could come back when Sonia wasn't around and—

"Hope," Dru snapped.

"Sorry." I tore my attention off the costume and walked up to the counter with sure, determined steps to face the firing squad—my business arch nemesis, today dressed in a business-casual attire of jeans and a white sleeveless blouse.

Sonia gave me a flat stare, clearly expecting nothing but disappointment and broken promises to come out of my mouth.

Having worked in the service industry for years before getting the Tea Cauldron, it was an expression I was well familiar with and fully prepared to counteract. I gave her my friendliest smile this side of I'd-rather-eat-a-lemon fake. "Good morning, Sonia."

She arched a single eyebrow.

I cleared my throat. "Miss Aguilar."

The other eyebrow joined the first, and I had the urgent need to shrivel up and die. One day, I told myself. One day I'd figure out the correct way to address her. Until then, I needed to stand strong and forge on.

"Sonia," I repeated in a firmer tone. "I need to talk to you about the Corner Rose."

Sonia's eyes rolled toward Dru in a slow, exaggerated gesture that gave the shop's costumes a run for their money. "You don't say."

"I've heard there is some interest by Tabbies, and I'd like to —" Her hand began to rise in a telltale stop gesture, and I rushed the rest of my words. "Lodge a complaint."

Her mouth pursed as her hand completed the trip. "Let me stop you right there."

By my side, Dru inhaled sharply. The tension in the shop ratcheted up by about a thousand percent.

"But it's within my rights as a business owner," I insisted before Dru's demon claws popped out and we finally found out if Sonia really hid a sword inside her cane.

"I don't want to hear it," Sonia said. "This is my private time. Bring it up at the next meeting."

That was funny, considering she'd had no trouble hearing herself talk PBOA business at my shop not that long ago. I opened my mouth to tell her just that when I noticed the purple and orange papers strewn across the glass counter.

"Are these the brochures for Halloween?" I asked excitedly. I grabbed one before she could stop me and *oohed* at the ghostly pumpkins and assorted Halloween details decorating the corners.

"The proofs," Sonia admitted grudgingly. "Check your details are right since you're here. Saves me a trip."

Ignoring Dru's pointed elbow in my side, I scanned the paper eagerly. Most paranormal stores in Olmeda were featured in the promotion, along with a couple of normal human ones, so as to not draw too much attention since we were still a secret from the world at large. Bosko's garish gift apparel shop had a place of honor on top, and I would bet the shop he hadn't spent an extra dime for it. The man was like the mafia boss of Olmeda's tourist trade and had one huge finger in every money-making pie.

I read down the list of shops until I found mine tucked away at the bottom. I didn't mind that—I was the newcomer and needed to pay my dues, but the typo was definitely a problem.

"My shop's name is spelled wrong," I told Sonia woefully. "It says Chauldron instead of Cauldron."

"Let me see." She snatched the brochure from my hands,

read the bottom of the paper, and made an angry noise. Muttering something about *first late, then wrong* and *next year we're using Paula's printer*, she clicked her pen to red and circled the typo a few times. Once done, she focused back on me. "Have you gotten anywhere with Cavalier?"

The question startled me. "We had dinner the other day at that French place by Balton Square and he's invited me to walk the dogs with him a couple of mornings before work." I wasn't about to tell her we hadn't had sleepovers yet or progressed beyond a few lingering goodnight kisses. Or admit that I was still coming to terms with the change in our relationship. The question was intrusive enough as it was; what business was our new dating life of hers?

Sonia closed her eyes, as if praying for patience. "The cemetery tour, Avery. I'm asking about the Halloween cemetery tour." She taped the paper on the counter with a perfectly manicured nail, pointing to a suspiciously empty spot. "There's still time to include it in the brochures."

"Oh, that." I brightened considerably. "I think we're slowly wearing him down. He insists he's thinking about it, but the strays are on my side." If my excellent proposals didn't convince him to open his cemetery for special Halloween night haunted tours, I was sure he'd eventually agree if only to shut Alex and Shane up about playing Garreth the Hound, Olmeda's number one Halloween attraction.

"Tick tock, tick tock. The clock is ticking. We need to know ASAP. By next meeting, if possible."

I bit my lip. The next PBOA meeting was on Thursday. I wasn't sure we had worn Ian down *that* much yet.

Wait a moment. Was this a test? I studied Sonia intently, but she gave nothing away. If I didn't get Ian to agree to the tours, she'd shut my complaint about Dru's ex down?

"Are we done here?" she asked.

"No," said Dru. "The Corner Rose—"

"Next meeting."

Dru and Sonia stared at each other so hard, I almost heard the electric boom of their glares clashing halfway.

Gently, I tugged on Dru's arm. "We'll bring it up at the meeting."

Dru narrowed her eyes one last time at Sonia, then allowed me to drag her away from the counter. Just as we reached the door, it opened, and I had to duck to avoid getting smacked in the face.

Hutton entered the shop, barely acknowledging us as he stepped aside to let us pass. A younger and more beautiful version of Ian, the local shifter alpha exuded power and grimness wherever he went.

Dru stormed out of the shop, but I paused to greet him.

"Hello, Hutton. How are things?"

"Witch."

Greeting and goodbye and a severe lack of respect all bundled into one neat word that still sounded like he meant to say it with a very different starting letter. Considering I had saved his furry hide a week ago, he seriously needed to adjust his attitude. I reminded him of this fact with a haughty lift of my chin.

"Good," he added like the words were being ripped off his throat. "Thanks."

Much better.

Dru was staring daggers at me from outside the shop, so I said my goodbyes and joined her.

"Can you believe it?" Dru fumed as we walked back to the Tea Cauldron.

It was hard to. After all the stress and hoops I'd gone through to make Hutton's alpha power potions, he should be treating me much better. He hadn't even paid me yet!

I brought out my phone and sent him a quick text reminding him of the bill. The fact I still had his number listed as Ass 2 brought me some satisfaction.

Grandma would not have approved of treating my clients this way. But then, for all I knew, Grandma might've had a private diary full of curses and code names for her most trying acquaintances.

"Hutton has some gall," I said.

"Not him. Sonia!"

Truthfully, Sonia's response hadn't come as a huge surprise, but Dru would probably sock me if I said that. "She should take this more seriously," I agreed.

"Did you do something to piss her off lately?" Suspicion filled Dru's voice.

Other than existing, apparently? "I haven't talked to her since the last meeting. I told you she hates me."

"Hmph."

My phone vibrated with an incoming text. Hutton.

Already paid.

Had he? Because my bank account disagreed. *Where?*

Same account as usual.

Must be the mythical account Brimstone and Destruction, my other dark magic client, also used to pay me. An account Bagley had obviously kept hidden from the Council. I asked Hutton for the account details, then gave my attention back to Dru.

"Look at it on the good side," I said. "At least she told us to bring it up."

"There is no good side. Sonia probably added it to her list of things to ignore next meeting just to mess with you."

While that was a distinct possibility, something told me Sonia wasn't that mean spirited. My natural optimism at work, no doubt. If you didn't believe the best in people, was there even a point in living among them?

"This way, we have a few days to work on our proposal," I told Dru. "We can gather information about Tabbies, maybe canvass the shops in the street, and come up with a list of reasons it'd be bad for the community if they took over the Corner Rose. Sonia will be impressed by all the paperwork."

"That's not a bad idea," Dru admitted.

"I'm not half bad at this business thing, you know. Runs in the family." The side of the family I had no blood connection to, but osmosis worked just as well. "I'll ask my sister for ideas."

"Your stepsister? The one who works for that big business management firm?"

"Yep."

"Fine."

"It hurts me you trust her more than me. You haven't even met her."

"She pulls in ten times your salary—that's all I need to know."

I sniffed loudly at that. "It's not the amount of money, it's what you do with it."

Dru laughed. "That inspires even less confidence in you."

"Buying Bee-Bee was *not* a bad investment," I argued, unlocking the shop's door.

"Sure. And what about the T-shirts that never sell?"

"Branding." I pushed the door open, and something rustled on the floor. A white envelope. "Oh."

Dru peered over me as I bent to pick it up. "What's that?"

"Someone slipped an envelope under the door while we were out."

"What does it say?"

I checked the front and back. "No address or stamps. Just

my name. Guess they used a messenger." I walked up to the counter and reached for a butter knife.

"Are you sure you should open it?" Dru asked. "What if someone has it in for you and spelled it somehow?"

Bringing the envelope up to my nose, I took a good whiff. "Smells like paper." Oftentimes, paper or cloth dipped into poison gained a slightly off smell. I angled it toward the ceiling light, but the envelope was too thick to see inside. "I think it's safe."

"Wait." Dru walked to the farthest corner in the shop, by the shelf of books, tarot sets, and crystals for sale. "Okay. Go ahead."

"No faith," I grumbled. I slashed the lid open and peered inside the envelope. A single card rested inside.

Carefully, I slipped it out and read the contents.

I'm ready to make an offer on the spellbook. Think of your price.

What on good Mother's green earth?

4

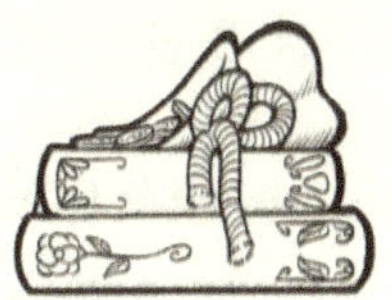

"Well?" Dru asked from the corner. "Are you feeling sick?"

"Someone's asking to buy a spellbook." I showed her the note.

She read the message. "Whose spellbook?"

Excellent question. "It doesn't say."

"Yours?"

I shook my head. Nobody would want to buy my spellbook —there was nothing special about it aside from the love and kindness my Grandma had poured into it. Certainly nobody who slipped anonymous notes printed on expensive card stock under the door and hinted that money wasn't a problem.

Good magic rarely called for excessive amounts of money, so it had to be dark magic related.

Which didn't clear up anything, since I was currently in theoretical possession of two dark magic spellbooks—Bagley's and Key's Grandmother's.

I doubted anyone was aware that I had confiscated Key's spellbook, so Bagley's was the logical choice. I had taken over her shop and her dark magic side business; therefore, I must have her spellbook.

Unfortunately for this eager buyer, while they had been correct in assuming I had gotten Bagley's spellbook along with the rest of the place, I had consigned said source of everything evil and foul to my backyard fire pit about an hour after discovering it.

There was no space in the world for that kind of item.

"I think they mean Ms. Bagley's dark magic spellbook," I said.

Dru looked two seconds away from rubbing her hands in glee. "How much are you going to ask for it?"

"Nothing. I destroyed it."

Her obvious disappointment was almost comical.

"Can you take care of the shop?" I asked. "And get started on our plan to chase your ex out of Olmeda?" I added to cheer her up.

Her face lit up with nothing short of evil delight. "Yes."

I thanked her and went out through the backyard. At this time of day on a Sunday, Ian would be at home, so I drove my Vespa to the cemetery, my heartbeats increasing as the distance decreased.

This thing between Ian and me felt both old and new. Comfortable and like staring down at the abyss at the same time. Part of me knew that I didn't need any excuse to drop by, but the rest of me felt more secure using the excuse of the card to explain the trip.

Would this ping-ponging of eagerness and nerves ever stop? I wasn't new to dating, but this felt like the major leagues compared to playing around in the park.

It felt real in a way few things had felt before.

And that scared the hell out of me sometimes.

I arrived at the cemetery without incident or Bee-Bee breaking down and found the side door open. I rang once anyway, to alert Ian of my arrival, and parked the Vespa inside the fence. Ian's house, a lovely two-story construction of warm brown and red bricks and slate gabled roofs, rested on top of a small hill overseeing the cemetery spreading on the opposite side. On my way up to the house, I crossed paths with a wiry man with pasty pale skin making his way down the slope.

He gave me a slight nod but didn't pause.

I waved at his back like an idiot.

Curious, I walked up the rest of the way to find Ian standing on his porch, busy on his phone, his free hand hooked on his jeans pocket, looking as harsh, forbidding, and impressive as ever.

My heart fluttered in my chest. I could eat him right up. Tall, broad-shouldered, with shoulder-length brown hair gathered back with a tie, and dressed in his usual all-black—black thin sweater, black jeans, black matte belt buckle, black boots.

A bark of greeting broke the spell, and I crouched to catch the white ball of supersonic fluff that was Fluffy.

She laved me with attention, and I petted her happily. Being in the presence of Fluffy cleansed my soul like nothing else could. There was so much goodness contained in her fluffy eagerness that I doubted Bagley had ever met her or all her evilness would've been washed right out.

"Hi, Ian," I said, straightening. The words came out breathless, and not just from the walk up the slope.

He pocketed his phone and took the steps down to the ground, one side of his mouth kicking up. "Hi, Hope."

Ah, his voice. I suppressed a shudder of delight as I allowed it to tingle its way down my spine. I wanted to follow it to its source, roll onto my tiptoes, throw my arms around his neck, and get lost in his mouth for a little while. Maybe continue with a proper roll on the grass on his lawn.

Really, this was getting out of control. I was twenty-six, not thirteen with my first crush.

"Who was that?" I asked, thumbing toward the gate.

Ian crossed his arms, and I noticed a distinct cooling of the warmth in his eyes. "My ex-partner's son."

"Ex-partner? The one who died?" The one people thought Ian had murdered, to be more specific. People could be so dumb. If Ian had killed his partner, the bounty hunters would've put him down. But the reputation served him well, so I doubted he put much emphasis on correcting the rumors.

"Yes."

A prickle of alarm made me tense. Had the son heard the rumors and come to cause Ian trouble? "What did he want?"

Ian shrugged. "Asked if I had anything left of him."

I studied his face, searching for any signs that he was downplaying the encounter, but beyond his usual granite facade, I saw no reason to believe he was lying or upset. I exhaled with relief. Good.

"Hey, Hope," Alex called from behind us. He and Key stood by the detached garage that Ian used as a workshop for his repair and restoration business. The white van with its adorable knight-and-dragon logo was parked right in front.

"Hi there," I answered loudly with another energetic wave. Fluffy backed me up with a bark, because she was the best. I was happy to see that Key looked happy, if still slightly shy, dressed in her usual jeans and sweatshirt. Her brown hair gathered in a ponytail made her look younger than her nineteen or so years of age.

From the other side of the van, Shane lifted his hand in greeting and walked toward the gate. The second of Ian's strays, he was a contrast to Alex's blond surfer looks with his tan olive skin, short dark hair, and black eye patch.

I turned to Ian. "You're working today?"

"Just doing some prep for the week."

It warmed my insides that Key was being included. Ian had

promised to give her a job on a provisional basis for a month, and I was glad to see he really meant to give her a chance rather than simply drag her along for thirty days, then give her the kick. The parallels with me and the shop weren't lost on me, and just as I meant to pass my six-month probation period with flying colors, so would Key.

With a dark magic user, truculent fire mage of an uncle as her only family in town, Key could use extra help to remain on the good side of the paranormal world. Working with Ian and his strays was the perfect solution for this.

Especially since I couldn't afford a second hire for my shop, and, to be truthful, I wasn't sure putting a penniless, innocent young woman within Bagley's reach was the best thing to do. Sure, Key had lied to me in an effort to get to my supposed dark magic items, but she'd had good intentions. She was a lovely, shiny egg easily washed, not a rotten one.

And speaking of rotten eggs...

"Have you talked to Hutton?" I asked.

"No."

The speed and assurance in Ian's reply didn't give me much hope for further brotherly reconciliation, but one had to try. "Maybe you should check on him?"

"Why?"

"There might've been repercussions from the alpha challenge. What if he's in trouble?"

"I'm sure you'll tell me if he is," he said wryly.

I hated it when he made sense. Not that it'd stop me. I checked our surroundings in case some sort of new paranormal creature had teleported onto the empty lawn around us and lowered my voice. "At some point in the future, we'll have to do the alpha power transfusion again. Your magic is powerful, but it won't last forever."

Ian looked even less impressed. "Hutton got my blood, my magic, and my help in the challenge. I'll keep my words."

Dealing with this man was like moving boulders sometimes. "One day."

He leaned down until our noses were almost touching. "One day?"

I poked his chest. "One day you'll see the light and admit you care more than you show."

"Show like this?" He gave me a fast peck on the lips.

Loud whistling made me jump back. Over by the garage, Alex was making kissy gestures while Key dragged him into the workshop. Fluffy, guessing it was a wonderful new game, barked and ran around us. Even Rufus woofed from the porch.

Flustered, I pushed Ian toward the house. "Let's go inside. I have something to show you." And, Mother Earth, was I happy Alex hadn't heard that one, or I'd never hear the end of it.

"Oh?" Luckily for me, Ian sounded genuinely curious and not in the least teasing. He allowed me to turn him around and we stepped onto the porch and inside the house.

Once out of prying eyes, I took my phone, brought up the photos I had taken of the envelope and the note, and showed them to Ian. He took the phone and studied the screen, then lifted his eyebrows in question.

"I went to visit Sonia this morning with Dru, and when we came back, someone had slipped that note under my door." Reaching over, I swiped to the photo of the note itself. "Read it."

I watched his eyes follow the writing, then my brain did a record scratch.

Wait, it screeched suddenly. *Did Ian just admit he cares for me more than he shows?*

What had been the words? I'd said, *You care more than you show*, and then he'd kissed me and said—

Ian put the phone back in my hands, and I stared at it like it was an alien object from planet What Just Happened.

"You think they mean Bagley's," he said.

With an effort of will, I refocused on the problem at hand. The note. Bagley's spellbook of dark magic horrors. "Yes. It has to be." I still hadn't told him about Key's dark magic family or the fact I was in possession of her grandmother's spellbook. I felt a twinge of guilt at the thought, but some things needed to stay private. I didn't believe for a second Key was a danger to him or the strays, and I didn't want to share her secrets without her permission.

A witch was meant to help her community, and sometimes that required secrecy. Who would trust me if I babbled my clients' secrets to my bounty hunter boyfriend? Key might not exactly be a client, but she was under my protection, and that was even more important.

"Who could want it?" I reached down to pet Fluffy, who was pawing insistently at my leg.

"The list is probably long," he answered with some amusement.

He had a point. Any number of people could be interested in Bagley's spellbook—frenemies, other dark witch competition, old clients. For all I knew, there was a healthy underground market for dead dark witches' spellbooks.

"Just tell them no," he added. "Or be honest and explain you destroyed it so someone else doesn't contact you again."

As if. "They'd never believe that."

"You *did* destroy it, didn't you?" he insisted, slightly suspicious.

I crossed my chest. "Scouts' honor."

"Were you a scout?"

"In my heart of hearts."

Ian snorted, a smile playing with his lips.

"You think they'll go away if I say no?" I asked.

"I'm sure Bagley received offers too. Use her reputation to your advantage."

"Don't bother me again or I'll slip snakes into your toilet?"

His rare boyish grin made an appearance. "Something like that."

I wasn't completely reassured, but he made excellent points. Whoever wanted the spellbook would have to go elsewhere for their dark magic fix.

For a few moments, I toyed with the idea of setting up a trap for the bounty hunters to catch this person and rid the streets from another dark magic user, but discarded the thought. If they got caught, bounty hunters might tell the Council about their claims of Bagley being a dark witch, and that'd open another whole can of worms that would end up with me out of a job at best and in Council jail at worst.

Being a good witch in a dark magic world really sucked some days.

Trying to distract myself, I studied Ian's cozy living room. It looked no different from the last time I'd been here a couple of days ago.

"You haven't put up decorations yet."

"It's early for Christmas, don't you think?"

I smacked his arm playfully. "Halloween!"

"Ah." He paused. "No."

"No, what?" I asked, all innocence.

"I'm not opening the cemetery for Halloween tours."

My pout of disappointment and sadness could've won contests. "But the strays will be so disappointed. They want to play Garreth so badly."

"They can take it up with the pack."

Hutton's young shifters were in charge of making scary

appearances as Garreth the Hound at strategic Olmeda spots during Halloween. It was a very contested role.

"And Key was so eager to redeem herself by giving the tours." I lowered my voice to a pleading whine. "She could really use a win." Especially considering how her last attempt at giving a tour had gone.

"I'm sure they can fit her at the haunted house. They're always short on people," Ian answered like the emotionless bounty hunter bastard many thought him to be.

"You're heartless."

He looked rather smug. For a block of stone. "I see my reputation precedes me."

"Hah. I know better." I poked his chest again, apparently my finger's favorite spot to be. "I'll wear you down."

His fast smile was nothing short of wicked sly. "You might need to work harder."

His words reminded me of Sonia. "Dru's ex-boyfriend is trying to get the Corner Rose for her parents. Did you know they own Tabbies?"

"Yes."

Of course he did. The man had probably run background checks on every paranormal in town, and probably more than a few humans. "She's upset about it. There's some rivalry between her and her ex, I think."

"No kidding."

Yes, that was a bit obvious. "She wanted me to complain to Sonia."

A knock on the door frame interrupted me. Alex and Key were waiting on the threshold, Alex with an unholy gleam of glee in his eyes, Key obviously wanting to be anywhere else.

"Are we interrupting?" Alex asked, grinning. Rufus ambled his way to get a few pets. After he was done with Alex, he sniffed at Key but didn't bug her.

"Nope." An idea occurred to me. I turned to Ian. "Hey, have you seen him around town checking out other buildings?" In his business, he dealt with a lot of buildings in Old Olmeda. Perhaps the Corner Rose wasn't the only shop Dru's ex-boyfriend was interested in. In fact, why should it be? The thought cheered me up considerably. If the man chose any other shop, even if we failed in our quest to kick him out of Olmeda, at least he wouldn't get Dru's chosen dream shop.

"Seen who?" Alex asked immediately.

I bit my lip, unsure if to admit the man's relationship with Dru. That was her private business to share, not mine.

"Someone's trying to buy the Corner Rose," Ian answered for me.

"And you don't like him?" Alex brightened. "Want me to follow him around, see if he's up to no good?"

"I'll help," Key added eagerly, no doubt thinking about her newly acquired hope of becoming a bounty hunter.

Fluffy yipped as if she, too, was looking forward to a very exciting evening of following and sniffing everything in her path.

Ian crossed his arms and shook his head. "You have work."

Alex frowned at the floor. "Yes, boss."

I had a feeling he wanted to feel useful, maybe because Shane usually was the one in charge of following people around. It wasn't my place to intervene, just as Ian had no say in how I conducted my business unless I asked for his opinion, but I couldn't just leave the poor guy looking like a drowned puppy.

Besides, it was my duty as the local witch to put my nose where it didn't belong.

"Maybe he could for a couple of days?" I suggested. "If the man does anything suspicious, it'll help our chances for the PBOA to reject his application."

"Is that why you went to Sonia?" Ian asked.

"Yep. She told us to bring it up on Thursday's meeting."

He looked thoughtful for a few moments. "I'll check him out."

"But, boss..." Alex began.

"No following."

Alex peered at me with sad, sad, Fluffy-level puppy eyes. He must've practiced at night in front of a mirror to get that level of authenticity.

Ian stepped in front of me. "No following. Do we have a problem?"

Alex's shoulders slumped for a moment. Then he inhaled deeply and straightened, meeting Ian's stern gaze. "No, boss."

"Good. Go back to work. If there's anything suspicious, I'll call you."

"Yes, boss," Alex exclaimed, sounding a lot more cheerful. He tugged Key down the porch steps and all but skipped back toward the garage area.

Ian turned his attention to me, his eyes accusatory.

I lifted my hands in surrender. "I didn't do anything." When the silence stretched and his expression didn't change, I asked, "Key's doing okay?"

"Yes, your stray is doing just fine. Same as when you asked two days ago."

And now we were both glaring. "She's not my stray. Witches don't have strays, they have interns."

Since Key wasn't working for me, she was obviously not one.

"Whatever you say, blondie."

"Oh, we're bringing out the big guns, huh?" I grabbed Fluffy and pushed her into Ian's face. "Fluffy, attack!"

Fluffy licked Ian's chin, her tail wagging madly.

Rufus woofed in displeasure, and I looked down at him. "Sorry, boy, you're a bit too heavy for me."

Ian wiped his chin and took Fluffy from my arms, settling her against his hip like she was a sack of potatoes. Fluffy didn't seem to take offense, her tongue lolling like she was having the time of her life.

I couldn't help but laugh at the picture.

Ian's eyes narrowed, and I leaned up to kiss his cheek on a dog-drool-less spot. "I'll call you later."

He tugged at the green strand in my hair. "Sure."

Ian wasn't a man of many words, but the contentment in that single one told me plenty. Feeling like a giddy teenager, I made my way out of the house and down the lawn.

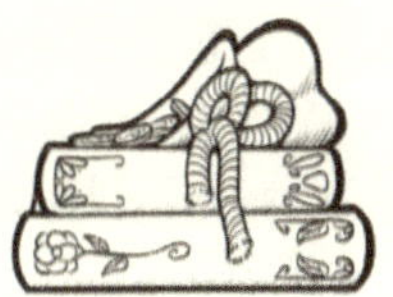

UNFORTUNATELY, the giddiness lasted until I returned home. The sight of the envelope on the kitchen counter and Dru's instant questions brought me back to earth with unerring aim. I relayed Ian's opinions about the note and told Dru he would look into her ex for anything suspicious we could use against him.

Later that night, after closing the shop and eating some grilled ham and cheese sandwiches for dinner, I took a closer inspection of the note and the envelope.

Ian might think the whole situation warranted nothing beyond a simple *no, thank you* without the *thank you*, but I had a nagging suspicion that it wouldn't be that simple. It was my first experience dealing with the dark magic spellbooks marketplace, after all. I had a right to be concerned.

A series of gurgles came through the sink pipes, and I stood to pat the faucet.

"Thank you, goldfish ghost. I appreciate the support."

A dark shadow peeked out, then slid right back in. Back when I'd done a spell to communicate with the ghost of the dead man in my bathtub, I had not only awakened Bagley but whatever haunted the pipes. My guess was someone's pet gold-fish. Dru thought it might be a rat. Ian was of the opinion that old houses made strange noises, but that was probably because he'd love for the Council to fork over money for him and the strays to check the pipes.

Since he had already given me deep discounts with the bathroom cleaning and other things, I couldn't blame the man.

After washing the dishes and tidying up the kitchen, I went into my bedroom to continue examining the note. It had been printed, so there wasn't anything to discern from the handwriting, and there were no other identifying features about the paper and envelope. Common brand—not Tabbies—and it hadn't been licked closed.

My gaze drifted to Grandma's spellbook. Was this note related to the strange warning the spellbook had given me after we'd solved Hutton's problem? That horrible zing of alarm and wrongness that still made my stomach sink whenever the memory crossed my mind? Holding the note in one hand, I placed my other palm on the book, bracing myself for the sting of dread.

Nothing. The fabric of the cover remained smooth, the embroidery comforting raised bumps under my fingertips. A familiar sense of clarity and goodness washed over me, and some of Grandma's words came to mind: If you only expect the worst, you will never find the best.

"Thank you, Grandma," I murmured.

I left the note on top of the envelope by the spellbook, hoping whatever evil intentions might be contained inside would be cleansed overnight. As I got ready for bed, I thought about the actual content of the note. How much did a good dark magic spellbook go for? Full of curiosity, I used the VPN to log onto the paranormal dark web marketplace and browse around. No spellbooks on sale, but that had to add to their rarity. They probably went for a lot of money.

It almost made me wish I did have the spellbook for sale. Almost.

It also reminded me that Bagley would've never felt the need to sell her spellbook, because judging from what I'd surmised about her dark magic prices, she'd been making bank.

Money that was floating somewhere, ready to be found and put to good use. Like, say, Dru's down payment for the Corner Rose. The idea perked me up immediately.

I checked my messages, but Hutton hadn't answered with the account he'd transferred the potion money to. Probably didn't want to leave proof of his evil purchases. I considered the time. Calling him now wouldn't put him in a sharing mood, so instead I sent a text to Brimstone and Destruction asking for the account he used.

Now it was time to do some research on Dru's ex-boyfriend.

He was easy to find. He held a high-level position at the company now, and his social media presence was strong. Lots of photos of him in different suits and a few in rolled-up shirt-sleeves that left no wonder how he'd been able to seduce Dru. His smile was always brilliant and his brown eyes warm, his posts strictly professional with no romantic dates to be found.

If I'd screwed someone over like he had Dru and who knows how many others, I wouldn't risk it, either.

I browsed back to my own social media and checked Ian's. He'd added a new photo today of some repaired moulding. Not exactly the kind of thing to bring one palpitations, but the obvious love he had for his business shone through, and that was enough to make my heart squeeze and leave a way more enthusiastic comment than the post required.

Reply to other's posts with what you wish to see for

your own.

Another very important tenet of witchhood.

———

Monday dawned still overcast and dreary, which meant I wouldn't get clients until later in the day. It gave me plenty of time to go on my money-finding adventure.

Unlike his alpha grouchiness, Brimstone and Destruction had no trouble answering my text about the payments with an email address. Just a sequence of numbers and letters that made no sense to me but were likely some evil internal joke for Bagley. First kill date and initials? Code for "gotcha, loser?" The possibilities were endless.

He also sent another text requesting one of his fake dark magic potions, so I told him to come Wednesday evening. He always insisted on witnessing the making of his potion, and I didn't want to interrupt my current quest for Bagley's money.

I went into the back to call Hutton. I expected to have to call him at least three times, but he picked up on the first try. It surprised me so much I blanked for a second on answering his rough, "What?"

"Good morning to you!" I said brightly.

"I'm hanging up."

Hah. "No, you're not." He had picked up too fast—he was curious about what I had to say. Or worried that the spell I'd done on him had horrible, unforeseen consequences such as the world had never seen.

"Witch," he said in warning.

"What account did you use to transfer the payment for the potion?"

"That again?"

"I enjoy getting paid for my work."

"I paid you," he said in outrage.

"Well, I can't find the money." I injected a note of innocent doubt into my voice. "Maybe you sent it to the wrong place?"

He inhaled sharply. "Are you accusing me of trying to scam you?"

"I wouldn't dare."

"You better not."

Seriously, how hard was it for him to simply spit out the email he'd used? Ghosts bled easier than this. "But can you just confirm the account for me?"

"Are you recording this?" he asked, full of suspicion.

"No," I said slowly. "I only want to confirm the email address."

He barked out a fast series of letters and numbers. "There you go. Don't call again unless it's urgent, witch."

He ended the call faster than my brain organized the data he'd thrown at me into a semblance of order. The numbers and letters matched what Brimstone and Destruction had sent me. Same account, then.

Now I had to figure out which service the evil spawn had used. Asking Hutton wouldn't do any good, so I messaged the fire mage again and settled in to wait.

Bagley was mercifully quiet as soft background music filled the shop, interrupted by the occasional honk and tire screech coming from the outside. To fill in the time, I got started on the Halloween decorations. Brimstone's answer came as I'd finished taping a mean-looking pumpkin silhouette to a windowpane.

As I accessed the payments site on the laptop, I wondered what the mage thought of all my questions. Had he guessed I hadn't inherited the money account along with the shop? Or did he want to be in my good graces since I was close to the local bounty hunter, who also happened to be employing his niece?

Someone trying to help me instead of blackmailing me into

helping them? That would be a first.

The payment service locked me up after three tries. Unsurprisingly, the "Forgot your password?" option sent an email to none of the accounts I owned. I tapped my fingers on the side of my favorite mug, the one my sister had given me as a birthday present a few years ago. It was shaped like a cauldron and had "Witch Vitamins" printed on the side.

My family might not know about the hidden world of para-normals, or be aware that I was part of it, but my witchy flair had been obvious from the start.

"Oh, no, my dear," came Bagley's concerned voice from the other side of the counter. "You forgot my password?"

I jolted straight. "You can see?"

She simply chuckled. "I can see many things, child."

Now she was going to dangle this password thing in front of me until the end of time. That's what I got for assuming she only saw what was in direct line of sight from whatever object she haunted. I considered taking the laptop to the back to continue my research, but it'd be a pain to set it back up if a customer entered the shop.

No, I decided with some pride. Not only would I *not* hide my actions from her, but I'd show her I didn't need her help to achieve my goal. I hadn't for Hutton's potion, and I wouldn't to find her secret stash of ill-gotten money.

"Now, dear," Bagley continued, "what do you say we come to a small understanding?"

"Let me guess," I said with no little sarcasm, "the password for a new body?"

She chuckled again. "No, dear. Nothing so radical."

"That'd be a new one," I muttered.

"We must start small. Make sure your power is up to it."

Great, even the evil mastermind was worried my power was too crappy to bring her back to life. "You're right, Ms. Bagley.

There is obviously no way I can bring your plans of world domination to fruition, so you might as well resign yourself to a life of haunting random chairs in my shop."

"Oh, silly. I'm sure your power is more than enough. Why, a little blood and you'd be surprised at what you can achieve!"

"Maybe in another life."

"Don't say it so flippantly," she said, suddenly serious. "Or you might end up like me."

Since I had no intention of killing people to use their blood to try to extend my life beyond death, I doubted that very much. "I'm pretty sure you ended up like you because of karma, Ms. Bagley."

"You mean I got a second chance at life as a reward for all the people I helped? Why, you might be right!"

"You just told me not to wish for another life," I pointed out.

"Tsk, tsk. Young people these days never listen. I told you not to leave the wish so open-ended. Precision is key where intention is concerned. Did your mentor teach you nothing?"

Oh-call-me-Tammy had, indeed, taught me nothing. Not that I was about to admit that to Bagley—I'd never hear the end of her offers to teach me *everything*. For a price.

"I know enough, Ms. Bagley."

"But you don't know my password," she replied, sly as a snake.

I cracked my knuckles. "I don't need it."

If I couldn't access her payment service account, then I'd figure out her actual bank account. Someone like Bagley wouldn't put all her money in one site, given all her dark magic clients knew the username email. More than one would try to hack it, so why leave her savings at risk?

No, Bagley would keep her money in an actual bank account nobody knew about.

It couldn't be a business account connected to the shop because if her dark magic side business were discovered and the Council took over, they could theoretically gain access to it, so why would she put her money there?

That didn't mean the Council hadn't discovered something related to it after Bagley's death without finding it suspicious. Her death had been unexpected; she wouldn't have had the time to hide her paperwork.

"Well?" the old demon witch asked sweetly. "What's your next move?"

"Glad you asked."

I abandoned my position behind the counter and retreated into the back with my phone. The archway to the back marked the end of Bagley's current reign of terror, so I stayed close, watching the shop through the bead curtain in case anyone came in.

As a rule, I liked to avoid reminding the Council of my existence while I was on probation, but things had gone smoothly for the last couple of weeks, and even my supervisor at the local Council branch had been pleased with my progress the last time we'd talked. I figured a short call wouldn't upend the balance.

At this point, you may wonder why I didn't simply drag the stool into the back and enjoy a few evil-witch-free hours of blessed solitude, but this way I knew exactly where she was. I had to be smart about my power of temporary exorcism over Bagley. If I took the stool out and Bagley remained silent upon her return, I had no way of knowing which object she had latched to.

That would make it hard if I *did* need her out of the way.

Besides, her being sat on constantly was a sweet payback.

The Council's automated system picked up, and I gave it my Witch ID number. After going through a series of menus, I was passed on to a real person.

"Montel's Council offices," a chirpy male voice answered. "How can I help you?"

"Hi, I'm the owner of the Tea Cauldron in Olmeda. I took over Theodora Bagley's shop in August this year."

"What can I do for you, Ms. Avery?"

I rubbed one of the naked bricks by the archway, as if the action would make me appear any more innocent through the video-less call. "I've come across some discrepancies related to the business accounts, and I was wondering if perhaps the Council found some extra documents pertaining the old shop's accounts while they cleaned up the place."

Since Ms. Bagley had died without heirs, the shop had returned to the Council. They had been the ones to clean up the building and get it ready for the next witch—me.

"What kind of documents?"

"Bank statements and the like."

"We're not allowed to reveal personal information."

"Of course not," I said demurely. "But you know how it is with old banks—it's hard to tell what's personal and what belongs to the business. I think some stuff might've gotten miscategorized."

"Noted," the man said in an understanding tone. "Anything else?"

"Not at the moment, thank you."

"I'll get back to you."

He ended the call, and I paced the hallway, relieved the conversation had gone as well as it could possibly go. Chances were they wouldn't discover anything, but treasure was often found in the crevices you didn't check.

And while the Council checked Bagley's stuff, I would continue my investigation down other venues. If I wanted to get the money for Dru before her ex got the Corner Rose, I couldn't just sit around and wait for people to call me back.

6

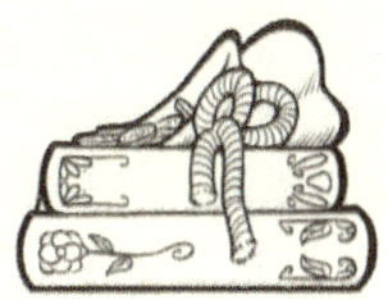

WHILE THE COUNCIL investigated whether they had found any extra bank statements, I'd focus on the banks themselves.

What kind of bank would Bagley trust with her hidden savings?

It had to be a bank with a local branch. Bagley had gotten the shop before internet banking was a thing, so she'd have had to open any account in person. Not a branch popular with the local paranormal community, though—she wouldn't want to cross paths with an acquaintance and risk them getting curious or overhearing something. She would keep the dark magic business totally separate from her front as the Council's helpful witch, pillar of the community, and widely beloved cookie-provider.

A bank in another town?

That seemed unlikely. Before the internet age, she must've gotten paid in cash, necessitating frequent trips to the bank. Even during the internet age, cash was bound to be a top two preferred payment method. People were bound to notice her going out of town on mysterious trips, and if someone saw her at a bank branch of another town, it would be even more suspicious.

But perhaps I was making things too complicated.

I called Key.

She answered almost right away. "Hope?"

"Are you busy?" Sounds of hammering rose in the background.

"Hope called," she told someone. "Taking a couple." A few moments later, the sound of a door shutting muffled the hammering. "Okay, I'm good. Do you need help with the shop?"

There was a note of caution in her voice that made me miss the times when she was dying to work at the shop. So what if that had been because she wanted to get to my nonexistent dark magic supplies? The thought still counted. "Nothing like that. I have a question about your uncle."

"Uncle Jeremy?" she asked, surprised.

"The one and the same. Do you know which bank he uses?"

"Uhm. No, sorry." She sounded genuinely apologetic that she didn't know, and suddenly I didn't feel so dejected that my shop wasn't as shiny as her new goal of becoming a bounty hunter like Ian.

"Do you know which bank his friends use? What's good for the less savory crowd?"

"I don't know. Want me to ask him?"

"No, don't worry. I'll figure it out." I didn't want Key more involved in the underground dark magic side of the paranormal world than she already was. Asking things about money was bound to get you noticed, and I'd rather people notice me over her.

"You sure?"

I reassured her, then called Dru. She took longer to pick up. A lot longer. Sometimes I thought she only did that to keep me on my toes because I was sure she found great joy in finding out what mess I'd gotten myself into every time I needed to call.

"Hi, Dru," I said as soon as she accepted the call. "Do you know what banks Lewis used for his personal stuff?"

Mr. Lewis, Dru's old boss, had been in cahoots with Vicky, who had been Bagley's secret dark magic intern, so it stood to reason if anyone knew about bank branches for the less savory paranormal side, it would've been him.

"His banks?"

"I'm—" The front door opened, hitting the melodic chime, and a middle-aged woman entered the shop. "One second." I parted the bead curtain and gave the woman a wide smile. "Welcome to the Tea Cauldron. Can I get you anything?"

The woman glanced around, uncertain. "I'm not sure..."

"We offer drinks to-go."

"Imma to-go you," Dru muttered through the phone.

The woman's face lit up. "Oh, that'd be wonderful. Thank you. Could I have the day's special?"

I hurried to make the peppermint-lavender-apple concoction and filled a recyclable cup. "Here you go."

After she paid and left, I lifted the phone back to my ear. "Dru?"

An ominous silence told me she'd hung up.

I was right.

With a heavy sigh, I called her again.

"Free now?" she asked dryly.

"Yep. So, about the bank accounts."

"The store had an account with Southguard."

It was the same bank I used for the Tea Cauldron. They really had some excellent terms for small business owners. "What about his personal ones?"

"That I don't know. Why?"

"I'm tracking down Satan spawn's money. I thought Lewis might've used the same bank."

A low chuckle rose from the haunted stool.

"You think I wouldn't have drained him dry if I knew?" Dru replied. "I have no idea what the jerk did with his personal money, but from what your BFF said, he had nothing left on any account. That's why the bank owns the shop now and Preston the bastard is about to buy it from them and open a shop in *my* shop and—"

"Yes, you're right," I said soothingly before she got more worked up and threw her phone at the wall and then made me pay for it. "No way he'd have told you that stuff. He was a devious son of a witch."

"Yes, he was," she answered, a lot calmer. "But now that I think about it, maybe his accountant might know?"

"He had an accountant?"

"For tax season. He always said doing numbers gave him a headache. Should've known something was up."

"Do you know which accountant?"

"Crane."

"Crane," I repeated, trying to imprint it into my brain. "Thank you."

"Is that all you need from me?"

"No."

"What else, then?" she asked caustically.

"I need your sunshine."

"My...sunshine?"

"The one you bring into the shop whenever you come through the door."

"Oh, shut up."

I laughed as she hung up, even though I was a hundred percent serious. I hadn't known how lonely owning my own shop could get until I'd opened the Tea Cauldron. Solo days like this one were nowhere near as nice as when I had friends around.

"Never trusted Crane," Bagley said. "The man is cold like a fish."

"The slug calling the snail slimy?"

"You make no sense, child."

"I thought it was pretty witty myself." I opened up a new tab in my phone's browser and searched for local bank branches.

"The Lord save us all if that's what passes as wit nowadays."

"I'm not sure. I think you'll get passed over on the way to Hell." I ignored the first bank on the list—mine—and clicked on the second one, then their phone number link. "Now, shush."

"Do not shush me, child. I'm several times your senior in age, power, and intellect."

"Shhh."

Bagley muttered, then remained quiet. Probably too curious to see what I was doing.

After a few minutes of holding music, a woman picked up the call, sounding a lot more bored than her Council counterpart. "How can I help you?"

"Yes, hello. My great-aunt passed away last month and I'm trying to close her accounts."

"Please come to a local branch with the death certificate and proof of relationship. Thank you for your call."

"The thing is, I'm not sure if—"

The call went dead.

Remember, Hope—perseverance is the name of the game. I tried the next bank. The wait time was shorter, but the operator didn't sound any happier, so I tried a new angle.

"Hi, my great-aunt recently passed away and I'm trying to

figure out if she had an account with one of your local branches. We haven't been able to—"

"Sorry, we can't corroborate whether an individual holds an account with us."

"The thing is, she died recently and we're trying to close the account, but we're not sure if—"

"Present a proof of identity and the death certificate at a local counter. Have a nice day."

He ended the call.

I stared at my phone, starting to get annoyed. The death certificate wouldn't be a problem, obviously, but the rest...

I peeked over the counter at the stool. "Did you even have a family?"

"Doesn't everyone?" She sounded quite smug.

"Why aren't they here fighting over your dead body?" Could I convince one of them to help?

The memory of Key presenting her top-quality fake driver's license at the bars during our Guiles and Romary escapade flashed through my mind. "Never mind. I don't want to know."

Could I hire the same person who'd done her ID to make me a fake proof of relationship? I'd still need to find the correct branch, but maybe if I went in person, it'd be easier to butter them up until they admitted whether Bagley had held an account.

Unless she'd used some sort of secondary business entity, so nothing was in her name.

Oh, Mother.

I dipped into the back to send Ian a text asking about Bagley's accountant. Now that I knew she was omniscient, it felt wrong to text him where she could see.

A few minutes later, the shop's door opened and Hannah came in, cheeks rosy as if she'd hurried over.

"Hi, Hannah," I exclaimed, warming at the sight of her eagerness to come in.

"Hello, Hope." She hung her jacket on the hanger by the door and came up to the counter with a folder in her hands. "How are things?"

"Most excellent now that my favorite repeat customer is here."

Hannah laughed. "What about the day's special then?"

"Coming up!"

I prepared her tea and served it in one of the special mugs reserved for my special clients.

She wrapped her hands around the mug and shivered. "Brr. It's cold today."

"Wonderful."

Business would pick up for sure.

"I brought you the photos." She tapped on the folder on the counter, then brought out a USB stick. "I printed a couple of my favorites, in case you want to hang them on the walls."

"You did?" I hurried to open the folder and gasped with delight.

The first print showed the shop by itself in full color, the brown bricks cozy and inviting, the multi-pane windows offering a hint of the warmth to be found inside. The second was the same but in black and white, making the building appear old and antique and like it had belonged in Olmeda since the beginning of time. The last print showed me grinning in front of the shop like a woman who was living her best life and her greatest dream.

"Hannah, these are amazing," I said, a little choked up. That last one was going on the wall for sure. "I love them. Thank you."

"No need to thank me. You paid me for the job." She blew

on her tea and took a small sip. "The originals are on the memory stick."

I took the folder and the stick and put them in one of the cabinets under the counter, away from any watery mishaps. "I'll guard them with my life."

"Don't go that far," she said with another laugh. "I have copies."

The door of the shop opened again, and I faced the newcomer. "Welcome..."

The words died on my lips as I saw who it was. The blond older teenage girl who had asked me for an illegal love potion back in Summer had entered the shop along with another friend. They were both dressed similarly in Olmeda's apparent teenage uniform of shorty shorts. At least they were wearing hoodies now.

Love Potion Girl ignored Hannah and fixed her intent stare on me. I didn't need a psychic to know she hadn't come for the day's special brew.

I pointed at the archway into the back. "In there."

The girls marched across the shop and into the back.

"Do you mind if I step out for a couple of minutes?" I asked Hannah.

She shook her head. "Don't worry about it."

Thanking her, I moved into the back, then shuffled the two teens into the kitchen.

"Why are you here?" I demanded.

Love Potion Girl tossed her hair back and crossed her arms. "Natalia needs a love potion."

I ground my teeth. This. *This* was what happened when you dealt with dark magic. It had a way to multiply and spread its rot. Never mind that I had given this girl a placebo and not an actual love potion, the damage still spread like the black death.

And the problem was, if I told Natalia that I no longer did the potions, they'd simply look for another witch. One who'd have no trouble charging them an arm, making her a *real* love potion, and then some poor soul would end up married against their will.

"I told you to keep it a secret," I said in my most severe tone.

Love Potion Girl rolled her eyes. "Don't wooorry. Natalia's a shifter."

Hutton would kill me if he learned I was selling dark magic to one of his pack. No, scratch that. He'd completely massacre me, full fangs and all claws kind of deal.

"Love potions don't work on shifters," I said, lying through my teeth. Hutton was an example that not only did real love potions work on shifters, they worked extremely well.

Natalia looked at Love Potion Girl in total panic. "Holly..."

Holly snorted. "She's playing hard to catch. That page said they work on every paranormal."

"What page?" I asked sharply.

"Look," she said. "You gonna make the love potion or not?"

"We should've ordered it online," Natalia said, all sad eyes and disappointment.

"No way," Holly said. "They're all a scam. I told you, her potion worked great for me and my sister."

"Fine," I said. "I'll make you the same potion I made for her." I pointed at Holly. "But it comes with some conditions. First of all, no telling anyone else. I don't care if they're your cousin or your second best friend." I showed them a very toothy, very evil smile. "If I learn you went to another witch or bought anything online, I will make a spell to cancel the love potions. Do you understand?"

Holly appeared horrified. "You can do that?"

"Of course."

"But I already paid!"

"Do it my way, or nobody gets lucky in love."

Holly and Natalia exchanged a look, then jerked their chins in agreement.

I fixed them with a stern glare and began counting with my fingers. "No telling anyone. No marrying within a year. No babies. Babies interfere with magic. Understood?"

Natalia nodded eagerly.

I held out my hand. "Where's the blood?"

She retrieved a small vial from her pocket and dropped it on my palm.

"Wait here."

I went back into the shop, apologized to Hannah, and crouched behind the counter to access my magic supplies cabinet.

The trick for placebo dark magic potions, I had learned, was to make them appear like the kind of potion the recipient expected rather than how it should look. For a true love potion, you needed unwilling blood—how the girl had gotten this much unwilling blood, I didn't want to know—so it stood to reason that a love potion made with it would look kind of bloody. And dark. Because dark magic.

Last time I'd used some flat soda, but I didn't have any at hand, so I used some of the blood-red syrup I kept for Brimstone and Destruction's fake blood potions and added some leftover tea from my earlier client. To top it off, I added a good amount of salt. The concoction should be disgusting enough to make anyone spit it out.

If I was lucky, Natalia would think love potions wouldn't work.

If Natalia was lucky, the person would spit it on her and then feel so sorry it'd start a conversation that would lead to a date.

I brought the vial into the back and put a tiny ward on the bottle so they knew I'd used some sort of magic on it.

Holly elbowed Natalia. "Told you she would do it."

"Nobody else," I reminded her sternly. "Or your marriage plans are done."

"Sure." She grabbed the vial and dragged Natalia out of the kitchen and into the shop. "Same price?"

Sighing, I followed. "Same price."

Hannah watched us with curiosity as Holly paid with her phone, but didn't have a chance to ask anything as Veva entered as the two girls left.

"I should get going, too," Hannah said, smiling as she brought out her wallet.

"Thank you again for the photos." I waved her money away. "On the house."

She thanked me and left, leaving me alone with Veva.

Veva Daly owned Cards & Destiny, a tarot shop on Marquesa street. We had met briefly when I'd been digging into Ian's parents' relationship, but I'd liked her immediately.

"Welcome to the Tea Cauldron," I said brightly.

She gave the room a slow nod of approval. "I like it. Very cozy."

"Would you like something to drink?" I pointed at the glass display. "Muffins?"

"Yes and yes, thank you." She sat on Bagley and studied the teas lining the back shelf among the T-shirts. "Earl Grey, please."

I made her tea, added some milk at her request, and presented it along with a banana muffin, my personal favorite.

Veva sipped the tea while she studied the shelf with all my tarot and occult stuff for sale. "I like your little nook."

I brimmed with pride. "Thank you. I thought it fit the shop's theme very well."

"What do you think about selling some of my tarot sets here on consignment?"

For a moment, I was left speechless. To collaborate with someone as integrated in the paranormal community as Veva was a dream come true. When others saw she trusted me, they'd start trusting me.

I swallowed the sudden lump in my throat. "I'd love to."

Veva set her tea down. "I was thinking that for Halloween—"

The back door slammed open, and a couple of seconds later, Dru burst through the bead curtain.

"He's here," she hissed, going to peer out of the window closest to the Corner Rose. "They're showing him the Corner Rose again."

Veva arched her eyebrows at me.

"Ex-boyfriend," I whispered.

"Ah."

All that needed to be said, really.

"About Halloween?" I said tentatively.

Dru muttered something else, plastering her face against a glass pane in an effort to get a better view of the street in front of the Corner Rose.

Veva gave her a pointed look. "Perhaps it'd be better if we talked about this later?"

"Let no others stop your plans, for they won't stop for you," I told her sagely. It was part of my morning affirmations list. One of my favorites.

"Well said. But in this case..."

My phone shook in my pocket with an incoming text, and I gave it a fast glance. Ian had answered my question about Bagley's accountant.

Desmond Crane.

The name nagged a memory into place. Hadn't that been

one of the men Lewis had pointed out during my first PBOA meeting? A wide man on the short side?

The shop's landline rang stridently, making me jump.

"Excuse me." I grabbed the receiver and used my most welcoming voice. "The Tea Cauldron."

"Hope Avery?" an electronic male-sounding voice asked.

"Speaking."

"Have you decided on a price for the spellbook yet?"

"What? Who is this?" The moment the words left my mouth, I wanted to take them back. It was obvious who it was, and I doubted they'd tell me their full name and address just because I'd asked.

"An interested party."

I turned my back to Veva and cupped a hand around my mouth and the receiver. "I'm sorry, I don't have Bagley's spellbook. There's nothing to sell."

"Who's Bagley?" the voice asked, a little snippy. "I want Hazel Oakes's spellbook."

Hazel Oakes's... *My* grandma's spellbook?

7

Six years earlier.

I STUDIED the book on top of the dining room table. It was one of those hardcover tomes wrapped in fabric instead of a paper dust jacket. Beautiful embroidered flowers on the pastel green fabric made me think of the kind of artisanal journals you found in farmers' market stalls and Etsy.

My mom sniffed into a paper tissue. "It was Grandma Oakes's journal. She wanted you to have it at seventeen. She also wrote you a letter. In case."

"Mom?"

Sniff. "Yes?"

"I'm twenty."

She waved that aside. "I hope you'll take good care of it, Hope. I know how much you loved your grandma."

A carousel of memories ran in my head—laughing in Grandma's garden, playing checkers together, eating grilled ham and cheese sandwiches at her kitchen table. Her light gray tombstone, looking strangely cheery in the cemetery among the flower bouquets. As an eight-year-old, it hadn't completely dawned on me at the time that I would never see Grandma again.

I didn't trust myself to speak, so I took the book and the letter up to my room, ready to go down memory lane.

Instead, a whole new world had been revealed, and I'd called the number at the bottom of Grandma's letter. The Council's number.

Present.

"I don't understand," I said into the phone.

"Think about it. I'm willing to pay top price. I'll be in contact."

The line went dead, and I stared at the receiver, utterly speechless. Why would anyone want to buy Grandma's spellbook? It was a family treasure for sure, but beyond my love for it, there was nothing special about it. Certainly nothing worth paying top price for.

Dazed, I tried to pay attention to Veva as she made suggestions for cross-promotion ideas between our shops.

Aware that my body might be present but my mind was somewhere else, the woman agreed to come by again in a couple of days and see if Hope had returned to planet Earth.

"What is it?" Dru asked the moment Veva was gone. "Who was that on the phone?"

My mouth opened and closed, then opened again. "It was whoever sent that note about the spellbook. They want to buy it."

"Bagley's?"

"Grandma's."

"*Your* grandma's?" Dru sounded skeptical, and I couldn't blame her. "Why? Was she a famous witch?"

"No. She was a nobody. She didn't even have a witch shop."

"Why would anyone want her spellbook?"

Why, indeed. Hearing someone else voice the question finally kicked my brain into gear. There was no reason anyone would want Grandma's spellbook, except for one.

"Someone's trying to mess with me."

Outrage filled me at the idea. How dare they?

Posting bad reviews, complaints, and leaving a ghost in my bathtub was one thing, but involving Grandma?

No.

Grandma was off limits.

"Why would anyone want to mess with you?" Dru asked, dubious.

"Same reason Vicky wanted me out of the shop? It must be someone interested in taking over Olmeda's witchy market."

Mentally, I ran through the list of suspects. Sonia, Hutton, Bosko, Wilburn, even Veva were all on the list—after Vicky and Key, nobody was catching me by surprise again.

Everyone was a suspect.

"The Council wouldn't just take it from you," Dru said.

"I'm still in the probation period. They can and will take it if they think I'm not up to the job."

Dru's eyes widened with sudden realization.

"What?" I asked.

She pointed at me, her outraged expression matching mine. "It's gotta be Preston."

I wasn't expecting that one, but, then again, *everyone* was a suspect. "You think so?"

"Yes. It makes perfect sense! He must've realized that I'd try to stop him from getting the Corner Rose, and as my friend and shop owner, you might get in his way, so he's trying to put you off your game, so you're too worried about this to stop his plans."

That sounded farfetched. "Did he have the time to research how to hit me where it hurts?"

"It wasn't a coincidence that you got the note the same week he shows up to check the Corner Rose. We don't know how long he's been interested in it." Her voice lowered to a dark whisper. "How long he's been studying us."

That made sense. The timing was too coincidental. My gaze strayed to the windows, and I gasped.

"What is it?" Dru turned around, and her sharp inhale was even louder.

Preston was crossing the street, walking toward the cars parked on the curb.

"Look at that," Dru exclaimed. "He leaves right after you get that call? Give me a break." Her ominous gaze met mine. "Time to follow his suspicious ass."

Her grim enthusiasm was contagious. "We need to figure out what he's up to," I agreed.

She charged toward the back of the shop. "Hurry up."

I flipped the sign to closed, bolted the door, and ran after her. By the time I emerged into the backyard, she already had the back gate open and was pushing the Vespa into the back alley.

I joined her on the street and watched her put on my helmet.

"I only have one helmet."

"I know," she said, then tapped her foot impatiently. "Hurry, or he's going to get away." Her eyes narrowed. "Are *you* going to let him get away with this?"

I huffed. I was most definitely not going to let him get away with anything.

If he was guilty of trying to mess with me, it'd only help us kick his butt come Thursday's PBOA meeting.

I sat on Bee-Bee, and Dru got on behind me. It started after a couple of tries, and I turned us around toward the Corner Rose. A few moments later, we were out onto the main street.

"Did we lose him?" I asked worriedly, scanning the cars for a blue one.

"There he is," Dru said, pointing ahead of us to a red Lexus pulling out into the street. "Bastard still driving the same car."

I nodded curtly and concentrated on following the car without being too obvious while Dru hunched behind me, muttering the whole time. Good thing she was a demon and not a powerful witch, or her intention would've made a mess of the streets around us.

About five minutes later, Preston slowed down and began rounding the same block, obviously searching for a parking space.

"Leave the Vespa there," Dru commanded, pointing at a few bicycles chained to a low fence.

As did as she ordered, and parked Bee-Bee in an open spot, then hesitated. Vehicular crime in Olmeda wasn't the highest, but still...

"Oh, don't worry so much," Dru snapped, reading my mind. "Nobody's going to steal this piece of junk."

I patted the Vespa's headlight. "Don't worry, Bee-Bee, you'll always be the prettiest piece of junk in my heart."

"Takes one to know one," Dru muttered as she took off the helmet and stuffed it in the compartment under the seat.

"I'm sorry," I said. "I was under the impression you wanted my help with..." I trailed off as Dru ignored me and ran up to the corner of the building. She peeked around, then beckoned.

"There he is," she whispered when I got closer. "Wonder where he's going."

In Old Olmeda, it could be anywhere, really. We followed him among the early afternoon throng of tourists toward

Balton Square. The shops here were small and picturesque, with three restaurants or bars per two lamposts.

Preston eventually took one of the popular side streets and went into Bosko's shop of garish vacation apparel.

"What does he want with Bosko?" I wondered aloud. No way Bosko would sell his shop, and the shop itself was a glorified hallway, anyway, not the kind of space Tabbies favored.

We crept closer and peeked through the T-shirts hanging in the entryway. Preston and Bosko were having an excellent man-to-man talk, full of laughs and entertainment.

I pulled her back before they caught us snooping. "What do you think he's doing?"

"The bastard," Dru growled. Her hands clenched and unclenched, and I checked her hair in case the telltale signs of her demon horns were peeking out. "He's buttering up the competition."

"His competition?"

"Yours!"

"Bosko's not my competition." I mean, sure, I sold T-shirts too, but mine were at least tasteful.

Dru threw up her hands and walked to the shop on Bosko's left, where she motioned for me to stand close to the display window. Catching on, I joined her and acted like I was super into the expensive local artisanal candles.

"He must've heard that we went to Sonia to complain," she explained in a dark tone, "so now he's ingratiating himself with other paranormal businesses so they don't vote against him."

"I wonder if Sonia told him about our intentions," I added just as grimly.

"She doesn't really hate you."

"So you say."

"And she doesn't hate *me*."

"That you know of."

"As much as I admire this suspicious side of you," Dru said, "being obsessed with Sonia isn't going to help us at all."

I grunted. Why wouldn't it be Sonia? *Everyone* was a suspect, no matter how unrelated to the problem they might appear.

"He's on the move," Dru warned.

I peeked over her shoulder and watched his back disappear among the tourists. "Let's go."

If Dru's ex-boyfriend was responsible for playing a joke on me and Grandma, he was going to pay dearly.

Preston's next stop was a sports store a couple of streets over. It specialized in yoga and home gym equipment.

"Is that one of the pack's stores?" I asked.

"Yep."

"What a cunning, devious man."

I couldn't help the slight note of envy in my tone. This should've been me, ingratiating myself to the local community instead of waiting for them to come to me. But it wasn't like I'd had the time, I reminded myself, trying to soothe the sad, teary emoji that was now my heart. I hadn't had the luxury to spend my mornings visiting people while running a one-woman shop.

After the shifter store, Preston dipped into a bookstore Dru assured me was run by humans, then walked back to his car.

Bee-Bee was thankfully still where we'd left her, waiting for us, and once again we followed Preston through Olmeda until he arrived at the private parking area of a small, lovely boutique hotel.

Dru snorted in my ear at the sight, which I took to mean Preston hadn't met an affordable chain hotel he wouldn't avoid.

We left the Vespa in a nook by a tree and settled to wait him out in a restaurant situated right across the street. The prices on the menu made me wish we'd lost Preston in the crowd.

"If he was seeking an introduction to the pack, I can call Hutton and warn him against him," I said.

Dru glared at the hotel like she was working out the best way to set it on fire. "You're with Ian now. Why would Hutton listen to you?"

Because if he didn't, I'd refuse to transfer Ian's power again. But Dru didn't know about that. She only knew Hutton and Ian hated each other's guts.

On the surface, at least.

"He might not like me, but I do supply them with all their potions. My opinion's gotta carry some weight."

Shifters and demons bought the most potions out of all paranormal creatures. Shifters were especially fond of memory potions, in case a human stumbled upon them shifting forms, and demons needed glamour ones to hide their naturally red eyes.

I squinted at Dru. Her eyes were the same beautiful brown as always. "Where do you get your glamour potions?"

She shrugged, still laser-focused on the expensive hotel across the street. "I have a stash."

"Hmm." I wasn't totally convinced. "Are you cheating on me with another witch?"

She made a noise of exasperation, as if my questions were intruding into her spy time. "Bagley had a sale in June. I got a bunch."

"You mean evil, dark magic witch Bagley, who killed people in her bathtub and used their unwilling blood for all her spells?"

Dru's head rotated ever so slowly until she was staring back at me. She blinked a couple of times.

"I'll make you a new batch," I said smugly. "On the house."

Her attention returned to the window, but her frown told me she was contemplating how much dark magic she had unwittingly consumed while drinking Bagley's potions. That and if it was worth abandoning her prime estate stalking spot to go into the bathroom and try to puke it out.

"I'll add a cleansing potion too." I had proven my point and could afford to be gracious, unlike the salads and soups that made our outrageously priced lunch.

A long time later, after the food and the free bread sticks were all gone, and there was still no sign of Preston leaving the hotel, and the waiter was clearing his throat near our table because there were people waiting outside, we gave up and went back to the shop.

As I told Dru, just because we hadn't caught him in the act, it didn't mean there weren't more ways to skin an ex.

She cheered up at that.

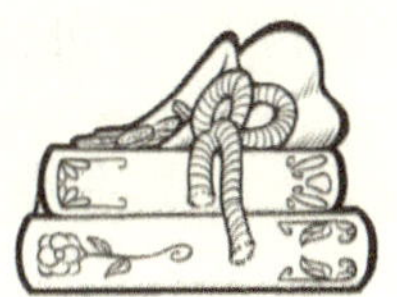

I LEFT Dru womaning the shop and rode Bee-Bee to Ian's current renovations project. It was a small, quaint old house that had recently come off the market and needed some love and care before the new owners moved in.

I knocked on the open front door, although I doubted anyone would hear me since rock music filled the air.

"Hello," I said over the music.

"Hey, Hope," Alex returned brightly. He was sitting on a ladder in the room to the right, applying a coat of white paint to the ceiling. Shane crouched in a corner, fiddling with another tray of paint. He lifted a hand, not bothering to turn my way.

"Where's Ian?"

Alex pointed his roller toward the back of the house. "Back there."

"Thanks!"

I took the main hallway, pausing to admire the wonderful work they'd already done in the kitchen, and found Ian and Key in the tiny fenced backyard. A couple of flags marked spots on the overgrown grass, and Key was on her hands and knees, her fingers digging into the soil, and her brow creased in deep concentration.

My chest swelled at the sight. I *knew* Key would be perfect for Ian's business.

"What are you guys doing?" I asked, way happier than seeing Key put to good use warranted. It probably had something to do with Ian standing in his all-black, his brow furrowed in deep thought.

"Working," he said.

Key looked up, her expression filled with determination. "Here. It's the last one."

Ian marked the spot with another flag. "Thank you. Clean up and see if you can help the boys."

Key nodded and ran inside the house, giving me a shy, happy smile on the way.

"Marking the position of dead bodies?" I joked, but only because Key had already checked my backyard for corpses.

Ian grunted, still studying the small expanse of grass and weeds. He pointed at a tree peeking over the fence. "Checking if the roots are messing with the pipes."

"You're welcome."

He fixed those green eyes on me that made me want to melt. "For what?"

My grin was smug and toothy. "For Key."

He huffed, but the ghost of a smile curved his mouth. "Did you bring us food?"

"No, but I brought you this." I produced an individually wrapped candy from my pocket.

Ian eyed it dubiously. "What's that?"

"An organic candy. Plum favor."

"Plum?"

"As close to black as I could get."

He laughed and took the candy. It disappeared into his jeans pocket. "Thanks. What new catastrophe brings you here?"

I opened my mouth, but he lifted a hand, cutting me off. "That bad? Do I need to sit down?"

"Not *that* bad."

"We better go inside."

I let him usher me back into the house and into the kitchen. He leaned against the central island, the top covered in thick plastic. "Tell me."

Since he was asking so nicely, I told him about the spellbook call, about Dru and my suspicions about Preston, and about our adventures following him all over Olmeda. To finish the tale, I brought out the folded envelope and note from my back pocket and presented them to him. I'd put them in a freezer bag.

He looked at the bag, then back at me, one eyebrow rising.

"To check for fingerprints or something," I said.

"Or something?"

"Maybe Rufus can follow the smell?"

"How many people have touched that?"

"Me, Dru, and whoever put it in my shop."

"You know Rufus is not a search and rescue dog, right?"

"He sure searches when it suits you, though." Like the time he had tracked me down in Guiles and Romary. I shook the bag. "Please?"

Without another word, he plucked the bag from my fingers and set it aside.

This was what I loved about Ian. He didn't make me or my ideas feel like annoying tasks he had to complete in order to humor me. He either was on board, or he told me what he thought of the plan to my face.

"Why would Preston want your grandmother's spellbook?" he asked, crossing his arms. He was wearing a faded black long-sleeved T-shirt today, and the movement brought the fabric taut across all the right places, making my mouth dry.

"To mess with my head. A distraction, so I focus on that instead of trying to stop him from taking over the Corner Rose."

"It seems farfetched and overly complicated. What if you just named a price?"

"I'm sure he'd make up something to stall the sale, then cancel it." I rubbed my chin, frowning deeply as I began pacing a tight circle in front of Ian. "Maybe it has nothing to do with me stopping him from taking over the Corner Rose." I remembered Doyle's tirade about expanding the Tea Cauldron the last time I'd talked to her in Montel. "Maybe he wants my shop so he can expand."

"I doubt it. The Corner Rose is big enough for Tabbies's purposes. Making a bigger store would make it lose its charm. It wouldn't attract as many tourists. And, even if those were his plans, the Council would never sell him the building."

He was right. "What if he doesn't know it belongs to the Council?"

Ian gave me one of his patented *c'mon, Hope, use that brain of yours* looks. I grimaced. "Yeah, all right, he knows." I sighed and leaned my elbows on the island by his side. "It's too coincidental for him not to be involved."

"Coincidences happen."

"But why would anyone else want Grandma's spellbook? It makes no sense."

"Are you sure there's nothing special about it?"

"As sure as my name."

"There might be some kind of code that you missed."

"Code?" Realization hit me. "You mean, like Bagley's ledger code?"

His expression softened. "Maybe."

"No." I shook my head hard. "No way. Grandma wasn't a dark witch."

"Hope..."

"No. Nope."

Despite my vigorous denial, I searched for the few precious memories I held of Grandma, most worn down to smells and feelings and hazy images taken as if someone had been standing behind us with a Polaroid camera at the ready. Nothing jumped out. Nothing that made my gut tighten with doubt. "Grandma was a good witch. The best witch."

"Then maybe the spellbook is worth more than you think it is?"

I gave him a rueful smile. "I love my grandma, but it only has a few simple spells and a lot of notes on common herb combinations."

Ian reached over to tug at my green hair strand, then lowered his hand to squeeze my arm. "The best option might be to wait until the person contacts you again, give them a price, and try to figure out who it is when they try to collect rather than assuming it's Preston."

I thought about that. As usual, he made an excellent point. "Everyone is a suspect," I agreed.

His mouth curved upward. "Even me?"

"You most of all." Suspect of burrowing into my heart, then leaving me behind, alone with only hazy memories to go by like Grandma had done.

I blinked, taken aback at the turn of my thoughts. Where had that come from?

"Something wrong?" he asked, studying my face.

"No, sorry." Being around him suddenly felt like too much. Like my skin was warm and chilled at the same time.

"Did you come up with some new plan?" he asked.

Yes, Hope. Plan to figure out who's messing with you. Focus. I gathered my wits and sent them forth with an encouraging shove. "Will you bring Rufus later, see if he can track the smell from the envelope?"

Ian straightened away from the island. "Let's do it now."

"Now?" I eyed the beautiful kitchen. "But the house..."

"The kids can take care of stuff for an hour. The dogs will be happy to see you."

And me them. I needed Fluffy to get me out of this strange gloomy well I'd inadvertently fallen into.

Fortunately, she did just that.

Unfortunately, Rufus picked no trail of whoever had slipped the envelope under my door.

———

Later that day, once we'd closed the shop, Dru and I lit the metal fire pit and proceeded to chill in the backyard. Fluffy lay down by my side as I reclined on one of two cheap camping chairs I'd gotten from one of Alex's buddies. Dru occupied the other, knocking back one of my diet sodas, while Key stood opposite from us, extending her hand forward like some kind of telekinetic super hero.

The back door light was turned on, so it was enough to see a clump of soil jump and flip upside down.

Rufus woofed appreciatively.

I'd kidnapped Ian's dogs under the pretense of walking them so he wouldn't have to.

"It's simply a very, very long walk, right, Fluffyfluff?" I told her.

Fluffy's tail gave a halfhearted wag.

Dru tilted the soda can toward Key. "What is she doing, again?"

"Mage training."

Key sent Dru a fast, irritated glance before remembering Dru was a demon, and would probably claw her eyes out if she annoyed her, and looked away. The clump flipped back into position, then burrowed slightly until the patch appeared undisturbed.

Her fist pump of victory was heartwarming to see.

Dru turned to me, her brow scrunching in confusion.

"The devil is in the details," I told her. To Key, I shouted, "Way to go!"

She grinned, then tried to lift the clump again.

"Remind me again why she's doing this?" Dru asked.

"She wants to be a bounty hunter."

"And how is flipping some dirt going to help her?"

"What if the bounty makes a run for it? Then she can make them trip."

"Well, damn," Dru said.

"What?"

"That makes sense."

"Thanks," I said smugly. "It was my idea she practice that." I had also offered Key the use of one of the shop's stools to practice burying big things deep into the earth, in case a bounty got out of hand, but she'd given me an odd look and said she wasn't ready for that step yet.

"But why is she practicing in your backyard?" Dru insisted.

"She felt tacky using the cemetery as a training ground."

Dru nodded in acknowledgment and took another sip of her soda.

"So, you want the Corner Rose to show your parents what you're capable of?" I asked.

She rolled her eyes. "What do you think?"

"That they made a big mistake by not giving you the job."

Dru snorted but relaxed against the chair. "They did."

"Do you ever visit them?" Ever since moving cross-country,

I missed my sister, mom, and stepdad, but I hadn't had the urgent need to visit them yet. Maybe because they hadn't understood my need to take over the shop, and I wasn't looking forward to an inquisition about how the shop was doing.

My sister, though. Her I missed fiercely. Emails and calls weren't enough, and I'd invited her to visit. Had even promised her I'd get an air mattress and she could take the bed.

"I haven't visited in a couple of years," Dru admitted.

"Not even for the holidays?"

"*Especially* not for the holidays."

I thought about that for a moment. "Ah, everyone in your family knows about your ex." No boyfriend, no baby, no job at the family business. No, family holidays couldn't be easy.

"I'd rather stick a fork in my eye than go to another family reunion. Weekend FaceTime is as much as I can take."

"Until you open your own shop?"

Her grim expression transformed into one of pure, evil glee. "Yes."

I lifted my soda can in her direction, and she clinked it with hers. "To showing our families what we're capable of."

"Damn right."

We took a sip of our drinks.

"How long did you go out with Preston?" I asked.

Dru made a face. "Six months."

That was a long time for someone to fake date. "Are you sure he was with you only to get closer to your parents?"

"He dumped me the day he signed on the offer." Her clipped words could've cut glass.

"Ouch. And you didn't see it coming?"

"Do I look like the kind of woman who would've stayed if she'd seen it coming?"

"Young love hides many defects," I agreed. "Didn't your

parents retract the offer once you told them about the reason he'd gone out with you?"

Dru answered with a stoic silence.

"You didn't tell them, did you?"

"Of course not," she snapped. "I was so embarrassed."

"So you packed up and moved here?" Realization hit. "You told your parents you were breaking up with him because you lost the job and needed to try out new places. You were punishing them for choosing him over you."

"For all the good it did," she grumbled.

"And he never contradicted your version of events?"

"Please. He probably thanked the Lord I didn't rat him out."

Even in her attempt at retaining her pride, it had worked out in Preston's favor. Had he been devious enough to plan it that way? Perhaps. No wonder she'd jumped on him as a suspect. Dru's theory about him being behind the spellbook scam was a lot more plausible now that I knew the details.

But I couldn't put all my bets on one person with only circumstantial evidence.

After taking another long, refreshing gulp of my drink, I brought out my phone and checked my list of suspects. It was depressingly long.

"What's that?" Dru asked.

"My list of suspects."

Her expression soured. "I'm telling you, it's the bastard."

"He's on top of the list." Literally. "See?" I showed her the screen.

Dru took my phone and swept upward. "You made it a to-do list?"

"Easier to cross people off."

She muttered something about someone saving her from his hell and kept browsing, then stilled. "Hope."

"Yes?"

"Why am I on the list?"

"*Everyone* is a suspect."

"You think I slipped you a note under the door while I was talking to Sonia with you?"

"You could have a partner," I pointed out. "Maybe you're back with Preston and are helping him mess with me. Hey, your demon horns are peeking out." I hurried to tap on the check mark by her name, and *Dru* was immediately crossed out as a done task. "There," I added brightly, "I just forgot to eliminate you, that's all."

"Am I on the list?" Key asked. She'd come around the fire pit to take a drink from her water bottle. I'd told her about the note and the call and asked her to keep an eye out for Preston. She'd looked extremely pleased at my request.

"Of course you're on the list," I lied.

Key brightened, obviously delighted to be included as someone worth investigating.

Dru pursed her lips but said nothing.

"What are you planning on doing?" Key asked.

"Yeah, oh great mastermind," Dru drawled. "What's your next move?"

I tapped my phone on my thigh. "Tomorrow, I'm going to talk to some people, see if Preston visited them, and try to get a feeling of where they stand about him."

"I already talked to some friends," Dru said. "They'll let me know if he makes any weird moves."

"Doesn't hurt for me to try too." It'd provide me with a good excuse to ask around about Bagley's accountant, maybe get an appointment with him.

"But what about the spellbook?" Key asked.

"I'm thinking about something Ian suggested—"

The distant ringing of the shop's landline interrupted me.

Key's eyes widened. "Do you think that's...?"

I shot out of the chair and scrambled into the building. I managed to get to the phone before the ringing stopped.

"Yes?" I asked, heart hammering in my ears.

"Have you made a decision about the spellbook?" the distorted male voice asked.

"I..." I searched for something to say. What had been the plan?

"It's simple. Yes or no, and name your price."

Simple? *Simple?* A sudden wave of rage filled me. "Fine. Five million dollars."

"Three hundred K."

Were they serious? Haggling like it was some random item at a pawnshop? "Grandma's spellbook is *not* for sale."

I slammed the received down. They could mess with me and with the shop, but how dare they mess with Grandma's legacy?

"Was that the bastard?" Dru asked from the other side of the counter.

A niggling of regret poked at my insides as I stared at the plastic phone and finally remembered my original plan. "Yes."

"What was it Ian said that you were going to try?"

My mouth drooped at the corners, and I gave Dru a soulful look. "Give the person a price, then try to figure out who they are when they send a payment method?"

Dru gave me two very sarcastic thumbs up. "Doing great, boss. Keep it up."

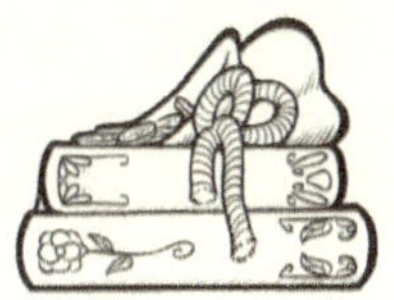

9

TRUE TO MY initial plans to investigate Preston's local meetings, I left Dru in charge of the shop and made my way to some of the paranormal-owned shops. It was a dreary day, but I chose to view the inconsistent drizzle as heavenly water nurturing my budding investigation.

I'd told Ian about my knee-jerk reaction to the caller when he'd come to retrieve his missing dogs, and he'd told me whoever it was would likely make another attempt at buying it. If not, they would simply try another tactic to mess with me, and that would help us determine who it was.

"Like the police needing more than one victim to catch a serial killer?" I'd asked him, hopeful.

He'd told me to try more science fiction and less of my sister's favorite romantic suspense books.

But basically, yes.

My first stop was Veva's shop. I owed her a visit after I'd treated her so unprofessionally the day earlier. To make amends, I brought her a box of muffins from Fairy Circle Cakes and a tin of Earl Grey. The pretty one I kept for decoration on the shelf because it helped with the cozy atmosphere.

Good friendships and successful business ventures required sacrifices.

Veva was delighted to see me, and we had a productive conversation until a regular client came in for a tarot reading.

According to Veva, Preston had yet to show his face in the shop, but she'd heard some rumors about his interest in the Corner Rose. She looked somewhat miffed when she learned he had visited other people's shops, but not hers.

Excellent.

I also used the opportunity to ask about Bagley's accountant.

"Do you know Desmond Crane?"

Veva made a face. "Are you going to hire him? He's not the easiest person to deal with. Knows his stuff, though."

"He's your accountant too?"

"Unfortunately."

"A necessary evil, huh?"

"Very unfortunately."

My next stop was Bosko's store. Bosko wasn't in, but his daughter was behind the counter. I introduced myself and invited her to visit the Tea Cauldron for a free sample of the goods.

She did not reciprocate.

Now a new owner of a beige bucket hat with googly eyes embroidered in the front to protect me from the rain, I added Bosko's daughter to my list of suspects and made my way to the same pack store Preston had visited the day before.

Luckily for me, Keith was the only one in the store. He was one of the shifters who had made an effort to come into my shop and strike up a conversation. In his late thirties, he was a solid block of a man with a friendly face and a cheery smile.

In a nutshell, the opposite of Hutton.

It was good to be reminded that not all shifters were rude, paranoid, and in need of dark magic.

Or were they?

I studied him closely, searching for any sign of evilness emanating from him. If only it were that easy.

"What brings you over?" he asked good-naturedly. Perhaps he was used to people eyeing him with suspicion. The prices on display *were* on the high end of the spectrum. "Need some equipment?"

I allowed him to show me their selection of yoga mats. A lot of witches swore by the daily practice of yoga to keep their spirit going, but I preferred a good dose of affirmations in the morning.

"Does the pack make a lot of money off these?" I asked, poking at a bright pink rolled sheet of foam.

"Our bestsellers," he said proudly. "The treadmills sell very well too. We offer free local delivery and setup. Are you interested in one? We carry one model that fits perfectly in smaller living rooms. Or we can order in for you."

My living room was of a good size, but I should really invest in filling it with furniture first. I told him as much.

"You want to go to Brock for that," Keith said. "The man is an artist with wood."

"Brock?"

"He has a warehouse out west. Look up his name on your phone, will show right up."

"That's probably too expensive for my finances," I confessed.

He laughed. "Ah, the curse of opening a store. Living on instant noodles and a mattress on the floor?"

I grinned. "Close enough. Speaking of money, what accountants do you guys use for the pack businesses? Is it Crane?"

His expression darkened. "He's the only choice, so yes."

"The only choice?" Olmeda wasn't that small. There had to be other accountants, even if they were unaware of the paranormal world.

"He's put everyone else out of business."

"I heard he's...unpleasant."

"He's the devil's own."

"But good at what he does?"

"Unfortunately."

That word kept popping up whenever Desmond Crane entered the conversation. I wondered if his apparent gift for accounting was the only thing separating him from sharing Vicky's grave in pack territory.

"I guess I should set up an appointment with him."

"Want me to call for you?"

"You? Why?" It didn't sound like they were friends.

"So he knows you have the pack's support and won't rip you off."

Aww. "That's so sweet, but there's no need." I had to maintain my neutral status and not show favoritism. If the paranormal population of Olmeda thought I was under the pack's protection, they might be too scared to come to me if they had any problem related to a shifter.

"Just say the word," Keith said, unperturbed by my refusal. "Now, about those yoga mats..."

I managed to extricate myself without spending money and moved on to check the bookstore Preston had visited as his last stop before driving to his hotel. Even though it wasn't operated by a paranormal—that Dru knew of—Preston had left without any purchase.

In my experience, people took longer to browse than he'd spent inside, so either he'd had a specific book or magazine in mind, or he'd met with someone. Could he have left some sort of message?

The bookstore was small and cramped full of secondhand books. Definitely the kind of store you entered intending to browse.

Very suspicious.

I ambled between two of the stuffed shelves, looking for anything out of place or any nook where one could leave a message. It was impossible. There were too many books ordered with no rhyme or reason, and even more haphazard stacks covered the floor.

For a moment, the disorder was so overwhelming that my heartbeats began to increase in pace and I felt the fabric of my T-shirt stick to my lower back under my light jacket. I suppressed a shudder and forced myself to move deeper into the shop until I reached the counter at the end. An old man sat behind a mahogany monstrosity with a cash register older than Grandma sitting on top.

He was reading *Sense and Sensibility*, which I'd have found endearing were my instincts not screaming at me to run out of here and return to my nice, dust-free, organized store.

Before I had a chance to speak, he grabbed a stick with a rubber pointing finger at the end and directed it toward a piece of paper stapled to the wall.

"One for .50, three for a dollar," I read aloud. "Really? That's cheap."

He harrumphed.

"I was wondering if you remember a man coming in yesterday? Tall, dressed in a striped dark blue suit."

The stick rose again, and for a moment I thought he was going to smack me with it, but at the last second, it pointed toward the wall again.

"If I buy three books, will you answer?"

"Not likely," he muttered.

"Six?"

"What about the entire store, so I can finally retire in peace?"

That seemed a bit extreme, so I politely refused his generous offer. "Mind if I leave some business cards for my tea shop in here?"

"Yes."

One had to try.

I thanked him and escaped the confined, dusty atmosphere of the shop.

"You over there!" someone shouted. "The one with the green hair."

Turning around, I saw a man advancing toward me with fast, angry strides. His cheeks were flushed and his eyes glittered with unholy rage.

"Do I know you?" I asked once he was within non-yelling distance.

People began giving us a wide circle. A couple stopped under an awning and brought out their phones, ready to become viral.

"Cut the crap, Avery," the man said.

Apparently, he knew me. "Uhm...?"

"What's this I'm hearing about you trying to undercut my haunted house business?"

Ooh. This must be Jim, the human who ran the haunted houses during Halloween. Vicky had complained about him for hours for not giving her the juiciest bits to play last year. If you ask me, the man should be thanking me for giving Vicky a bigger target than him to focus her dark magic on, instead of yelling at me in the middle of the street.

"I'm not trying to undercut your haunted houses."

"Oh, yeah? Then why are people telling me Cavalier is organizing his own haunted attraction and is going to steal my workers?"

Oh, boy, Ian was going to love that one.

On the other hand, if the city was convinced the haunted tours were as good as done, wouldn't that help my chances of convincing him to do them? A little one hundred percent organic, victimless guaranteed, carefully applied peer pressure never hurt anyone.

"He's not going to organize a full-on haunted house," I said. "But we're hoping he might open the cemetery for special tours."

"And who's going to work those tours, huh? Who is going to perform as the ghosts walking around? Who's going to be in charge that drunken idiots don't veer off course? Who will take care of the tickets? Who will do the research and planning and write the script? Who's going to be in charge of controlling the lights and the fake smoke?"

That...was a lot of things I hadn't thought about. Would he mind repeating himself so I could make a list, I wondered. "He won't poach your people, I promise."

"You're not Cavalier!"

"But you came to me, right? He'll only use any of your workers if you have to turn people away. Think about it—you won't have anyone complaining that they didn't get a job this year if you can send them to Cavalier."

His eyes narrowed. "What's stopping him from offering better pay and my guys going to him first for a job, *then* coming to me if they don't get it?"

"Yearly taxes on a city block of property?"

Jim appeared slightly mollified, so I pressed my advantage. "Think about it. It'll be an opportunity for cross-promotion."

"How?"

"It wouldn't be that long of a tour. He can send everyone to your houses once they're done with the tour and are thirsty for more jump scares, and you can send your overflow to the cemetery so people don't get bored and leave bad reviews."

"The lines are a headache," Jim admitted.

"See? Perfect!"

"And you're sure he won't try to steal anyone?"

"I'm sure." What had he said? People to play ghosts, tickets, to keep guests in line, and what else? Ah, yes, smoke machine and lights. We probably didn't need the machine or the ghosts, especially if Shane and Alex played Garreth the Hound. Would Dru be willing to help with some of the tasks? I didn't see her giving a tour or waiting patiently to yell at drunk tourists to get back into the marked path, though.

"Are you listening?" Jim demanded.

No, not really, I realized. "Sorry, what?"

"I said," he enunciated as if I'd just learned English yesterday, "that if I find out Cavalier is messing with me, I'll make sure of paying *you* a visit."

"Why me?" Now that I thought of it, why was he approaching *me* instead of Ian?

"You heard me," Jim said with grim finality, then spun around and stalked away.

It seemed Ian's reputation had grown among the human side of Olmeda as well as the paranormal one. Lucky, lucky man.

The encounter had scattered my thoughts, so I went to check my suspects' to-do list and refresh my memory when I noticed I'd received a new text.

Heard you were looking for deliveries.

I frowned at the message and checked the sender. I didn't recognize the number.

What kind of deliveries? I wrote back, clamping down the

immediate knee-jerk reaction of telling whoever it was that no, *I* made the deliveries.

Mess up once, shame on a passionate nature and the love for one's Grandma. Mess up twice, time to retake meditation.

After waiting for a few minutes, I cut my losses and went back to the shop. I'd decide who to approach next in a more productive environment than the middle of the street.

The reply arrived when I was halfway home.

The special kind. Willing to lose this one for the correct price.

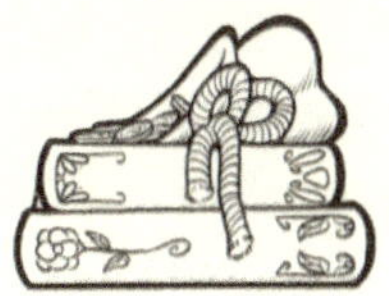

Special kind was obviously magic. Anonymous sender meant dark magic. But why would anyone lose a delivery for a price?

The answer smacked me in the face as I opened the Tea Cauldron's front door.

Whoever this person was must be the dark magic delivery guy I'd been looking for two weeks ago but hadn't been able to find. They must've heard of my interest and now wanted to earn some extra money by offering to lose this new delivery. As the local dark witch, it stood to reason I wouldn't want out-of-town dark magic dealers reaching potential clients.

Any entrepreneur worth their salt would see this as an excellent opportunity for profit. A local dark magic businessperson helping another dark magic businessperson, for a fee.

The shop was busy, so I didn't have the chance to tell Dru about my inquiries and the text until much later.

Using a lull between customers, I resumed hanging up the Halloween decorations.

"It's gotta be the bastard," Dru said, handing me some more tape to fix an orange-and-black garland to the top of the window. "He probably ordered some kind of potion to poison everyone who's against him buying the Corner Rose."

"You might be overthinking things," I said. I jumped off the windowsill and observed my work. "What do you think?"

"You have to take the offer so we can set up a trap."

I gestured toward the garland and the other pumpkin and witch silhouettes taped to the window. No spiders for me. I shuddered. Fake webs were as far as I was willing to go. "I mean, about the decorations."

"Very pretty. Now, answer that text."

I dragged the box of decorations to the other window. "How do you propose we set up a trap?"

My phone rang, and I checked the caller ID. "Oh, hold on. It's Crane. I left a message earlier." I hurried to accept the call. "Hope Avery speaking."

"Is this—" A female voice cleared her throat. "This is Desmond Crane's office calling back about a consultation appointment."

"Yes?" I asked eagerly, glancing at Dru. She was checking her own phone, a miffed expression on her face. I hadn't shared my hopes about Bagley's money with her yet, cautious for a change. To give her hope, then take it away if I couldn't find the account or access it? Now, that was cruelty beyond words.

"We have an opening tomorrow morning."

"That'd be perfect, thank you."

"Ten-thirty. There are directions on our webpage."

Crane's assistant hung up, and I resumed my decoration work.

"You're going to work with him?" Dru asked, doubtful.

"Everyone uses him."

"He's annoying."

"So I heard."

"We can use Ian."

I paused mid-taping another cardboard pumpkin. "As an accountant?"

Dru let out an exasperated sound. "For the trap. He's still a bounty hunter. If we"—she finger quoted—"hire him to catch whoever is buying the dark magic, he can haul Preston's ass to bounty hunter jail. Or worse." She licked her lips, and I swear her stomach growled.

Bloodthirst aside, the idea had plenty of merit. Unfortunately, it wouldn't quite work. "That will put a spotlight on me, if the bounty hunters check who put in the petition. I can't risk them taking notice of me or the shop."

"We can set it up as an anonymous tip."

"Whoever Ian catches will start naming names to get out of trouble. If they catch the person delivering the potion, he'll know it was me who blabbed and will serve my head on a silver platter."

"Hmm." Dru pursed her lips. Today they were painted black, like her mood. Should I suggest she use the shop's official black T-shirt uniform to complete the look?

Did I want to live?

After weighing *logo T-shirt* against *continued existence* on my inner priorities scale, I decided to stay silent on the matter.

"The plan needs work," she admitted in a mutter. "But you should answer the text, anyway. What if they give the offer to someone else?"

"There's no other local dark witch." Hopefully. The thought of another undercover evil witch slinking around Olmeda waiting for her time to shine made me break out in a sweat.

A mother and a kid stopped by the other window, the kid pointing up at the decorations with enormous, awed eyes. The mother asked the little girl something, and the kid nodded. They approached the front door.

Dru fixed me with a glare. "We'll revisit this later."

She retreated behind the counter as the mother and kid entered the shop.

"Muffin," the girl exclaimed, pointing at the glass display.

The mother smiled at us. "Hi, could we have some green tea, a glass of water and a muffin?"

"Muffin!" the girl repeated, all eager delight.

Dru rearranged her expression into a rare, genuine smile. The sight was a balm to the soul—it was good to have evidence she was not all hard edges.

"Sure, honey. Chocolate, plain, or banana?"

The girl's forehead scrunched up in deep concentration. "Chocolate!"

Dru dealt with their order while I continued decorating the second window. The whole time, I sensed the kid's fixed stare on my back, and it made want to try harder.

Turning toward her and her mother, who had moved to the table by the shelf, I held up a pumpkin and a witch hat silhouettes. "Pumpkin or witch?"

"Witch!"

I grinned at her enthusiasm and taped the black cardboard to the window. "You like Halloween?"

"Yes!"

My phone vibrated, and the caller made my grin broaden.

"Hi, Ian," I said.

"Did the person call again?"

"Not yet," I replied cheerfully.

"You sound happy. What are you doing?"

"Talking about Halloween."

He immediately hung up.

I laughed.

The next morning, I arrived at my appointment with Desmond Crane fifteen minutes early. He sounded like the kind of guy to slam the door in your face if you were one second late, so it paid to be prompt.

His offices were near Balton Square, part of a renovated old building with a real estate firm occupying the first floor. The small reception area was clean and accessorized in warm beiges and off-whites. It reminded me of a doctor's office rather than an accountant's.

Not that I had much to compare it with, having never needed an accountant before now.

To my surprise, I was ushered into his office at ten thirty on the dot. I'd expected to be left hanging around for ten to twenty extra minutes as a show of power. A kind of *I'm the only paranormal accountant in town, so what you gonna do, huh?*

Desmond Crane was a short, stocky guy wearing a cream-colored suit and a severe expression on his wide face. He rose to give my hand the fastest, jerkiest shake in the world, then immediately grabbed a wet wipe and wiped his fingers.

I wanted to point out that if he simply didn't offer to shake hands, he'd save a lot of money in wipes, but I kept my mouth shut. Maybe he was making a point.

"What can I do for you?" he asked in a curt tone that told me he had better things to do than stand here at his place of work and interact with his clients.

"As you know, I've taken over Ms. Bagley's shop."

"Everyone knows that, yes."

"I understand you were her accountant?"

"I'm everyone's accountant."

Not mine. Again, I kept my mouth shut. Except Crane simply stared at me, growing irritated at the lack of words coming out of my mouth, so I opened it again.

"I was wondering if I could have her bank information? There seems to be a discrepancy."

"Are you a family member?"

For a second, I genuinely considered lying and saying I was. It'd make things so much easier for everyone involved, including me. Ultimately, though, this man could probably see through any fake identification I had Key's guy make. "No. But the accounts involving the business are of importance to the Council and the continuing business of the shop, and if she funneled any of the profits toward any private account, that falls under the purview of... Of..." I raked my brain, searching for any other official-sounding words to add to my diatribe. "Of me as the new owner of the Tea Cauldron."

There. Perfect. My chest puffed up with pride.

"Have the Council contact me with a court order. My client's information is private."

"But Ms. Bagley's dead."

"And you are not her next of kin."

My gaze drifted to the rest of his office. No filing cabinets full of folders I could search, no tantalizing hints of boxes chock-full of account details. The room was small, immaculate, and with nothing but an open shelf, the desk and chairs, and a few framed diplomas on the wall.

In short, nothing that warranted a possible break-in and search. Maybe they kept the paper files in another room?

It wasn't as if the Council would pressure Crane without proof, and the only thing I got was that all my dark magic clients were paying somewhere, and that somewhere wasn't my bank.

Not the kind of thing the Council would approve of.

"Are you taking on new clients?" I asked.

"Personal or business?"

Was that a trick question? "Business. For the Tea

Cauldron."

"April will take care of the details. She will send you an email with the contract and our banking details."

"I'd like to see the terms first."

He fixed me with a stern look. "We have a standard, non-negotiable contract. If you don't like it, find someone else." The *and good luck with that* was implied.

"And your fees?" I ventured.

"Detailed on our website."

"Could you, uh, remind me?"

He took a business card from the top of a stack and pushed it my way. "Website."

Well, this was going great.

"Do you like books?" I asked, noticing the old leather-bound tomes on the shelves.

"Books?"

"Old tomes, spellbooks." I made a vague gesture with my hand. "That kind of thing."

"I'm an accountant, Miss Avery, not a witch."

I studied his reaction closely. "No need to practice what's inside to collect them."

"You have ten minutes left in your one-hundred-fifty dollars consultation," he warned in chilling tones. "Is there anything else *business related* you'd like to ask me?"

I tried not to choke at the price. If that was an example of his fees, no wonder everyone disliked the man. "Was Bagley a client of yours for long?"

Crane opened the laptop on the desk, and for a moment, I thought he might be checking on something. But when he simply ignored me and kept typing, I realized he was simply multitasking on my dime.

"Surely you can answer that much?" I asked, beginning to sweat.

He kept his mouth shut and simply waited me out, the contents of my bank account ticking down reflected on his eyes like a doomsday clock.

"Do you recommend I file any side income with the main shop's business or that I open another entity for those?" Whatever advice he gave me would be the same advice he'd given Bagley. It might help narrow the possibilities.

"Depends on the income. Please talk to April if you wish to use us for your personal filings as well as the shop's."

"It's a different contract?"

"Yes."

With a whole other set of fees, no doubt. "Is there anything special I should keep track of?"

"April will send you a list of documents."

April better be getting paid well. In fact...

I stood and smiled brightly. "I guess this is all I needed to ask today."

"Good to do business with you, Miss Avery." Standing, he offered me his hand.

With anyone else, I'd have saved him the trouble of wasting wipes, but now that I knew he could afford them... I shook his hand and placed my other on top of his for maximum coverage.

He narrowed his eyes and tried to shake me off. I held on for a few seconds, then allowed him freedom.

I heard him mutter a few obscenities as I turned and made my way to the door. Outside in the reception area, the woman behind the desk looked up with curiosity.

"Hi," I said in my friendliest tone. "Mr. Crane said you could send me the contract to my email address?"

"Yes, of course. What's your email?"

I gave it to her and watched her enter it on her keyboard. "Say, did Ms. Bagley ever come to the offices? The old owner of the magic tea shop?"

April pushed her glasses up her nose. "Oh, no. They corresponded by email. We have a very robust online system for our clients," she assured me.

Did Ian know any hackers among his bounty hunter buddies? Something worth looking into. "That sounds lovely. Say..." I leaned in closer. "You see that new guy in town around? The one who wants to buy the Corner Rose."

She glanced at Crane's door. "Oh, yes. He came by last week for a consultation."

My heart almost stopped. "Consultation? He hasn't bought the shop yet, has he?" Were we too late?

"Oh, no. I don't think so. He asked me if Mr. Crane ever goes to the PBOA meetings or if he sends me."

"What's your take on him? Preston, I mean. I'm a little concerned, since I might end up being his neighbor."

She frowned deeply, as if recalling the encounter. "He was very polite. Very charming."

I'd keep that last part for myself when I reported my discoveries to Dru. "Did he ask for the contract, too?"

"Oh, no, not yet. He said he'd be in contact."

That made me relax slightly. Preston was obviously still fishing for support and not in actual business talks. I paid for the consultation, thanked April, and hurried back to the shop.

I was unlocking the front door when the man himself made an appearance, as if he'd been waiting for me to show up. For Dru's sake, I hoped he'd been waiting a long time.

"Miss Avery?" Preston asked in a smooth-as-silk tone. "I'm Elijah Preston. Could I have a word?"

I had two options. I could stay self-righteous and kick him out or try to squeeze his plans out of him through a careful application of sugar, honey, and witchy charm.

Years of working in the service industry made the decision for me. I pasted on a fake smile and invited him in. Hopefully,

Dru would see this like the age-old strategy it was rather than a complete and total betrayal.

He followed me inside and sat on Bagley while I pulled up the blinds and flipped the shop sign to open.

"This is cozy," he said with genuine approval in his voice.

Hah! Genuine. As if. "Thank *youuu*." There was an art in elongating that *you* without sounding downright mocking, and I was nothing if not an artist. "Would you like something to drink? The day's special?"

He studied the blackboard on the shelf. "Rooibos? Sounds delightful."

I went around the counter and busied myself with the water urn. Once the tea had steeped in, I poured some cold water to make it lukewarm. Waiting for beverages to cool down was a true-and-tried delay tactic, and I didn't want him to stick around for that long.

"Muffin?" I asked politely.

"Can't afford it." He patted his middle section with a rueful pout, making sure I noted the way his white shirt molded to his perfectly flat stomach under his open suit jacket.

My bland smile could've made salt weep. "What brings you here, Mr. Preston?"

"I've been visiting some of the local establishments." His grin was blindingly white and proof of regular dentist visits. "I thought it was high time I visited yours, seeing as how we might be neighbors soon."

He had probably skulked around for days, waiting for the opportunity to charm me when Dru wasn't around.

"That's so sweet of you. Is the purchase final, then?"

He laughed. "Not quite yet. It seems I need to jump through a few more hoops." The curve of his mouth turned sly, and he leaned in. "But I don't see myself having much trouble clearing them."

So, this visit was a warning more than an attempt to charm me. Or perhaps two for the price of one. "I see. I suppose I had it easy myself, being a Council witch and all. Witch shops are too important to depend on other people's approval."

He sipped his tea to hide his reaction to the huge, completely amazing ball I'd served his way. Dru would be proud. Grandma, perhaps not so much. Bagley would probably rate my performance later and find it lacking dark magic.

"Of course," Preston said, putting his glass down. No cute mugs for him. Plus, I happened to know Bagley had haunted that particular glass not long ago. Dru would most definitely approve. If she knew that Bagley haunted the shop.

I really should tell her at some point.

"Witch shops are an integral part of the community," he continued. "Setting up Tabbies right next to one would be a great honor."

"Do you practice magic yourself?" I asked matter-of-factly.

"Oh, nothing as important as what you do here," he said with some humor.

My gaze sharpened. "With the right spellbook, any spirit mage can do a lot of good."

"Books were never my thing."

And a million gasps were heard around the world. "Could I interest you in some starting titles?" I gestured toward the bookshelf in the corner, never taking my eyes off his face.

He gave it a cursory glance, then returned his megawatt smile to me. "Maybe another time."

The mention of spellbooks hadn't provoked any kind of reaction or acknowledgment of his evil deeds. Dru wasn't going to like that. But then, the man had to be a fantastic actor to fool Dru into entering into a relationship with him just to get closer to her family.

Preston took a few big gulps of his tea, then put the glass

down. "Tasty," he said as he stood. "But now I should get going. Do you mind if I come around later this week for another chat?"

"Go ahead," I said, sugary sweet. "I'd love to get to know you better."

Too thick? Nah. The man was probably used to people stumbling over themselves to get on his good side and his dating app.

"Wonderful. I'll see you then."

Not a minute after he'd paid and left, Dru entered the shop.

The timing was so perfect, I wondered if he'd somehow put a tracking app on Dru's phone.

"Preston was just here," I said before she learned it from one of her many contacts in the paranormal community.

"I know," she snapped. "What did he want?"

"Checking out the competition, I think."

"Did he ask about the spellbook?"

"No. I brought up spellbooks, but he didn't blink an eye."

Dru began pacing. "We need more information to take to the POBA if we want to stop him from getting the shop."

"I agree."

The door opened, and chimes filled the air. A man entered the shop, and I did a double-take. There was something odd about his face, and I couldn't fully register his features. A glamour potion?

He bolted the lock and flipped the sign to closed.

"Uh, excuse me..."

The man turned and brought a gun from inside his bomber jacket. He gestured toward the archway.

"You two, get into the back. Now."

Oh, good Mother Earth. We were getting robbed!

11

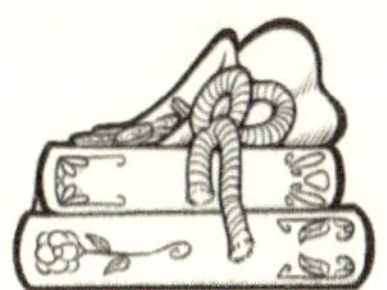

Dru and I exchanged glances.

"I *will* shoot you," the man warned in a low voice. "Move."

We filed obediently out of the shop into the back hallway. My gaze darted around, looking for anything I could use to defend us. Could I move fast enough to grab the broom out of the closet? But what good would that do against a gun? I believed the man's threat—with a glamour potion that strong, he could shoot and waltz out of here. No camera would record a sharp image of him, and nobody could give a description of his face.

Dark magic glamour for sure.

And as usual when I ended up in these kinds of situations, my freezing potion was upstairs in my nightstand. Maybe it was time to invest in a can of pepper spray.

Ahead of me, Dru clenched and unclenched her hands, a bit of pointed nail showing through. She nodded toward the kitchen. No need for her to tell me she was going to make a go for it once we were in close quarters.

She slipped inside and disappeared from view, flattening herself against the wall by the door.

The man let out a heavy sigh and pressed the barrel of the gun against the back of my head. A chill ran down my spine. I had failed to move fast enough, and my magic was all but worthless against a piece of metal—I needed flesh-to-flesh contact.

"Nice try," the man said. "Make a move and the witch's gone. Get to the other end of the kitchen, demon."

Dru cursed and did as he asked. The man shoved me inside, and I stumbled forward to end up next to her.

I expected him to close the door and lock us up, but he followed us inside the kitchen.

"The cash is all in the shop," I said tentatively.

"I don't care." His gun moved toward the counter. Dru tensed, ready to leap, but the gun returned toward us in the next second. "Put your phones over there."

We placed our phones on the counter.

"Push them into the sink," he pressed.

I pushed the devices until they clanked into the metal sink.

"Tie the demon up."

"I don't have any rope," I said.

The man dug into the pocket of his jacket and tossed me a ziptie. "Use that. *No* magic."

Yeah, right. Even as I moved behind Dru, I awakened my magic. If I made a spell weak enough to pass undetected—not an impressive feat, given my power level—he would never know. Even the weakest of spells might give us the upper hand down the road. But what could be useful in this situation? Without herbs or moon water, my options were limited, and I had to act fast.

"Turn around so I can see," the man snapped.

Dru turned around, and I put the ziptie around her wrists.

"Make it tight."

Or course. I called on my magic, trying to keep it down to the barest of murmurs.

Let this *tie*—

"I said, *no magic*," the man exclaimed, shoving me aside. He checked on the ziptie, then pushed Dru down. "Sit down."

Dru snarled, but sat on the tiled floor.

The man retreated a few steps.

"Now, witch," he said, "bring me the spellbook, or the demon dies."

I froze. "The spellbook?"

"And no tricks. I'll know if it's fake."

A lump formed in my throat. Of all the things I had expected, this wasn't it.

"What are you waiting for?" he snapped.

"I don't have it with me," I lied, trying to hide my wobbling lip.

"Liar. Witches always do. Bring it, or I'm shooting a different part of your friend every fifteen seconds."

Dru's attention was fixed on the man, her eyes sharp, missing nothing, waiting for the opportunity to strike. But guns could do a lot of damage very easily, even to a demon in her full form. No spellbook was worth Dru's life.

"Fourteen. Thirteen."

"I'll bring it," I squeaked, dashing out of the kitchen.

Now I had a chance to get the freezing potion.

I burst into my room and snatched Grandma's spellbook from the dresser and the potion from the nightstand. Unfortunately, I didn't have a landline phone upstairs, so no chance to call Ian for help.

Pulse hammering in my ears, I returned downstairs and made my way silently to the kitchen. The man had retreated out of view, which meant I'd lose precious time peeking in and aiming the freezing potion.

I approached the door at an angle until I could see Dru. She was still focused on the man. Mentally crossing my fingers, I popped into the room and threw the potion in the direction of her gaze.

He ducked, and the bottle flew by his side, barely missing him. The thin glass broke on impact and froze half my kitchen wall.

Dru shot to her feet and made to rush him, but he recuperated fast and aimed the gun at her face.

"Stop."

Dru stopped mere inches away from the barrel of the gun.

"Back to the corner."

She did as he told her, her movements jerky and angry, outrage simmering in her eyes, and I hoped that was directed at our robber, not my lack of aim.

"Where's the spellbook?" the man asked.

I brought it up. "Here."

"Put it there, then go to your friend." He indicated the counter by the sink.

I placed the spellbook where he'd pointed, feeling tears well up at the sight. Grandma's spellbook had been my lifeline whenever I felt lonely, empty, or close to giving up on our dream. It had reminded me of her goodness, that good things must exist in the world, and that wishes couldn't come true unless you sought them out.

What was I going to do without it?

"Move back," the man ordered in irritation.

I did, but my fingers lingered on the worn green fabric cover with its beautiful embroidered flowers.

The man grabbed my shoulder and tore me away, sending me stumbling backward. On unsteady feet, I joined Dru and peeked down at her bound wrists. She had her claws out and was trying to reach the plastic tie to rip it apart.

Focus, Hope. Grandma would've given up her spellbook a thousand times over to save someone. Her spirit remains with you, in your heart and in your magic, not with a handful of papers glued together.

I would mourn the loss of the spellbook later.

No, I told myself with sudden resolve. There would be no mourning. I would figure out how to track this bastard down and get Grandma's spellbook back.

The thought wiped away the burning in my eyes and settled my churning stomach into deadly calm. This guy had no idea of what was in store once he left this room.

Unaware of my silent vow of revenge, the man kept his gun trained in our direction while flickering his gaze down to the spellbook. He opened it and flipped through some of the pages.

"What is this? A joke?" he demanded, returning his full attention to us. "I said to bring the spellbook. Hazel Oakes's spellbook."

I swallowed at the anger in his voice. "That's her spellbook."

"Stop trying to mess with me."

"But that is Grandma's spellbook."

"This is not the spellbook," he barked. "Bring it *now.*"

At my shocked blank stare, he moved the gun back to Dru. "Twelve."

"But..."

"Eleven. Ten."

"That's the only spellbook I have!"

He narrowed his eyes. "*Nine.*"

I moved in front of Dru. No way I was letting her get hurt because of me. "I'm serious. I don't have any other spellbook."

"Hope, move," Dru whispered behind me.

Like hell.

I heard her shuffle on the floor, and the man's gun moved slightly. I summoned my magic. I wasn't sure of what I could possibly do with it, but I would do it. No Hazel-Oakes witch was going down without trying.

"*Eight.*"

A thick black shadow shot out of the faucet. A giant tentacle smacked the man right on the head, sending him flying into the opposite wall. The gun went flying. The man hit the brick temple-first with a loud thwack, then crumpled down to the floor, unconscious.

A deadly silence gripped the kitchen.

My mouth fell open, my gaze going from the man to the dark tentacle slithering back into the faucet, back and forth, back and forth, like a grand prize was on the line.

"Holy shit." Dru choked out. "Is that a *tentacle*?"

"Goldfish ghost?" I asked in a weak voice. "Is that you?"

The tentacle stopped its retreat, its blunt end hooking onto the edge of the sink.

Swallowing hard, I moved closer. It seemed to be waiting for me to say something. For a tentacle, it appeared suddenly...shy.

I patted it awkwardly. "Thank you, goldfi—uh, kraken ghost."

The tentacle vibrated at my touch, then snapped back into the pipes. Gurgling noises of happiness reverberated behind the wall.

"You have an octopus living in your pipes?" Dru asked, her voice shrill.

"I...I thought it was a goldfish's ghost."

"*Why would you have a goldfish's ghost in your pipes?*"

"It's... It's a long story." I stared at the sink for a few blank moments, my heart ricocheting inside my chest, then something inside me snapped into action. I grabbed one of my cutting knives from the cutlery drawer and hurried to Dru's side. Crouching behind her, I began working on the ziptie.

"Explain. *Now*," she demanded, sounding a lot more like herself.

Thank the Mother.

I told her about the ghost in the bathtub, not caring she'd already heard this part, then about Bagley coming back to haunt the shop, and the noises in the pipes, and the small hints of shadow I'd seen come out of the faucet ever since I'd done the spell.

The moment her hands were free, Dru shot to her feet, rubbing her wrists. She snatched the gun off the floor, checked the safety, and slipped it into the waist of her jeans. Then she gave the man a kick in the side and rounded on me.

"Bagley's been a ghost in the shop this whole time?" she whispered. "And you didn't tell me?"

I looked at the man, alarmed. "Uh..."

"What?" She kicked him again. For good measure, I expect.

"Nothing."

"Why didn't you tell me there is a dark magic witch haunting the shop?" She hunched, looking around. "Is she here?"

"No, she can't go beyond the first room."

And maybe I should've lied because her glower returned to me, upped by about a thousand. "Explain yourself. Why didn't you tell me?"

I smiled weakly. "It didn't come up in conversation?"

Her hands went to her hips. "Try again."

"I was going to tell you, but Bagley's always quiet when people are around, and I didn't want her to bug you if she discovered you knew of her existence."

Dru huffed. "Sure, Hope." She pointed at me with a finger. "This conversation is not over. *Don't*," she added in warning as I took on a kicked puppy expression.

"Sorry," I mumbled, rearranging my features back to normal. "What do we do with him?" I gestured at the man.

"Tie him up."

"Do you think he needs medical attention?" I'd read if you fell unconscious from a hit to the head, you likely had a concussion.

Dru kicked him again. Gleefully. "Does it look like I care?"

Fair. I rummaged through the cupboards for some packing rope, then tied his hands tight behind his back. At least he wasn't bleeding all over my kitchen floor. That was good.

Blood is hard to wash off grout.

Dru cut some more rope and got to work on tying up his ankles. I left her to that task and retrieved my phone from the sink.

Time to call for reinforcements.

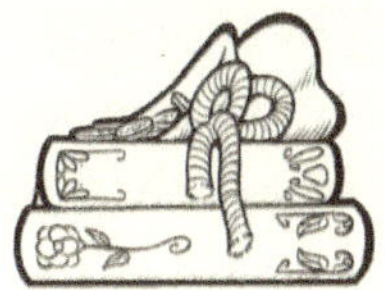

12

IAN PICKED up after a few rings.

"Hello, Hope."

His voice was warm and a little sinful and made my toes curl and wish I was calling for any other reason other than…

"Hi, Ian. Someone tried to rob us at the shop. Well, me."

"What?" he snapped, all warmth gone. "Are you okay?"

"Oh, yes, we're good." I glanced down at the man, still unconscious. "We got the robber all tied up. What should we do with him?"

Dru mouthed *backyard*.

I covered the phone and whispered, "We're *not* burying him in my backyard." This murder house had enough ghosts as it was.

"Hold on," Ian said.

I heard him walk down a hallway and Fluffy's excited barks. Ah, I'd caught him home. A few moments later, the door of a car slammed shut, and a motor started.

"I'm on my way. Tell me exactly what happened."

"A man using a dark magic glamour came into the shop and tried to take Grandma's spellbook at gunpoint."

"At gunpoint?" He didn't sound shocked so much as wanting to make sure he had the facts straight.

"Yes. He made me tie Dru up and go get my spellbook."

"Go on." Loud honking sounded in the background. Rufus gave one of his rare, deep barks.

"Drive carefully," I said fretfully. Which was weird because I never fretted. I stared at problems right in the eye and refused to let them overtake me. A strangled giggle made it out of my chest. "I'm sorry. Adrenaline crash."

"Concentrate on the facts. The man made you get your spellbook. What happened next?"

Facts. Yes. That's right. I inhaled deeply. "I brought him Grandma's spellbook, and he said it was the wrong spellbook." The reminder of the scene made me snatch the spellbook up and hug it tightly to my chest.

I'd been so close to losing it. To losing Grandma.

So close.

Now I wanted to weep instead of giggle.

"How did he know it was the wrong spellbook?" Ian asked.

"Someone must've given him a description. He flipped through some of the pages and told me to get the real spellbook."

"And then what happened? Did you use your magic on him?"

"Oh, that's right! When I went up to get Grandma's spell-book, I grabbed my freezing potion," I said proudly.

Dru snorted. "And then you missed."

"He ducked! It wasn't my fault."

"I see," Ian said. "So that didn't work. Did you use your magic then? Or did Dru get free? Is that how you overpowered him? Do I need to tell Shane and Alex to bring the cleaning supplies?"

"No, no. The man threatened to shoot Dru if I didn't give

him the correct spellbook, then a tentacle shot out of the faucet and smacked him against the wall."

A long silence ensued. Dru rolled her eyes and shook her head but took a step away from the sink.

"A tentacle shot out of the faucet and smacked the man against the wall?" Ian repeated, as if he wanted to get the facts straight but was afraid he'd heard correctly the first time.

"Remember my goldfish ghost? Turns out it's a kraken."

"A kraken," Ian repeated flatly.

"It's an octopus," Dru snapped. "You have an *octopus* haunting your pipes."

"It saved our butts," I told her. "It gets to be a kraken."

"I'm going to need God's help at this rate to stop myself from strangling you. Are there any other ghosts hanging around? Spider in the attic?"

"I don't have an attic."

"Are you sure? Maybe it's a ghostly one."

"I'm sorry I didn't tell you about Bagley," I said, contrite. "I thought it was for the best."

"It was," Ian said on the call.

I showed the phone to Dru triumphantly. "Ian agrees."

"Cavalier doesn't have to work here. He doesn't get a say."

"Fair." I returned the phone to my ear. "By the way, Dru has the man's gun, so be careful with what you say."

Ian humphed. Dru looked like she wanted to slug me with said gun.

"I'm almost there," he said and cut the call.

I pocketed the phone. "He's almost here."

"You didn't need to call him." Dru poked the man with her foot. "We could've gotten rid of him by ourselves."

"How?"

Dru's gaze drifted toward the window into the backyard.

"Don't start."

"What? Key said there's nobody buried there. Plenty of space."

"He's not even dead!" *Wait...* "Is he?"

We both glanced down.

"We should probably check," I said.

"Sure. You go ahead."

I returned the spellbook to the counter and crouched by the man's head, pressing two tentative fingers to his throat. I couldn't feel a pulse, given I had no idea of where to check for that, but his skin felt normal and warm.

"I think he's alive."

"Too bad."

Dru did have a way to keep her grudges going. Grandma was a big believer in forgiveness, and so was I, but one had to admire Dru for sticking to her convictions.

Clanging against the backyard gate announced Ian's arrival. I hurried to let him and the dogs in.

"He's in the kitchen," I told him, grabbing Fluffy and hugging her tight for a good dose of her cleansing wonderfulness.

He told the dogs to stay and walked into the building without another word. I put Fluffy down and hurried to follow. Fluffy was a ball of kinetic energy, but she was well trained. She sat by Rufus's side, tongue lolling expectantly.

"I'll introduce you to my new pet later," I told her before stepping inside. "Don't worry, though. You're still first in my heart."

Fluffy yipped in agreement.

Inside the kitchen, Ian was crouching by the man, studying him intently.

"Do you recognize him?" I asked.

"I can't see through the glamour," he said dryly. "It's a potent spell."

"Dark magic."

"Yes."

He patted the man's pockets, and I scrunched my nose. On the other side of the man, Dru made a similar face of disappointment that we hadn't thought of that earlier.

Ian found nothing in his pockets or shoes. No wallet, no hotel key, no potions, not even loose change.

"Always be prepared," I said with approval. It was all good and well to be confident in the success of your plans, but that didn't mean you shouldn't do due diligence in case things went sideways.

"He must've stashed his things somewhere else before coming in," Ian agreed.

"We could use Rufus to track where he's been."

Ian got to his feet. "A glamour potion this strong masks everything about you, not just your face. There won't be a smell for Rufus to follow."

Ian's shifter nature enhanced his senses in human form, even olfactory ones, so I had no trouble believing him.

"No wonder we couldn't get anything from the envelope," I murmured unhappily.

"You think he sent the envelope?" Ian asked.

I blinked in surprise. "It has to be. There can't be two different people looking for Grandma's spellbook."

"In my experience, people who send notes and make polite phone calls aren't the same kind of people who do robberies in broad daylight."

"You think it's two people working together?"

Dru coughed a *the bastard*.

"I'd rather not assume," he said. "Where's the spellbook?"

I pointed at the counter. "Over there."

Ian picked up the spellbook and examined the front and back covers, handling it with the utmost care. To anyone else, it was a book, not even that beautiful or old, but seeing him treat it like a museum antique made me choke up all over again.

He put it down and opened the cover to investigate the interior, then he tensed, his eyes widening for a nanosecond.

"What is it?" I asked.

"Your grandma was Hazel Oakes?"

"Yes. Why?"

He flipped the pages but said nothing, as if he was buying himself some time to organize his thoughts.

"What is it?" I pressed. "Why did you flinch?"

His features took on the stonelike quality I was so familiar with. "I need to show you something."

The robbery had shocked me, the threats to Dru panicked me, but the mix of his expression and those words? That chilled me to the bone.

"What's wrong? Tell me."

"Not here."

I glanced at Dru. The urge to see whatever had made Ian turn into cold stone was nearly overwhelming, but best friends came first. "We can't leave Dru alone here with him. What if he has friends?"

Dru's mouth twisted in a grimace of displeasure, as if it hadn't occurred to her until now that someone might come to help the man and she wasn't thanking me for putting the idea in her head.

"I'll take care of it," Ian said. He made a quick call. "It'll be a few minutes. You're keeping the gun?" he asked Dru.

She crossed her arms. "Sure am."

Ian nodded, and I was again surprised by the matter-of-fact quality of his decisions. Dru had the gun; Dru got to keep the gun. It was of no interest to him.

You had to admire a guy who respected the right to finders keepers.

I moved closer to where he stood by the spellbook until we were almost touching.

"Thanks for coming," I whispered, pressing my arm to his.

"If you guys start making out, I will shoot you," Dru said from the other side of the small room. "Hey, does Ian know about your ghosts?"

If he hadn't, he did now. I sent Dru a look of warning.

She shrugged. "Just checking."

More like payback. Ah, well. I deserved it.

"Yes," Ian said.

"All of them?"

"Yes," he repeated.

Dru appeared less than impressed. "You told your boyfriend before you told me, the person who actually works here?"

"It was his grave dirt that started everything," I pointed out.

Her lips curled. "Please."

"Bagley's playing a game," Ian said, unbothered by the fact that Dru had probably just added me to her list of grudges, and it'd take me a few lifetimes to dig my way out of it. "She would've never revealed herself to you because you're a demon, not a witch, and she knows you're too smart to believe in her lies."

I snapped straight. "Hey, now."

Dru flashed me an evil grin. "No, please. Continue."

Ian rubbed his chin. "That's all there is to it. You're not a witch and not likely to help her find one to continue her plans, so while you are of no use to her, part of her might wonder if you know of her existence and are faking it or not. It's good to keep her busy with small guessing games like that rather than the big picture."

"She has plans?" Dru asked, a little aghast. "What kind of plans?"

"She wants a new body," I said.

Dru shivered. "Creepy."

"Yes."

We fell silent, and the longer we waited, the more I worried Ian had called the strays to help out. As much as Shane and Alex had proven themselves with Vicky and Mr. Lewis, it wasn't right to keep putting them in danger. This man had used a gun. If he had a friend coming to help him, they might have a gun too.

I bit my lip, about to ask Ian who he'd called, when someone clanged on the gate.

Ian went to open it and returned with a familiar figure.

"You!" I exclaimed in outrage.

The Crawler's berserker bouncer filled the kitchen's entry-way. "I'm here."

I turned to Ian. "Are you sure we can trust him? What if the man has a mage friend?"

"I kept you out of the club, didn't I?" the berserker gloated.

"Only because I didn't really try."

He strode in and loomed over me, an evil smile stretching his mouth. "Oh, *really*?"

Hmph. As if I was going to cower at this. "More powerful people than you have tried to intimidate me, big guy. Unless you want to look behind your back every day for the rest of your days, I suggest you tone it down."

His grin turned wicked. "I'd like to see you try to tone me down, witch."

My magic might not be big enough to take down a berserker of his size, but I wasn't losing this staring contest. A witch had to stand strong and claim her territory.

"This is Mark," Ian said. "He does jobs for the bounty hunters sometimes."

"Jobs the shifters and witches can't deal with on their own," Mark drawled while wriggling his eyebrows.

"Or maybe they would if you let them into your establishment," I countered.

"I don't make the rules."

"Mark will stay guard until the man regains consciousness," Ian continued as if there wasn't a duel of wills happening in front of him. "Let's go." He walked to the back door, then paused. "Or we can stay here and wait together."

"No," I said, not breaking eye contact with Mark. "I'm going."

I walked backward, bumped into the wall, then stepped into the doorway proper.

"I'll be back," I warned. "Don't mess with my stuff."

Mark lifted his hands. "Wouldn't dream of it."

I glowered at him one last time, then hurried to join Ian in the backyard.

"He's a good sort," Ian said once we were in his SUV and driving. "Helpful."

"Not to me," I muttered. I should put up a no-serkers sign on the shop's front, then invite one of his rival berserkers in. That'd teach him not to play favorites while I conducted important investigative business. "Where are we going?"

"Home."

And that's the last thing he said until we parked at the cemetery and he ushered me into his house. He had me sit on his comfortable couch and told me to wait. The living room was as cozy as always, made up in warm wooden colors and with a big fireplace dominating one wall. An astronomy book sat on the glass coffee table, and I pulled it my way.

Ian didn't talk much about hobbies, but I'd caught him staring up at the sky a few times. I wondered if he had a telescope upstairs and if that's how he spent his nights.

I wondered if his bedroom had a skylight to watch the stars as he fell asleep.

He reappeared a few moments later with a big file box in his hands, which he placed on the floor. After sitting by my side, he began rummaging through the box.

"What's that?" I asked.

"My ex-partner's files."

My brain rewound to three days earlier and my fleeting meeting with his ex-partner's son. "I thought you said you told his son you had nothing left from him. You lied to him?"

"My ex-partner had no sons."

My mouth opened and closed. "Secret baby?"

"He had no living relatives. I checked."

Weird, but I'd have to ask about that later because he finally pulled out a thin folder and handed it to me.

"What is this?" I took the folder from him.

He didn't answer. He simply sat so rigidly I'd break a finger if I tried to poke him.

Unease running down my spine, I placed the folder on my knees and opened it.

Grandma's smiling face looked back at me.

13

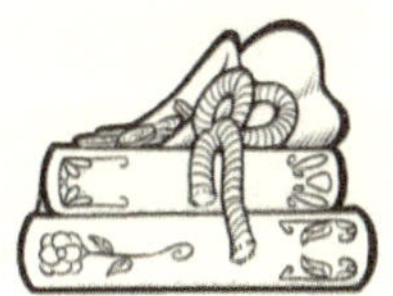

MY HEART STOPPED BEATING. For a few moments, my body reeled in confusion, unsure of what it should concentrate on. Restarting the beating of my heart? Inflating my lungs? Shocking my neurons back into continuing their job of bringing information back and forth?

Then, at least, it settled on my limbs, and with excruciating slowness, I reached out to touch the Grandma's headshot pinned to the inside of the folder's cover.

"What...?" I heard myself say in a whisper of a voice, half shock, half wonder.

All those hazy memories of Grandma took shape in sudden, stark relief, the blurred edges reforming and filling in with the image in front of my eyes. The idea of her, for so long a dimming memory, returned in full force, filling my chest with so much yearning it began to hurt in earnest.

My gaze unwillingly abandoned her image to rest on the other contents of the folder. A couple of pages and a few more photographs. I browsed through these, enthralled.

Grandma putting a grocery bag into an old blue car I'd completely forgotten about until now. Grandma coming out of a drugstore dressed in a green cardigan over a flowing black dress. Grandma talking with another woman, a big smile on her face.

I moved the photographs aside and read the first paper—a form with Grandma's name and date of birth, address, and a few other personal details. The second page contained a detailed list of Grandma's usual haunts annotated with times of visits—grocery store, drugstore, library, community center, florist, and so on. The kind of thing someone who was following someone else would make notes about.

Realization set in.

"Ian?"

"Yes." His voice was cold and hard and like he was bracing himself for something to break on it.

"Why did your ex-partner have a file on my grandma?"

"I don't know."

I glanced at him sharply. His expression was set in stone, his gaze focused ahead rather than on me or the folder on my knees.

"Grandma would never hurt anyone. Why would a bounty hunter have a file on her?" My voice increased in pitch. "Why was he following her? She wasn't a criminal. She'd never do something bad enough to get a bounty hunter involved!"

I stopped, trying to calm my breathing.

Ian looked at me then, his lips firming even more—something I would've thought impossible—before answering. "Not all people chased by bounty hunters are bad people."

Returning my attention to the folder, I flipped through the papers and the photographs, my hands shaking ever so slightly. "Why is there so little information?" I scanned the initial page again in case I'd missed something the first time around. "Why doesn't it say why he was following her?" I pointed at the box. "Is there more in there?"

Ian held me in place before I lunged for the box. "This is all there is."

"How do you know?" I demanded, trying to shake off his hold on my arm.

"I've been through all the files. Trust me, this is all there is."

"How can I trust you? You waited until now to tell me about Grandma's file!"

He flinched, and I regretted my harsh words immediately. That Ian operated on a need-to-know basis was something I'd understood from the very beginning. Being mad at him for it now was quite stupid.

And yet.

With fast movements, he retrieved Grandma's folder, put it on the table, then dumped the box of files on my lap.

"Knock yourself out."

I took him at his word and began pulling files out and checking them. By the third one, I knew he was right, but something egged me on to keep checking.

"I've read every file in that box," he said. "There's nothing else about your grandmother."

I'd have expected those words to come with an edge of pity or any sort of emotion, but his monotone voice made me abandon my box quest to study him. Ian could out-granite actual granite anytime, but even by his standards this was a bit too much. Was he nervous? Stressed? Something was off here.

I set the box aside and touched his leg. His muscles were rock solid under his black jeans. A literal marble statue.

"Why didn't you tell me?" I asked, my voice a lot softer than expected.

His features finally twisted—a slight grimace of irritation. "I didn't know your grandmother was Hazel Oakes."

Now that was almost as big a shock as the discovery of the

file. "You didn't run a background check on me when I took over the shop?"

He snorted, and something in me loosened at this show of humanity.

"Of course I ran a background check on you. Your father isn't listed on your birth certificate, and your mother never married before your stepfather. I didn't know your father's family name was Oakes."

"Oh." That made sense.

Suddenly, I couldn't take it anymore. He looked so stern and irritated at himself and guilty that I threw my arms around him and hugged him tight.

"I take it back. I do trust you."

He squeezed my arm. "Good."

Before he could do anything else, I stood and began pacing the rug on the other side of the low table.

All right, so there was a bounty hunter file on my Grandma. This couldn't stand, even if the bounty hunter in question had been dead for a while.

If he'd suspected Grandma of something, who said someone else didn't too? Maybe that's what all the spellbook business was about—someone had mistaken Grandma for a dark witch, and that's why her spellbook hadn't passed muster for our robber.

I had to clear Grandma's name. Restore her reputation.

The need burst inside me with the strength of a thousand Fluffys clamoring for attention.

"How do you learn more about old bounties?" I asked.

Ian watched me walk back and forth. "You don't."

That made me pause. "Aren't there records somewhere? Payment records? Hiring notices? We could see who paid your partner for the job and go from there."

"Yes, but it won't work for this."

"Why not? Is it because I'm a witch? They won't share information outside of bounty hunters?"

"This wasn't an official job."

"What do you mean?"

"Some bounty hunters pick up side projects."

"Like spying?" I thought of the man tied up in the shop's kitchen. "Or stealing?"

Ian wiped all expression off his face. "Stealing. Sure."

I gasped with comprehension. "You mean a hitman! They take extra jobs as hitmen. Your ex-partner was a hitman?"

Ian raked his hair with one hand, dislodging some locks from the hair tie keeping it gathered back. "Yes."

The word had come out unwilling and uncomfortable, and I wondered if it was the first time he'd admitted to it out loud. If Ian had been paired with this man right off the bat as soon as he'd joined the bounty hunters. I couldn't imagine how hard it would've been to find that your partner—your mentor for years—had turned out to be a hitman on the side.

Maybe it wouldn't have been hard for someone else, but for Ian? You could see his righteous streak from a mile away. Just look at how he'd taken care of the strays and given Key a job.

No wonder he was always so prickly when I joked about hitmen.

"Is that how he died?" I asked. "While he was acting as a hitman?"

"Yes."

The conversation was clearly making him uncomfortable, so I returned to the part that mattered.

"Why would anyone hire a hitman to go after Grandma?"

"I don't know."

Horror filled me, and judging from Ian's sudden tension, it must've shown all over my face. "Oh, no."

He tensed, ready to jump up and come to me, but I lifted a

hand to stop him. With the other, I brought out my phone and called Mom.

She picked up fast.

"Hope, honey? What is it? I'm still at work. Did something happen?"

"Mom, how did Grandma die?"

"Grandma?"

"Yes, Grandma."

"Why?" Mom sounded confused. "Is it her death's anniversary? Did I miss something?"

I stifled my impatience. Waiting for others to catch up was an opportunity to take in their feelings and respond in kind, I reminded myself. "You didn't miss anything, Mom. I just need to check on something, and I wanted to make sure I have my facts straight."

"Oh, I'm glad. Your grandmother died of a heart attack, honey." A note of pity entered her voice.

"You're sure she didn't die of something else and you didn't tell me like you didn't give me her book until I was twenty?"

"You're still mad over that? It's been six years!"

"Not mad, Mom. I just want to make sure it was a heart attack and not something worse you didn't want me to know about. I don't need to be protected from the truth."

"It was a heart attack," she said firmly.

"All right. Thanks, Mom."

"When are you going to visit?"

"It won't be for a while. I'm too busy with the shop."

"You can leave it in your assistant's hands for a weekend. The world won't end."

Mom didn't know about the probation period, and it was hard explaining it to her. In her world, either you started a business, or you worked for someone else. There was no tryout middle ground. "I'd rather wait a few more months. I'm sorry, Mom. Gotta go."

I ended the call and faced Ian. "Grandma died of a heart attack."

But my relief died as fast as a boulder trying to fly. I scowled even as he gave me a knowing look. "But if someone used dark magic to provoke one, a human doctor wouldn't know. Did your partner use dark magic?"

"*Ex*-partner. And I don't know. I only discovered these"— he gestured toward the box and the folder—"after his death."

"Why would he keep files about his illegal jobs? Anyone could find them and nail him to the wall with them."

"He was old school. He liked to keep notes."

I knelt on the rug and turned Grandma's folder my way to check the contents again. The date printed on the back of the photographs gave me pause.

"These were taken a year before her death." I poked at the numbers.

Ian leaned forward to read them, and another thought occurred to me. "Did you ever follow up on the people in the other folders?"

"Some," he said. "But there was nothing to be done. Duncan was already dead."

Duncan. It was the first time I'd heard him mention his ex-partner's name. Could I do some digging of my own without Ian knowing about it? Would Dru know anyone in the bounty hunters?

Later, though. Returning Grandma's reputation to its innate state of goodness came first.

"Someone paid him to spy on Grandma then...nothing?" I checked the page with the locations and dates. "It doesn't seem like he followed her for too long. A week at most."

"The bounty must've ended."

"Why?"

Ian shrugged. "Whoever hired him might've changed their mind. They could've hired someone else or run out of funds."

I didn't like the thought that there might be another hitman out there with Grandma's bounty. I tapped Grandma's headshot clipped to the cover. "Can I keep this?"

"You can keep it all."

As usual, Ian's straightforwardness was a shot to the heart. Of warmth this time rather than irritation. "The whole box?"

"Don't press your luck."

I grinned. "So, someone hired your ex-partner to spy on Grandma, then rescinded the job? Or maybe whoever it was simply wanted a report of Grandma's daily goings and your ex-partner gave them that? But why?" I got up and began pacing again. "Could it have something to do with this spellbook business? It seems too coincidental."

"It only seems coincidental because of the file. This happened twenty years ago. That's a long time if someone wanted your grandmother's spellbook."

I followed his train of thought. "And if someone had wanted Grandma's spellbook back then, they'd have hired your ex-partner to steal it, not to follow her around." I spun toward him. "Unless!"

"Unless?" He sounded wary, as if I was in the habit of sprouting wild theories and plans.

He should know better by now. *All* my theories and plans were sound and foolproof.

"Unless," I continued, "all this following around was prep work for the actual break-in, but the bounty got canceled before he got to do it, so he cut his losses and returned home instead of going through with it."

My experience of being around Ian in his more "professional mode" had told me that bounty hunters did the job they had been hired for with little deviance.

"That's possible," he admitted.

See? Foolproof. "But *why*? Grandma would've never practiced dark magic."

"You saw her perform magic?"

I shrugged, unwilling to admit to the haziness of most of my memories of her. "Of sorts."

"You lived full time with her?"

"Visited during some weekends." I lifted my nose at him. "I know where you're going, and it's not going to work."

He arched a brow. "Oh?"

"Grandma was too kind, too good a soul to practice dark magic while I wasn't around. I would've felt it."

"You were a kid."

"Kids sense some things better than adults."

His mouth kicked up at the corners. "All right. So, *assuming* your grandmother didn't practice dark magic, but that this is still tied up to the current spellbook business." He gave me a pointed look meant to remind me what he thought about assuming in general. "Could she have owned someone else's spellbook? Perhaps someone in her family who practiced dark magic?"

I thought of Key's grandmother's spellbook hidden in my closet. "Grandma would've destroyed it. Unless she didn't know it contained dark magic spells?"

"I doubt your grandmother was that clueless."

"Maybe she never opened it. Maybe it's one of those ornate things with a lock and she didn't have the key."

"Where did it go then, after her death? To your father?"

Excellent question. "I'll have to call Mom again to ask."

My phone rang. It was Dru.

"The thief is awake."

14

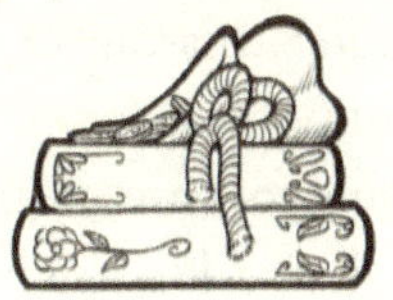

By the time we got back to the shop, Shane had joined the festivities. I wondered how he'd found out about our problem, since Ian hadn't touched his phone since we'd left earlier.

"Boss," Shane said. He was sitting on the counter by the sink, and I wondered if Dru had told him about the kraken.

Mark the berserker was leaning against the wall by the window, and Dru had brought a stool from the shop to sit in a corner. The thief sat on the floor in the other corner, still tied up and glaring at everyone with defiance.

Considering Rufus was sitting two inches away, growling in a scary rumble, I was unwillingly impressed.

Fluffy trotted up to us from the shop—someone had pulled down the blinds—and I petted her absentmindedly.

"Can you do something about that?" Mark the berserker pointed at the robber's face. "It's giving me a headache."

I rolled up my sleeves. "Sure."

"Touch me and die, witch," the robber said.

Rufus snarled.

I grabbed a spray bottle from one of the cupboards and sprayed moon water on the man's face.

"What the heck," he sputtered. "What was that?"

"It helps for cleansing," I explained. Then I pressed my hand to his forehead, calling on my magic.

Let this *glamour* come to an *end*.

Magic thrummed down my arm, concentrating on the palm of my hand. Like electricity making connections, it jumped from atom of moon water to atom of skin, burning away the remnants of the glamour potion.

"Oops," I said, veering forward, my legs turning into instant noodles—the cooked, floppy kind. The spell had taken a lot more power than expected to destroy the glamour. That had been one strong potion.

Strong arms caught me and pulled me up. Ian helped me onto the stool Dru vacated, and I sat with a sigh of relief. Fluffy trotted up to me, a distressed look in her eyes, and I summoned enough energy to move my foot enough to nudge-tell her I wouldn't be joining her at the cemetery just yet.

Mark immediately stepped forward and took photos of the thief.

"What are you doing?" the man demanded. The glamour dispelling had revealed an average adult male face on the gaunt side. Not the man who had claimed to be Ian's ex-partner's son.

"For the wall of honor at the bar," Mark said with his usual glee.

"Wall of honor?" Dru asked before I could.

"They have photos of idiots caught messing with bounty hunters at the Crawler," Shane said.

"Wait? You've been in the Crawler?" I asked, outraged. "But you're a shifter!" I pointed at him and turned to Mark accusingly. "He's not even twenty-one."

Mark looked Shane up and down and shrugged. "He looks twenty-one to me."

Shane grinned, a rare occurrence that made him appear even younger. "I'm twenty-one."

I looked at Ian, waiting for him to back me up, but he had moved to stand by Rufus's side, unperturbed by our banter.

The sight of him looming over the thief reminded everyone in the room of why we were here, and we all grew quiet and serious.

"Who hired you?" Ian asked.

The robber pressed his lips together and glared back.

Rufus snarled again, but the man didn't budge.

Dru stepped up. She lifted a hand with a flourish, and five sharp nails snapped into existence. "Allow me."

The robber harrumphed. "You wouldn't dare."

"Hope," Dru said.

"Yes?"

"Bring me one of the shop's T-shirts."

For reasons beyond me, the request made me suddenly giddy. "Really?"

"I don't want to get blood on my blouse."

Shane jumped off the counter. "I got plastic sheets in the van. Save us a lot of time in cleaning afterward."

Ian gave him a sharp nod. "Go."

"Stop," I said.

Everyone turned to look at me, surprise on their faces.

I focused on the man tied up on the floor. "Did they pay you well enough to be tortured?"

The man glared back, and I dismissed it with a wave of my hand. "Yes, yes, robber's pride, etcetera, etcetera. It's not like we don't already have you packed up and ready to go. Are you seriously going to go down fighting for someone who couldn't do their own robbery? If you just tell us, I swear we'll tell everyone we beat the information out of you." I lifted my pinky finger. "Scout's honor."

The man cussed. "Whatever. I was hired online."

"Where?" Ian asked.

He gave us a web address.

"Username?"

"String of letters. I don't remember. It's all anonymous. It's on my phone."

"Anonymous my ass," Dru muttered. "Preston is more like it."

"And where is your phone?" Ian asked, unfazed.

The robber glared at Ian but said nothing.

Dru waved her sharp nails. A couple of cute horn ends poked out through her curly hair. "Sharpened this week and eager to go for a drive."

Rufus backed her up with a growl, eager to get in on the action.

"In an old mailbox," the man said with a growl. "Pink house in Mills."

I snapped my fingers with recognition. "The cute, old one that needs a new roof and some weeding?"

"Yes," he gritted out.

"I know where it is," I told Ian with a triumphant smile.

"We all do," Dru said dryly. "We've lived here longer than you."

Mark let out a mean chuckle while Ian asked for the password to the robber's phone. I chose not to reciprocate with a scorching remark right that moment. But in two days, when it came to me in the middle of the night? That would be another story.

"Why did you think it's the wrong spellbook?" I patted Grandma's book, still lying on the counter. The familiar touch remained as comforting as always, and the sensation lifted a huge weight from my shoulders.

There was no way on Mother's green earth that Grandma

had been a dark magic user or a willing participant in keeping a dark magic spellbook.

It wasn't in her nature, just like it wasn't in mine.

"I was given a description of the interior," the man spit out.

Interesting. "What was the description?"

"It should be filled with alchemist symbols."

"Say what?" I asked, blankly.

"Alchemist symbols," he repeated, louder and slower. "You know, that crap to turn stuff into gold and all that. I looked them up online."

"Why would a witch's spellbook contain—" Oh. *Ooh.* If someone thought they could convert lead into gold, dark magic would be a good way to do it.

"If there was a spellbook containing the secret to turn things into gold," Ian asked in his best bland tone, "you don't think it'd be better guarded?"

"It's not my job to check if it works or not," the man replied. "My job was to get it, that's it."

From his tone of voice, he didn't believe the conversion was possible either, but someone obviously did. And if I was right, and this was the same reason Ian's ex-partner had been hired to check out Grandma, why the twenty-year wait?

I tested my legs, found they'd returned to solid consistency, and pushed myself off the stool. "Time to go."

They all turned to me.

"Where?" Dru asked.

My gaze flicked to the robber. It felt rude admitting I wanted to get his phone and dig around his contacts for whoever had hired him.

Ian saved me the awkwardness by addressing Mark and Shane. "We won't take long. Can you handle it?"

"What am I," Dru muttered, "the soggy veggies side dish?"

"You're the backup," Ian answered, not missing a beat.

Dru seemed content with this. She blew on her sharp demon nails and smiled smugly at the other two men. "Problem?"

Mark grinned appreciatively. "No, ma'am."

Shane crossed his arms. "Sure thing, boss."

"Let's go," Ian said, walking out of the kitchen.

I followed him into the backyard, Fluffy trotting along.

"I'm sorry, Fluffy," I told her, full of regret. "I think this is a bipedal-only operation."

Fluffy whined softly and put both front paws on my knee, as if to demonstrate she could pass as one if she wanted to.

I scratched between her ears. She probably wanted another grand adventure like the one we'd had over a week ago around Guiles and Romary's clubs. "Next time, I promise. Now, be a good girl and stay to cleanse the house, okay?"

She sat down on her butt and gave me a woeful look.

Feeling like the worst person in the world, I fortified myself and closed the gate behind me.

"Don't laugh," I warned Ian when I noticed the amusement in his eyes.

"Wouldn't dare." He tilted his head toward the exit of the back alleyway. "Would you like to lead?"

"Ha, ha. Very funny. I know you've all lived here forever and I haven't. But since you insist, yes. Yes, I will."

Chin up, I strode by the Corner Rose's backyard and toward the street beyond. Ian followed, his movements a lot more relaxed than they'd been since he'd seen Grandma's name on the spellbook's pages.

The house our unfriendly robber had used to stash his phone wasn't far, tucked inside a quiet side street, and it took about a five-minute walk to get there. The single-family house was small and lovely, right out of a doll magazine, and likely abandoned. A "For Sale" sign had been hung on the front fence since before I'd moved to Olmeda, and it made one wonder how much the owners were asking since it hadn't sold yet. Old Olmeda was prime real estate.

Ian yanked the rusted mailbox open, and a bit of metal went flying onto the street. Grandma wouldn't approve of this wanton property destruction.

"Should've used a hairpin," I murmured, peeking inside. A phone in a thick plastic case rested on top of a thick mountain of ancient leaflets.

"Do you have a hairpin?" Ian asked.

Since I didn't want to be told *then shut up*, I chose not to answer and grabbed the phone, taking care to avoid the arachnid squatters.

"It's a phone," I confirmed.

"Astute."

"Yup." Turning the phone to inspect the back, I saw it was one of those cases that came with a cardholder. A hotel card key and a folded ten-dollar bill had been stored inside.

I took out the bill and handed the phone to Ian. "Here, hold this."

Ian immediately took possession of the phone, slipped the card key into his jeans' back pocket, and inputted the password our captive had graciously provided.

I felt around the back of the gate for the lock.

"Hope?"

"One second." I pushed the gate open and hastened across the short flagstone path and up the two steps onto the porch. After pushing the bill under the screen door, I returned outside and locked the gate back up.

Ian blinked, baffled.

"To pay for the mailbox," I explained.

Instead of rolling his eyes or laughing, he simply pocketed the phone and said, "Let's check out his hotel room."

And this was why he was the best.

"Did you find anything on his phone?" I asked as we began walking toward Old Olmeda's center.

"It's a disposable phone. He only has a few text conversations. I'll take a better look later at home."

I trusted him to have more experience than me digging around someone's phone, so I didn't ask to give it a try. Between one thing and another, the morning had turned into the evening, and the usual crowds were filling the most popular streets. I rubbed my stomach, feeling suddenly ravenous.

Without breaking his stride, Ian took me by the elbow and nudged me toward a hole in the wall with a burrito counter.

"What?" I asked, confused.

"I heard your stomach. What do you want?"

I ordered the first thing I read. "We need to hurry," I whispered worriedly. "We don't know when whoever hired that guy will try to check in."

Ian paid for the burritos and passed me one. He'd ordered the same thing. "Surely, a smart, resourceful witch like you can walk and eat at the same time?"

The dare in his tone made me laugh. "You're on."

I unwrapped my burrito and took a good bite. Delicious, if a bit too spicy.

I know, I know—shameful. But we don't all get to choose the taste buds we're born with.

To my surprise, our robber was staying at a nice chain hotel not far from John B. Fieldman Park in one of the better parts of Old Olmeda.

"Not what you expected?" Ian asked, a note of amusement in his voice.

"Not really. I thought it would be more...motel with flickering neon signs and creepy old man as the manager."

Robbing paranormals must pay well for him to afford this. No wonder Ian's ex-partner had gone rogue.

"We're not in the fifties anymore," Ian said.

I waited until we crossed the elegant lobby and taken the elevator to ask, "Did you get to stay in places like this when you bounty hunted?"

"The accommodations were mostly acceptable."

"Who paid for them, you or the clients?"

The elevators opened, and we walked down the blue-carpeted hallway.

"Depends on the job."

"That's convenient."

"And tax deductible."

Ian found the room and inserted the key. The door opened without a glitch, and we stepped inside. It was a nice modern room with just enough space to walk between the wall, the bed, and the desk situated under the window.

"Check the bathroom," Ian said. He paused for a moment, then added, "Maybe you can revive a ghost to tell us something."

"Ha-ha. You're hilarious, but I doubt I'm lucky enough to come across two murder bathtubs in my lifetime."

Right?

I eyed the bathroom door warily.

Behind me, Ian chuckled deeply as he rummaged through the suitcase stashed by the desk.

I should be mad at his teasing, but the fact that he was teasing made me want to sing. A thawing Ian was a wonder to see, and I was glad he had something to concentrate on rather than the fact that his ex-partner and mentor hadn't been the best of people.

Humming, I entered the—ghostless so far—bathroom and checked the items on the counter. The usual hotel freebies and a small black bag containing toothpaste, some first aid supplies, and a bottle of painkillers. A razor and a toothbrush rested in a glass by the sink.

Nothing suspicious under the counter or in the shower, either. I'd have checked the toilet cistern too, but it was one of those integrated inside the wall. Too bad. I'd have loved to awe Ian with my smart thinking.

I came out of the bathroom to find him checking under the mattress.

"Just the usual bathroom stuff," I said. "You?"

"Just the usual repairman," he said.

This man.

Walking up to him, I tapped his shoulder. "Ian."

He turned to look at me. "Yes?"

I gave him a fast kiss. "You're cute."

His grin was heart-stopping. "So are you." He returned the peck, then studied the room thoughtfully.

Copying his stance, I observed our surroundings. "I suppose it was too much to expect to find a notebook full of notes about his evil, dastardly deeds."

"He probably keeps those on the phone."

"You said it was a burner."

"It might have enough." His attention returned to me. "We're going to have to let him go."

I made a face. "I know."

The law-abiding citizen in me cried in disappointment, but if we took the man to the bounty hunters, they'd investigate Grandma for the possibility of dark magic. It would destroy her reputation and put a spotlight on me and the shop. I couldn't afford that, especially since I still had a listing in the dark marketplace and kept giving people fake dark magic they thought was real.

Bagley might be dead, but her legacy was proving hard to obliterate.

"I'll warn some of my contacts," Ian said. "They'll keep an eye on him, in case he takes other similar jobs nearby."

And that was as good as it was going to get.

"What's next?" I asked.

"You tell me."

I thought about it for a few moments, then the answer became obvious.

"Your ex-partner's fake son."

"Yes," Ian said simply.

If Ian's ex-partner's file on Grandma was tied to the recent interest in the spellbook, what did that say about a stranger passing themselves as his ex-partner's son and asking for anything he left behind?

"He might've wanted the file on Grandma—the timing is too coincidental. But how are we going to find him?"

Ian gave me a slow smile.

15

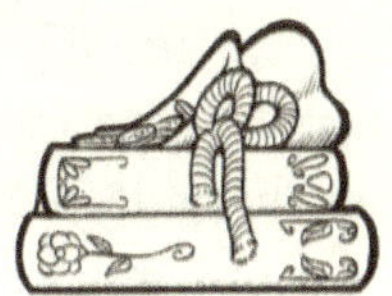

"You know how to find him?" I asked excitedly.

"I had Shane follow him," Ian said.

I clapped my hands. "Genius!" Then I frowned, remembering Shane leaving after the stranger and Alex's sad puppy eyes. "Next time you should use Alex, though."

"Alex is good at other things."

"Gotta let your boys fly, Ian."

"Are you going to lecture me on how to employ my workers while you dump your stray on me?"

Key was totally not my stray, but I got his point. "We better get going before your ex-partner's fake son realizes his robber got caught."

"*If* they're related," Ian reminded me. "It could be coincidental."

I patted his arm. "Sure. Where is he?"

We left the hotel and made our way back toward the narrower streets full of shops and restaurants and tourists. We reached Guiles and Romary, but rather than going deeper, we took another street and arrived at a fancy hotel built out of three old mansions merged together. It reminded me of the

Three Sisters, if they had ended up in the same family rather than different ones.

Haunted for sure.

The man behind the gleaming reception desk smiled at us.

"Welcome to Hargrove House. I'm afraid we're booked full tonight, but we might have some openings for next week. Would you like to make a reservation?"

I expected Ian to transform into a super friendly tourist and charm the man with friendly smiles and an overdose of honey, but he retained his usual serious, inscrutable expression.

Bounty hunter, I reminded myself, not smooth chameleon spy.

"We would like to leave a message for Joe Miller," Ian said.

"Room number?"

Ian turned toward me, as if it was the most natural thing in the world that his girlfriend would know about it. Look at that, the man did have some acting chops after all.

"I'm not sure," I told both of them, scrunching my forehead for added effect. "I don't think he mentioned it, did he?"

"Let me see..." The man began typing on a keyboard hidden from view. After a few minutes of scowling at the computer screen, his expression cleared and his mouth drooped with the weight of bad news.

"I'm sorry. Mr. Miller isn't a guest at this moment."

Mystery Man must've given Ian a fake name. I touched his arm, all outwardly worried. "Oh, no. How are we going to find him?"

Ian brought out his phone and browsed through his pictures. When he settled on one, he showed it to the hotel man. "Are you sure he's not here? Perhaps he made the reservation under his company's name."

The man squinted at the phone, then shook his head. "I don't recognize him. I'm sorry."

"Perhaps someone else booked him?" I asked, adding a hopeful note to my voice I didn't even need to fake.

I was *so* good at this.

"I'm sorry, ma'am. I'm the only one here at the moment." His eyes narrowed with slight suspicion, as if only now he was finding our questioning odd. "Can I help you with anything else?"

We thanked him and left the hotel.

"Fake name," I said. "He anticipated you being suspicious and went to a random hotel, just in case."

"Yes."

"Can I see the photo?"

Ian held up his phone.

I angled his hand to get a better look and jolted. The photograph was a still taken from a security camera showing Ian's front door and porch. "You have a camera on your porch?"

"Yes."

"No wonder you made the hotel man suspicious." Nobody searching for a friend would have this kind of photo. Although... I brightened. "Can we use face-recognition software on this?"

"This is not the movies."

It had been worth a try.

"So, it's a dead end." Disappointment flooded me. How were we supposed to find who was behind believing Grandma had a dark magic spellbook? The robber had failed, but Mystery Man might send another. If we didn't nip this in the bud, the information might spread and Grandma's reputation would be torn to shreds. All her lifelong efforts to be good and help her community would be wiped away because someone made a simple mistake.

Ian squeezed my arm. "We'll figure it out."

I nodded sharply. "Yes, we will."

We returned to the shop to find Mark and the robber gone and Alex standing in their place, a bag of chips in his hands. Fluffy and Rufus were out in the backyard.

"Bouncer dude said he and his friend will 'help' him out of town," Alex said.

"Did you find the bastard?" Dru asked.

"I'm not sure your ex is involved in this," I said. A few calls to rattle me was one thing, but hiring someone to go after the spellbook went well beyond pranks. Someone had serious interest in this supposed alchemist's spellbook, and that person being her ex was a bit too coincidental, even for me.

Dru pressed her lips in a way that said *my ex is totally involved*.

"Why did your grandma have an alchemy spellbook?" Alex asked.

"She didn't," I said firmly.

He lifted his hand and the bag in a peace gesture. "Sorry, boss. Just wondering."

"Why would anyone think your grandma had an alchemy spellbook?" Dru asked.

That was the golden question, wasn't it?

"Is there any chance that your grandmother's family is more powerful than you think?" she asked. "What do you know about your ancestry?"

"Nothing much," I admitted.

"You could be secretly a super witch," Alex said eagerly. "A lost heir of a powerful family or something."

Shane, back to sitting on the counter, kicked his leg.

"What?" Alex demanded. "It could happen."

Ian ignored them and asked, "Is there anyone you can ask on that side of your family?"

"No. It's always been just Grandma and me. I'm sure all her relatives aside from me and dad are dead."

"What about your father? Maybe he'll know something?"

"He left when I was a baby and we never heard back from him."

"I can track him down," Shane said.

"Thanks, but no need," I said with a sour smile. "If he'd wanted to get in contact, he would've. I'm not hard to find."

"Could it be him who wants the spellbook?" Dru asked.

I frowned. I had no way of knowing what kind of man my father was, so theoretically, it could be possible. "Seems like going through a lot of effort when he could simply walk in and ask for it."

"If he did that and you refused to give it to him, then you'd for sure know it was him when he hired someone to steal it," Dru pointed out.

"You have a very suspicious mind."

She shrugged. "It makes sense."

I thought back to the man I'd seen leaving Ian's house. Could he be my father? I abandoned the notion immediately. Way too young.

But could Dru be right? Could my father be involved? Even though I'd promised to myself that *everyone is a suspect* was my new motto, the coincidences were starting to be a bit too much if I added my father to the pile—Dru's ex-boyfriend arriving in town at the same time someone put a hit on the spellbook, and also at the same time someone attempted to pass as Ian's ex-partner's son.

I was getting a headache just thinking about all the moving parts.

"We're going to need a murder board," I muttered.

Alex munched on some chips. "We got a couple of leftover white plastic planks from that job at the old firehouse."

"Want me to bring them, boss?" Shane asked.

Ian shook his head. "I doubt Hope's father is involved. If he knew about the spellbook, he'd have tried to get it long ago."

"Maybe he did get it," I said. "Maybe he found it before he left, and nobody realized. That's why everyone still thinks Grandma had it. Maybe Grandma never knew she was in possession of it. It might've been in some trunk in the attic."

"Secret super-powered witch," Alex said.

I wished. "I'm definitely not a super-powered witch. Doing a big spell completely wipes me out."

"Are you *sure*?"

"There's a test."

Everyone snapped to attention.

"There's a test?" Alex repeated, clearly for the suddenly attentive audience.

"Yup. I keep a couple in case a local teen witch comes into their power."

"Take it," Alex urged.

Shane nodded. Ian tilted his head in a thoughtful manner. Even Dru appeared interested.

"Fine. But it's not going to reveal anything amazing."

"You never know," Alex said eagerly. "I bet your powers have been dormant until now! Hold on." He brought out his phone and sent a text. While still holding the bag of chips in his other hand. Talk about powerful. "Let's wait for Key."

Shane tensed, his one eye narrowing.

Oh, boy. I glanced at Ian, but he seemed unaware of the possible drama developing under his nose. Ah, well. He had basically told me to mind my own business earlier where the strays were concerned. Nothing to be done but wait and watch. Gleefully.

Mark arrived before Key could.

"What did I miss?" he said, out of breath.

"We're testing to see if she's a super witch," Alex said happily.

Great, now it was a party.

"Her?" Mark focused on Dru. "A demon-witch mix?"

Alex laughed. Dru fought a grin but lost. Shane shook with silent mirth. I didn't dare look at Ian.

"Me," I snapped, feeling my cheeks heat. "I'm the possible super witch."

The berserker's snort told everyone what he thought about that, and for a moment, I wished I *was* secretly a super witch so I could rearrange the features on his face from where I stood.

Breathe in, breathe out. Those who think less of you simply do not know the full extent of your greatness. It is not your job to educate them if they won't educate themselves. Let them fall into the pit of their ignorance and then remove the ladder.

I gave Mark one of my best customer-facing smiles. The one they knew was fully fake and there wasn't a damn thing they could do about it. "Those who doubt only do it out of their own self-doubt."

He wriggled his eyebrows. "Nice try, super witch."

Tonight I was making a super witch spell just for him for whenever he came around to restock on potions. Nothing Grandma would disapprove of, of course, just a small reminder of who was boss witch here.

A clang on the back door announced another new arrival. Sonia? My third grade teacher? At this point the possibilities were infinite.

Almost immediately, thunder cracked in the distance, and I groaned internally. This was why you asked the universe, not dared it.

"I'll take care of this," I said before anyone could move.

I all but ran into the backyard and jerked the gate open. The evening had gotten darker while we had been waiting inside, making Jeremy the mage, a.k.a Brimstone and Destruction, a long, looming shadowy being. Right on brand.

"Busy today. Come in a couple of days," I said.

His mouth snapped closed, then his brows dipped deeply, giving him a scary, malevolent expression I was sure he practiced in front of the mirror. "You told me to come today."

With everything that had been going on, I'd forgotten our appointment. Immediately contrite, I gentled my voice. "I'm sorry. Something came up and I can't make your potion right now." I glanced over my shoulder in a meaningful gesture. "I have *company*."

Jeremy the mage took the hint immediately. Stiffening, he backed away. "I will return tomorrow." He pointed at me. "There better not be any more delays."

"There won't," I promised.

He spun on his heel and walked down the alley. Another crack of thunder marked his departure. Behind me, Fluffy let out a sharp yip of surprise.

I closed the gate, turned, and saw Mark and Alex's faces plastered to the kitchen window. Hopefully it was dark enough that they hadn't gotten a good look at Brimstone and Destruction. Deciding to let them simmer in their curiosity for a few more moments, I crouched and gave Fluffy some much needed affection. On both sides.

"I'm sorry, Fluffy," I whispered. "I'll tell thunder man not to do that when you're around."

Rufus woofed in agreement, and I gave him some head scritches before walking back inside. This time, I left the back door open so the dogs could come and go at will. The poor things deserved the freedom after waiting patiently for so long.

"A client. I told them to come back tomorrow," I said the moment I stepped into the kitchen. Ian had been standing in the door, blocking anyone from trying to follow me. Too bad he couldn't clone himself and stand at the window too.

Everyone took me at my word, and nobody appeared unduly curious. To my great relief no more uninvited guests arrived before Key did, out of breath as if she'd run the whole way over.

Her eyes widened at the assembly, and she swallowed hard. "Uh."

I clapped my hands, gaining everyone's attention. "Let's do this."

"Are you really a super witch?" Key whispered as we moved into the shop.

"That's what we're about to find out," I said, injecting some sunshine in my voice for the benefit of my audience.

They might think it a possibility, but I had no doubts my powers were nothing special. I had taken the test several times—once when I'd first figured out I was a witch, excited to see the extent of my magic, and again when I'd joined the Council officially.

Others might've been disappointed by the less-than-impressive results, but I was fine with it. Greater power did not correlate to being a better witch.

It's all in the kindness, not the power.

Grandma's wisest words, as far as I was concerned.

We spilled into the shop, and I went behind the counter to grab a power testing kit. I poured some moon water into a small glass bowl, then opened the packet with the sterilized lancet.

"This is the test?" Alex asked. He picked up the paper strip and examined it under the ceiling light. "It looks like a pee test."

Shane smacked his arm. "Don't touch it."

Alex's expression filled with alarm, and he dropped the strip on the counter immediately. "Oh, shit, I'm sorry. Did I mess it up?"

I chuckled. "It's fine. You won't contaminate it. It only reacts with spirit power."

"Cool," Key said by my right. Ian stood on my left, while the rest crowded on the other side of the counter, leaning in eagerly. So eagerly, Mark was all but lying on top of it. Even Fluffy pawed at my leg, picking up on the anticipation saturating the room.

I was starting to feel like a fungus culture under the microscope.

One of the gorgeous ones that looked like a forest or a bouquet of flowers.

"How does the test work?" Ian asked. His voice carried none of the eagerness on display on everyone else's faces. It helped ground me, because...

Because a tiny, tiny part of me had begun to wonder.

What if?

What if I was a late bloomer power-wise? What if I was a lot more powerful than I'd thought?

Would I remain the same witch or be forever changed? Would Grandma's lessons still apply?

"I mix my blood with the moon water," I explained, almost absentmindedly, "then I dip the strip and activate the spell contained within."

Giving myself no more time to doubt my own power, I prickled the tip of one finger with the lancet, waited for a big bead of blood to form, and dipped it into the bowl. Wisps of pink spread through the liquid, faster than they might in normal water, as if the moon water knew what to do with a drop of willing blood and was eager to perform.

I cleaned my fingertip with a small square of sterilized gauze —also part of the kit—and tried to put a small bandage on top.

"Let me," Ian murmured. He took the bandage from me and deftly covered the pinprick with it. It brought back memories of me tending to his hand wound two weeks ago. Memories of his warm skin under mine, of realizing he had been dating me without me knowing. Of our first kiss.

A furnace came to life deep inside my belly, its flames licking slowly up my chest, into my cheeks. I told it to shut down. This was not the time.

"I'll activate the strip now," I said firmly to my audience as well as myself.

Time to concentrate.

I dipped the strip of thick paper into the bowl and tried to concentrate. Having seven pairs of eyes wholly focused on me was unnerving, and as little magic as this spell required, it still needed my full attention. My full intention.

Power of the *spirit*.

Magic tingled from my fingers into the paper, awakening the small ward laid there by someone a lot more powerful than I. It sucked on the magic greedily, returning the favor with a soft tickle against my skin, letting me know that it had received my offering and was eager to get to work.

I let go of the strip. It floated on the surface, attracting the pinkish wisps of blood like a magnet.

"Cool," Alex whispered.

Even Mark looked impressed.

After a minute or so, the moon water stood transparent again, and the strip of paper had become slightly pink. I picked it up and shook some droplets off.

"Is it done?" Shane asked.

"Yes." Moving the kit's instructions to the middle of the counter, I placed the strip by the color chart. From barely pink to fiery red. Weak to strong.

Immense relief filled me. No super-secret late blooming power. I was still me.

Dru made a sound of aggravation. "Waste of time."

"We should do another," Alex suggested, sounding quite disappointed.

"Not going to help," muttered one of the stools.

Shane immediately snapped to attention, his single-eyed gaze scanning our surroundings. "What was that?"

"Nothing," Ian said firmly, and proceeded to shoo everyone out of the room, the building, and, hopefully, the rest of my week.

Smiling at the faintly pink strip of paper, I cleaned up, chastised Bagley, and met Ian in the hallway, Fluffy trotting by my side.

For a moment there, the universe had threatened to upend itself. Beyond me losing the shop. Beyond failing my duties. Even beyond being unable to clear up Grandma's legacy.

But then it had righted itself again, reminding me that anything could be achieved by the strength of one's will, not power.

My smile broadened. Happiness filled my chest like a sudden explosion of blossoms.

I was still me.

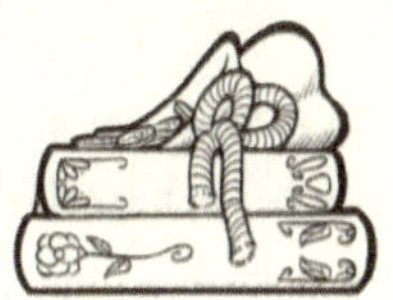

16

IAN WENT out to take the dogs for a short walk and returned with a couple of drinks and a large pizza. My stomach growled at the sight, the burrito long forgotten.

I'd cleaned the kitchen and returned Grandma's spellbook upstairs while Ian was out, so we made ourselves comfortable on the backyard chairs, eating the pizza in the ambient light coming from the hallway.

"Thank you," I said. I took a good bite of the slice of cheese and pepperoni and it absolutely melted in my mouth. Olmeda might be known for its fried chicken, but its pizza was the pinnacle of perfection.

Ian nodded and took a swig of his beer. He looked delectable as he relaxed on the camping chair, his face upturned toward the sky.

I followed his gaze. The city lights were too strong to show much, but as I waited, pinpricks of light began peeking out here and there. Watching the stars together made for an easy, intimate atmosphere. Same spot, same position as my earlier girls' night, yet so different.

I would never admit it to the girls, but I think I rather liked this one better. Especially with Fluffy sleeping on my foot and Rufus keeping sentinel by Ian's side as he petted him absent-mindedly.

Cozy.

Perfect.

"Grandma wasn't evil," I said.

"I believe you."

Fluffy yipped sleepily, adding her support.

Rufus said nothing, which I understood—he was a suspicious sort like his owner, so he likely also subscribed to *everyone is a suspect*.

"Why now?" I asked, returning to the question that had been bugging me since I'd seen Ian's ex-partner's folder. "Why wait twenty years?"

"Remember, it might be unrelated."

"Not likely."

"But not impossible. Someone looking for Duncan's files might have nothing to do with the spellbook. And both might have nothing to do with the bounty related to your grandmother."

I drank my diet soda, welcoming the fresh bubbles running down my throat. "This is the part in thrillers where you yell at the characters for not making the obvious connection." My sister's books had taught me as much.

"This is real life. Coincidences happen."

"It's also the part in movies where you yell at the blonde for going down into the basement alone."

"I can see why that would worry you. Have you thought about dying your hair?"

"I tried full green once," I admitted. "But it was a bit too much."

"Have photos?" He sounded strangely interested.

"Maybe. What are you willing to pay for them?"

"What about a trade?"

I sat at an angle to study him better. He was still looking up, a small smile playing with his lips. This was a rare relaxed side of Ian I hadn't seen before, not even during our first real date, and it warmed my insides that he was choosing to show it to me here in the murder house, surrounded by strange ghosts while eating pizza after a hard day's work of interrogating bad guys and searching hotel rooms.

"What kind of trade?" I asked.

"I'll show you mine if you show me yours."

My cheeks immediately burst into flames. "I see."

He turned his head to arch his eyebrows at me. "Hair-wise."

I tried to look very prim and proper. "Of course."

He huffed a laugh.

"Wait, do you mean you dyed your hair green?" I scooted the chair closer, nearly upending the box we'd brought out to use as a table. "Show me!"

"I've never dyed my hair."

"What then?" I studied his dark-brown wavy hair gathered at the back of his neck. "Oh! You used to keep it short?"

"Yes."

"Show me!"

"You first."

I dug out my phone and browsed through my old pictures on the cloud. It took me a few minutes, but I finally found them. I'd been twenty, about the same time I'd gotten the small koi tattoo on my back. My hair had been longer then, falling past my shoulders.

Ian took the phone from my hand and studied the photo intently. It was a silly selfie done right outside the hair salon with me grinning widely at the camera. He swept sideways, and another selfie appeared, this one with me winking exaggeratedly. The next one was a photo of me and Nicole taken at the marina on a lazy Sunday afternoon. I remembered the moment clearly —I had joined my sister for a family outing, and her husband was the one taking the photo, my crying niece in his free arm.

I snatched the phone from Ian before I got all weepy. "Your turn."

He made no move to take out his phone.

"Did you just con me?" I asked with mock outrage.

He drank more beer, his smile obvious now. "I don't have them with me."

"Unfair!"

"We didn't agree on a time frame."

Oldest trick in the book. That'd teach me.

I nudged Fluffy. "Fluffy, attack!"

Fluffy burrowed her head deeper into her paws.

I gave Ian a dignified look. "She will attack tomorrow."

Ian glanced at the white fluffball with obvious affection. "I'm sure she will." He leaned his head back to stare at the sky again. "You can see the photos on our next date."

The word date coming out of his lips brought a small thrill to my system. I was still unused to hearing it. Fast kisses and easy conversation over food was one thing, but dating? It both thrilled and scared me. Ian was a few years older than me. He was serious and unwavering. There was a weight to his decisions that told me he thought about them long and deep before making them.

Dating Ian wasn't a light summer fling. It wasn't a "fun as long as it lasts" kind of deal.

I had gone through a couple of those before, and the fun never lasted that long. It soured and became annoying, and one party always stayed way longer than they should've.

That party might've been me.

I was bad at reading the room sometimes.

My sister blamed my natural optimism. My mom was of the

opinion that I'd never been seriously invested in them, so of course I couldn't see when things went wrong—my heart simply hadn't cared that much.

Both had a point.

But this thing with Ian felt different. The small sparks whenever we touched felt different. The kisses felt different. The fluttering in my stomach whenever he focused his total attention on me felt different. It felt more real. Like it had meaning. Intent.

Magic.

That's how it felt. Like a spell weaving its way into my life, around my heart. A well-honed, well-crafted spell full of intent. His intent.

It rendered me powerless to resist.

And that felt like the scariest thing on earth.

Reaching over, I tentatively touched his hand. He immediately flipped it to interlock his fingers with mine.

The sparks burst into life. The warmth. The precipice that told me I better make sure I wanted to jump in because once I was fully committed, I wouldn't be getting out.

But precipices and holes were only scary because they opened into a pit of darkness, and Ian was offering me the sky.

I grinned at the pinpricks of light so far above us.

Grandma would approve.

"I'm sure the bounties are connected—Grandma's and the spellbook," I said with conviction. Mostly because it was mind-boggling to think she was involved with two bounties for two different reasons. "What are we going to do next?"

"I'll ask around Duncan's old contacts."

"See if his fake son has been visiting others?"

"They might know who he is."

"Smart."

"What about you? What will you do now?"

I thought about it for a few long moments. "I'm going to do the same, I think."

"Ask Duncan's old contacts? I don't know. They might get suspicious if two different people nose into their business."

Laughing, I shushed him. "I'm going to ask Grandma's old friends, see if they remember anything odd about the year before she died."

He squeezed my hand. "Are you sure you're up to it?"

Wistfulness filled me. "I came to terms with Grandma's death a long time ago. I'll be okay. Thanks for asking."

He lifted my hand to place a kiss on it, as if to remind me that no thanks were necessary. Not between us.

Sadly, no more kissing followed. We finished the pizza and our drinks, then returned inside to clean up.

To my surprise, Ian asked if I minded if the dogs stayed upstairs with us.

"With us?" I repeated blankly.

"Do you have extra blankets?" he added unhelpfully.

"Uh."

"I'll stay in your living room."

"Uhh."

His eyebrows made perfect arches. "I assume you still don't have a sofa? I'd rather have something between me and the floor."

I swallowed hard. "You're spending the night?"

"I'm not leaving you alone tonight. The man might have an accomplice ready to attempt another go at the spellbook."

"Thank you. You can, uh..." My ears were burning now. "We can share the bed."

He gave me a quick kiss. "I don't mind the floor. You take the bed."

Dazed, I retrieved some blankets from the landing's closet and handed them over, then watched him prepare a makeshift bed in my empty living room, put out water for the dogs in the kitchen, and lie down on the blankets without bothering to undress.

An hour later, as I lay on my bed, unable to sleep and staring at the wall separating the bedroom from the living room, I still didn't know what to make of it. A sign of respect? A decision to take things slow for his sake as much as mine? A lack of interest?

Whatever it was, I couldn't figure out if I was relieved or disappointed in his decision, but part of me insisted this was such a missed opportunity, and that part was making me sad.

No opportunity is missed. They simply reform into new ones. Still...

So much for only one bed.

————

The soft murmur of rain woke me up the next morning before my phone did. That, and the noise of water splashing in the bathroom sink.

Goldfish ghost?

No, it was a kraken, and—

I sat up with a snap. Ian!

Shoving the covers aside, I stumbled out of bed and onto the landing. Ian stood in my bathroom in all his shirtless glory.

Hard pectorals and hard biceps with a scattering of small, old scars. *Forearms.*

My mouth went dry. I had seen Ian shirtless before, and the sight never ceased to impress.

No opportunity is missed, I reminded myself. *See? Now you get to have this forever burned into your memory.*

"Good morning," he said.

Without another word, he bent over the sink, cupped water

into his hands, and returned to washing his face and neck. He had grown some stubble overnight, and it looked good on him. It accentuated the harshness of his features, turning him from someone you'd better we wary of to straight *cross the street if you see him coming* material.

"Coffee?" I croaked.

He dried himself with my hand towel and I decided then and there not to wash it ever again. "Please."

I dragged myself into the kitchen, unconcerned by the fact that I was still in my oversized sleeping tee. This was how I'd met Ian for the first time, after all—the ship of him seeing me at my worst had long sailed.

Fluffy greeted me eagerly with small, short barks as if aware we might have neighbors. Rufus let out one of his customary woofs and stared dejectedly at the floor and his nonexistent bowl of food.

Obediently, I filled two bowls with dog food and got started on Ian's coffee.

As I waited for the coffee to brew, I approached the sink.

"Good morning, Kraken."

Gurgling sounds reverberated through the drain.

"Do you really have an octopus ghost in your pipes?" Ian asked from the doorway, startling me. He had put his black sweater back on but still walked barefoot.

He looked good like this. In my kitchen. Cozy. Nice. Sexy.

My thoughts must have been obvious on my face, because he walked up to me and gave me a chaste, lingering kiss.

"Good morning," he repeated against my lips.

I grinned. "Good morning."

"Your ghost?"

"Oh, that's right." I patted the faucet. "Kraken, come out, meet Ian."

A dark drop formed at the end of the faucet. It grew and

grew until a blob the size of my fist hung from the end. Two small white eyes blinked up at us. A ridiculously cute small tentacle popped out of the blob and extended tentatively.

Oh, my goodness. "It's a tiny kraken," I choked out, extending my finger toward it.

"Hope," Ian warned.

I waved his concern aside. If the ghost had wanted to hurt me, it could've at any time before now.

The tiny kraken poked my finger once—a strangely solid push—then it retreated inside the faucet. Thumping echoed from the pipes.

I turned to Ian with a triumphant smile. "See? Harmless."

Ian had a very strange expression on his face. With a sigh, he grabbed his coffee and muttered, "Not for the thief yesterday."

"That's because he was a bad man." I looked down at the dogs. "Always feel free to maim the bad guys."

They responded with sharp barks.

"Your dogs approve."

"My dogs will do anything for food."

I washed and dressed while he drank his coffee, then accompanied him downstairs and into the shop.

"You're sure you don't want to stay for breakfast?" I asked, disappointed our cozy time together was coming to an end.

"I need to get back before the strays come in." He gave me a pointed look. "All three of them."

I ignored that and unlocked the front door. "Are you sure you want to leave the dogs here?"

"Yes."

Thank the Mother. The thought of staying alone today after the last day's events was daunting even for my naturally optimist *surely I can't be as unlucky as to get robbed twice in a row* side.

Ian lingered next to me, as unwilling to open the door and end the moment as I was.

Then he pulled me into his arms, all controlled strength and intense eyes.

My breath caught in my chest. This was it. This was what I had secretly hoped for last night—the heat in his gaze, the squeeze of his hands, the heat of his body, the melting of my insides. The way his mouth parted. The way he leaned down, all promise and intent. All magic.

"Awww. Are you two going to have a Hollywood good-bye kiss?" Bagley asked.

And poof, there went the magic.

Ian released me, grabbed the stool, and dragged it toward the hallway.

"Look here, young man," came from the stool. "I was only encouraging you."

He hesitated halfway through. "May I?"

"No!" exclaimed Bagley.

I thought about it for a second, then nodded.

He put the stool firmly on the other side of the bead curtain, then returned, grabbed my hips, pulled me close, and brought his mouth down on mine.

My arms went around his neck as the kiss became deep, fierce, demanding, harsh, and everything in between.

He ended it as fast as he'd begun it and left the shop, leaving me a breathless puddle of mush.

Eventually, I managed to flip the sign to open, draw up the blinds, and make it around the counter to prepare for the day.

And since Bagley was now out of the picture for a little while, I was free to enact my plans without the evil hag interfering or learning too much.

Let the *Grandma was not evil* campaign begin.

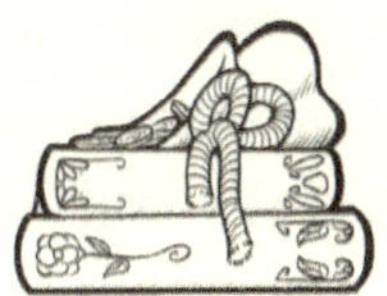

17

ASKING Grandma's old friends back home would be the way to go if I wanted to prove her innocent. Unfortunately, visiting Grandma's town for a fishing expedition was out of the question. Halloween was fast approaching, and If I disappeared for a few days, Sonia would take notice.

The Council might also not look kindly if I abandoned the shop for that long, especially during the probation period. Dru was good, but she wasn't the witch in charge. I was.

A witch's duty came with great responsibilities.

On top of that, I'd promised Dru to help with the Preston issue, and from the way he was buttering up the paranormals in town, it was promising to be more of a fight than I'd expected.

I began nibbling on the last banana muffin, pondering my options.

If a trip wasn't possible, could I do some long-distance questioning instead?

The problem was I had no idea who her friends had been. It had been too long, and I had no old letters or contact lists from Grandma.

Mom might remember something, though.

I checked the time, made a mental time conversion, and figured it was safe enough for a morning call.

"Hope? What's wrong?" Mom asked straight away. I was going to get a complex if she kept assuming something was off every time I called.

"Nothing's wrong, Mom. Good morning!"

Mom groaned. "Who did you inherit that sunny morning attitude from, because it surely wasn't from me."

"As you keep telling me, the Fae stole your real baby and left me behind."

She laughed. "They sure did. Now, what is it so urgent that you're calling this early on a weekday?" Her voice sobered. "Does it have something to do with your grandmother? Are you still bothered by her death?"

"Who is it?" my stepdad asked in the background.

"It's Hope."

"Ah. Tell her hello from me."

"Hello, Dan," I said loudly.

"Hope," Mom chastised. "My ear." To my stepdad she said, "She says hello."

"Mom, do you know who Grandma's friends were? I'm thinking of doing something special for her birthday."

"Her friends? No, sorry, honey. I know she had a few friendly neighbors, but I didn't spend long enough with her to know about her friends. Wait, no. I remember another lady of her age who used to hang around sometimes when I dropped you off. Let me think."

She mulled on this while I opened a new note on the laptop, ready to write down names.

"I think it was...Miranda? Mandy? Something with an M and an N in it."

I typed both names dutifully, if a little disappointed that's all she remembered. "You don't remember her last name?"

"Oh, no way. It's been way too long. She seemed nice, though. Otherwise, I wouldn't have left you alone with them."

"Of course not."

"Your grandma was a good woman, Hope. I hope you know this. No matter how your father turned out, it was of no fault of hers. She loved you very much."

"I know, Mom." I blinked away the sudden wetness in my eyes. "Thank you."

"I'm sorry I can't help you more. You could come for a visit and drive over, if you're bent on finding her friends. I'm sure they still remember her."

"I can't afford the time off right now."

"I see."

From her tone of voice, she clearly saw none of it.

"What about her belongings?" I asked. "Grandma's I mean. Do we still have anything left from her? A couple of boxes in the garage?"

"None that I know of. Her lawyer donated everything except for her journal, which went to you."

The mention of a lawyer perked me up. "Do you remember the lawyer's name? Did you keep their business card?"

"No, sorry, hon. We only interacted a few times."

"That's too bad."

"What you're trying to do is very nice, Hope. But don't worry too much if it doesn't pan out, okay? Your grandma wouldn't have liked you to stress about her."

"I promise I won't. All happiness, no stress."

"That's my changeling."

"Ha-ha. If you remember anything, you'll let me know?"

"Of course. Mind if we continue this later? Dan is pointing at his watch and giving me dirty looks."

I laughed. "Sure thing, Mom. Love you."

"Love you too."

She ended the call, and I considered the two names on the screen. Admittedly, not much to go on, but bigger cases had been solved with less information.

Or so true-crime TV had led me to believe.

My next step consisted of approaching the investigation into Grandma's past from the magical side, so I spent a few minutes going through the Council's public directory until I found a phone number for Grandma's local Council branch.

As was the case for Olmeda, Grandma's town didn't have its own Council branch but was under the oversight of a bigger city.

The automated system picked up right away, and I made my way through its labyrinthic pathways until I reached a real person. Different Council branches might pride themselves on their local flavor, but at their bureaucratic center, they were all the same nightmare.

I greeted the woman on the other side of the call, gave her my name, and explained my business. "I'm looking for information about a local witch by the name of Hazel Oakes. She died eighteen years ago."

"I'm sorry, Ms. Avery, but we can't divulge our members' information."

Which reminded me I still had to look into Bagley's accounts. Between spying, robberies, and tossing hotel rooms, it had slipped my mind. "I understand, but I'm her granddaughter."

At least this part I wouldn't have to fake.

"I'm sorry. We can't give any kind of information over the phone. If you could come in person, perhaps we could arrange something."

"That's not possible at the moment. Isn't there anything I could access online? I'm mostly interested in any intern she might've had, or other local witches she might've entered a coven with."

"As I said, that's highly private information."

"Would it help that I was registered at your branch in the past?" Until the move to Olmeda, that's where I'd maintained my Council membership. "Hope Avery, registered by Hazel Oakes at birth."

"Hold, please."

Tinkling music filled the call. Very Zen. Very on brand. I eyed the merchandise bookshelf in the corner. Maybe I should add some music. Did anyone buy music CDs anymore?

The soothing music stopped abruptly, and the witch returned to the call.

"Ah, yes, I see your membership file, Ms. Avery. I still need to corroborate your identity, though. Could you send a photograph of yourself holding your Council ID clearly visible?"

She rattled an email address. I took a selfie with my ID, then emailed it to her. A few minutes later, she called me back.

"Everything seems in order, Ms. Avery. What files would you like to access? We haven't gone fully digital yet, so I might be unable to send some things, you understand. For those, you'll have to come in person."

"I understand." I gave her a list of requests—known friends, partners, interns, any warnings on her file—and my thanks, then hung up.

What next?

My mind went blank.

Very blank.

Was this all I could really do to clear Grandma's name? A call to Mom and a request for old records?

But what else could I do? The bounty hunters would have no idea about who had hired Ian's ex-partner, since it had been off the books. I had no access to face-recognition software or the time to run around showing Mystery Man's face to passersby in case anyone recognized him, and Ian was in charge of searching the robber's phone.

An unwelcome thought slithered into my head.

Maybe there was little to do because there was nothing to discover.

The truth was, good magic didn't put you in a hitman's file. Didn't make you a robber's target.

How depressing.

Sensing my mood, Fluffy whined from the archway, and I went over to give her some pets, then brought her back upstairs. Rufus stood at attention at the top of the stairs. Since it was still raining, the dogs were confined inside, but it had felt cruel to close the door on them.

Fluffy brought me her favorite current toy—a knotted up old T-shirt—and I bent to grab it so I could throw it for her.

Instead, Fluffy dodged my hand and swirled hard, letting go of the T-shirt at the same time. It flopped to the floor a few inches away from her, but from the way she looked at me, all expectant tongue lolling, you'd think she'd just broken the world's hammer throwing record.

"Maybe you have," I told her. "Maybe you're the best T-shirt thrower in the world."

She went to the T-shirt, then back to me, tail wagging madly.

"You want me to fetch the T-shirt for you? Is that it? Are you trying to cheer me up, Fluffy?" I blinked furiously and hugged her close. This dog was going to be the death of me.

Rufus let out a low woof from his position by the steps.

"You're the best too, Rufus."

He was content with this and dropped his head onto his paws. After making sure their bowls were full, I returned downstairs feeling quite energized.

Fluffy was right. Just because things appeared obvious, it didn't mean they were the truth.

Just because what I'd done so far appeared to not be much, it didn't mean it wouldn't have far-reaching consequences.

Work smarter, not harder.

With that, another idea occurred to me. Grandma hadn't had social media accounts, but her friend might now. A search for both names and Grandma's town returned several pages of hits, but I wouldn't let the number defeat me.

For the next couple of hours, I checked the results between customers.

At about midmorning, a clap of thunder startled me. It was still raining and gloomy, but other than the day he dumped Key on me, Brimstone and Destruction wasn't known for being a morning person.

Luckily, it was during a lull in customers, so I flipped the sign and scurried to the back. The steady rain drenched me immediately, and I hurried to open the back gate.

Brimstone and Destruction stood under a giant black umbrella lined with black lace.

"Witch," he intoned.

"You're early," I accused. "I could've had customers."

"I have an appointment tonight."

And my customers were apparently not his problem.

Nothing to do but let him inside. Like a vampire.

He walked in after me and stopped at the sight of Fluffy and Rufus peering from the stairs.

"Dogs," he said.

"Dogs," I agreed. I pointed toward the kitchen. "In there."

He eyed the animals warily and slid into the kitchen, putting as much space as possible between himself and humanity's best friends.

Was Brimstone and Destruction, fire mage of Olmeda and well-known among the criminal class, scared of dogs?

I fought a grin.

Once inside the kitchen, he focused on me and used his most truculent voice to say, "Prepare my potion."

As I collected the ingredients to make a show of preparing his potion, his attention never deviated from me. Anyone else would've glanced around, curious, but not him. It probably had something to do with his deals with the dark side of the paranormal world, where curiosity might get you killed. See nothing, hear nothing, get out as fast as you can.

Time to put that to the test.

"Have you heard they're selling the Corner Rose?" I asked.

"I am not here for chit chat, witch."

And yet chit chat he'd have to endure. I placed some herbs and clear quartz in a circle on the counter. "I heard you might have some competition moving in."

He stiffened. "Competition?"

"The man interested in buying it? I saw him talking to several...*people.*" The hint that these people moved in his circle might seem heavy handed, but Brimstone and Destruction enjoyed over-the-top performances. Hence me making a show of producing his potion.

"Bah." He sniffed. "That man is not one of us."

"Are you sure? He might be trying to lie low then strike once he settles in."

"Then he'll be a lamb among wolves." He showed me a full smile, all wicked angles and lots of teeth. As soon as I'd obviously given it the appreciation it deserved, the smile snapped out of existence and he said, "Now prepare my potion, witch."

To underscore his point, he produced a tiny flame in the palm of his hand.

"Yes, sir." I eyed the flame warily, and wondered who

would win in a fight, Jeremy the fire mage or Kraken the pipe ghost. I wasn't exactly scared of Brimstone and Destruction—not anymore, anyway—or believed he'd rat out my dark magic business to the Council as long as I was good to Key, his niece, but it was good of him to remind me I had no idea how his clients put his fire power to use.

For all I knew, he could be a human incinerator for hire.

I shuddered at the thought and finished preparing the ingredients for the fake potion. Making a big production of it, I mixed the fake blood into the transparent vial already filled by an extra-strength energy drink and some moon water, all the while pouring my magic into it so he'd sense a potion was being made.

Be *true* to the *goodness* in you.

I wasn't sure if my spell would work on him, but one had to try.

Once the potion was ready, I carefully passed it to him. As usual, the satisfaction he showed while he examined the dark red contents made me mentally knock on wood that he'd never figure out I'd been scamming him the whole time.

"So the man interested in buying the Corner Rose is not interested in poaching your territory?" I had to make sure.

Brimstone and Destruction pocketed the vial, exited the kitchen, and walked toward the back door, giving the dogs an abrupt wide berth as he suddenly noticed they'd stepped down into the hallway.

"Many have tried over the years, witch. And he is not one of them."

With those parting words, he grabbed his lacy black umbrella and saw himself out.

I turned to Fluffy and Rufus. "That's disappointing. Dru won't like it."

They made dog noises of agreement, then I shooed them back upstairs and reopened the shop.

Having Brimstone and Destruction confirm Preston's involvement in the dark paranormal world would've helped our case immensely. On the other hand, I was glad he wasn't, because figuring out a way to tell everyone he might be involved in shady business while not revealing *I* might be involved in shady business would've proven to be a feat.

Still, I spent the rest of the day preparing a list of cons to present to the PBOA until Ian arrived in his SUV to take me to the meeting.

18

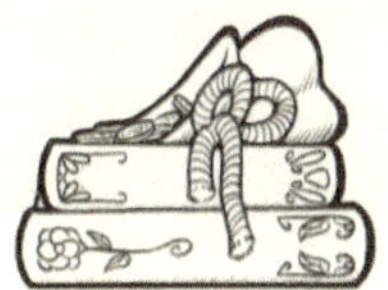

To nobody's shock, Dru joined us for the PBOA meeting. The room was already half full by the time we arrived. Veva was here, as were Desmond Crane and other familiar faces. I brought my usual offering of grilled ham and cheese sandwiches to the side table and grabbed one of the top triangles. After taking a big bite, I munched with obvious enthusiasm.

"Yum," I said loudly before taking another bite. "*So* yum."

Ian, who was used to my weekly performance, moved away to find an empty seat in the last row—his favorite position in the room.

Dru, who had never come to a PBOA meeting with me before, stared at me like she was deeply regretting her decision to move to Olmeda.

"What are you doing?" she demanded in a harsh whisper.

I finished the sandwich and liked my finger clean like a theater actor trying to get seen from the last row. "I'm tempting people into trying my sand-witches."

"Why do you care if—wait. Did you just say sand-*witches*?"

"Good, huh?" I said with a conspiratorial wriggle of my eyebrows.

Dru spun on her heels and stalked away. She sat on a first row seat, slammed her small purse on the chair next to hers, and ignored me.

"Sand-witches?" I asked Bosko as he ambled nearby.

He grunted, poured himself a coffee, and kept on walking.

"They go with everything," I called after him.

"I'll have one," said a friendly voice.

"Keith!" I grabbed the tray and offered it to him. "One hundred percent handmade." And, unlike my predecessor's PBOA cookie offerings, dark magic free.

He picked one up and ate half in one bite. "Not bad. Could be warmer."

"But at least it's not freezing, huh?"

"Touché."

I scanned the crowd. "Hutton here today?"

"Over there." He pointed toward the farthest corner from where Ian was sitting.

Hutton and his trademarked glower conversed with a tall woman dressed in a dark blue business suit I didn't recognize. "Who's that?"

"Monique. She owns a temp job agency downtown."

"They're friends?" As I watched, the woman crossed her arms and began tapping her low-heeled shoes. "Never mind, no need to answer that."

Keith chuckled. "The boss can be tough, but it's for the pack's benefit."

That, I believed. Hutton might be mean and rude and would rather steamroll people over than have to listen to them, but I couldn't deny he always had the pack's wellbeing in mind.

"I'll see you around, Hope," Keith said before moving away.

Nobody else was close, so I took the time to study the crowd again, taking special notice of anyone I hadn't seen before, or anyone who was acting awkwardly. And, especially, anyone who might be trying to study me while I wasn't paying attention.

I couldn't discount the chance that fake ex-partner's son, a.k.a. Mystery Man might be in league with someone in the audience. While it appeared to be a one-man operation on the surface, we had no way of knowing how many people were involved.

Everyone was a suspect.

I rued the necessity of moving away from *kindness over power* but consoled myself with the fact that it was only temporary. It had to be.

The door in the back by the small raised stage slammed open, marking Sonia's arrival. I rushed to Dru's side as people scrambled to find a seat and snatched her purse up, sitting right before Desmond Crane tried to get the seat. He glared at me, but Dru shooed him away.

I hoped that didn't mean I was in for a rough awakening come tax season.

He chose another seat, and a few seconds later, Sonia arrived at the folding table on top of the stage and dropped her massive pile of folders on top.

"Find a seat already," she barked.

We all swiveled to watch a young man stumble over someone in his rush to reach an open seat in the middle of the row.

"Sorry, Sonia." He plopped down, his face crimson under the weight of our stares.

Like a well-organized flock of sheep, we all turned back toward Sonia.

She propped her cane against the table and made use of the chair. In a few economic moves, she had the first folder open and a sheaf of papers squared in front of her.

"We have a few things to discuss today. First order of

business—"

Dru elbowed me hard, and I yelped.

Sonia's gaze bored through me so thoroughly it was a miracle I had any internal organs left. "Yes, Avery?"

"Nothing." Dru kicked my leg, and I corrected myself. "I mean, I'd like to make a complaint."

"Later."

"Yes, Sonia." I leaned into Dru and whispered, "Are you trying to get me in trouble?"

"Anything else to add, Avery?"

Ah, crap. I'd forgotten I was sitting in the first row. "No, Sonia."

"Then shut up."

I clamped my mouth shut.

"*As I was saying*, first order of business is Halloween. Has everyone approved the proofs?" She looked up from her papers and narrowed her eyes at some poor soul sitting behind me and Dru. "Yes, Bobby?"

An older man sporting a thick beard, a flannel shirt, and a mean frown was shaking his head. "I haven't gotten it yet."

"I sent it to the newsletter."

Newsletter? My hand crept upward until it entered Sonia's narrowed field of vision. "What is it, Avery?"

"I'm not on the newsletter, either."

"Check your spam folder."

I opened my mouth to tell her I always checked my spam folder, and I had never seen an email from the PBOA, but decided to die on Dru's hill later on rather than this one.

"Anyone else not receive the proofs? Belinda?"

"I sent back some changes, but I'm not sure if you got them," a woman said from the other side of the aisle.

"Do you expect me to answer every email?" Sonia asked in a dangerous voice.

"No, Sonia, but there was a mistake in our address and if it isn't corrected then how are people going to find us?"

Sonia made a note on a paper. "I will recheck later."

"Thank you, Sonia," the woman said with obvious relief.

"Who is that?" I asked Dru in a low whisper.

"If you can't be bothered learning your fellow PBOA members, Avery," Sonia said, "don't expect to get far in this community."

How had she heard that? She wasn't even a shifter!

Or was she? The question was going to keep me up at night.

"The shop keeps me busy, but I'm trying my best to get to know everyone." I turned to the crowd and produced one of my brightest smiles.

A few chuckles and friendly smiles met my proclamation. From the second row across, Veva gave me a nod of approval.

I gave Sonia a pointed look. *See?*

Sonia's right eye twitched, but she moved on. "We need to have these at the printers by Sunday, so *please* make sure no more changes are needed." She scanned the attendance and focused on Hutton and Keith. "Garreth the Hound?"

Hutton's scowl didn't change. By his side, Keith gave Sonia a thumbs up. "All ready."

"At least something's ready," Sonia muttered, making another note on her paper. "What about the cemetery tours?"

"No," said Ian, loud and clear from the last row.

Sonia glared at me.

I lifted my hands in a *what can you do?* gesture.

She lifted a brow in a perfect *figure it out* arc.

"Working on it," I mumbled.

"Work harder," Sonia said, then added to herself something that sounded a lot like, "Since you can't smarter."

Someone stood with a question about the banners and flags that were supposed to go across some of the narrower streets.

The Tea Cauldron sat opposite a series of private houses with front yards, so no banners for me. But maybe we could do some of the flags? I made a mental note to email Sonia about it later —I was within cane-throwing range, so I didn't want to chance writing a reminder on my phone.

As Sonia moved on to the next topic, I tried to study the attendees without rousing suspicion, which was hard since I was sitting in the first row. Nobody was paying me undue attention other than the occasional glares from Hutton and the natural curiosity by some of the other business owners who caught me staring at them.

A few points of discussion later, Sonia opened the floor for questions, and I jumped to my feet before Dru attempted to break my ribs again.

"Yes, Avery?" Sonia asked.

"I'd like to make a formal complaint about Tabbies buying the Corner Rose."

Loud murmurs filled the room, and Sonia clapped her hands to quiet everyone.

"Explain."

I mentally reviewed the list of cons I'd come up earlier in the day and with Dru during the drive. "I think Old Olmeda should remain in the hands of small business owners. It's not a place for more big chains—we already have enough of those."

Assenting murmurs rose behind me.

"Old shops full of history like the Corner Rose deserve a personal touch that simply can't be achieved by a chain like Tabbies," I continued. "If we allow them to open, what's stopping every other big company from also opening a local store? Soon there will be nothing quaint or unique about Olmeda. It'll look like every other town out there. Visitors will stop coming and our tourist trade will dry up."

Bosko stood, nodding vigorously. "Lady's got a point, Sonia."

His agreement was a bit of a shock, and I hoped it didn't show on my face.

"Yeah," said another man. "Don't want the town to be filled by big conglomerates that only care about the bottom line." He slammed his chest. "Our shops have heart."

"Oh, c'mon. It's just a paper store, not some evil conglomerate," a woman said. Dru glared at her, no doubt adding her to her personal list of revenge targets. "I've met with their guy. He's a nice boy."

Keith snorted. "Janet, you think every man below the age of forty is a 'nice boy.'"

Laughs and snickering spread along the room.

"Screw you, Keith," Janet said hotly.

"Friday night. My schedule is empty, baby," Keith answered with a wink.

Sonia clapped for attention before Janet's head exploded. "Anything else?"

"Yes." I squared my shoulders, turned, and gave everyone an earnest look. "Places like the Corner Rose deserve to be in the community's hands. Would you really give it to a newcomer over someone local?"

"Why not?" asked Bobby. "We gave you the witch shop, didn't we?"

He totally got me there. "That was different. The shop reverted to the Council after Ms. Bagley's death."

"I don't see the difference," Janet insisted.

"Yeah," said someone else. "What's the difference?"

"Yes, Avery," Sonia said in sugary sweet tones. "Please enlighten us."

I met Ian's gaze. He arched his brows, as if daring me to show these people I meant business.

Oh, I'd show them the meaning of business.

"First of all," I said loudly, "the Council is not a chain. Second of all, the shop was not stolen from a local witch interested in taking over." It had totally been, but they didn't need to know about that. "Third, the Council sought permission before giving it to me, didn't they?" I added, glancing at Sonia over my shoulder.

Sonia agreed, almost unwillingly. "They did."

"That's a bunch of crap," someone else said. "What's your problem with Tabbies, anyway?"

"The Corner Rose is right by my shop."

"So what?"

"So, I don't think Tabbies opening there is a good idea. It'll bring down the neighborhood's quality."

"I agree," Bosko said. "It's bad business having one of those super modern chains around."

"Shut up, Bosko. You wouldn't know good business or good quality if it spit in your face."

"Tell that to my bank account, Bobby."

Laughter filled the air.

Sonia clapped again.

A couple of rows behind me, Veva stood smoothly. "If I may?"

Sonia gestured for her to continue.

"We may not have had a choice in the person taking over Bagley's shop, but I think we can all agree that having fresh blood in the community is for the better." My mouth started to droop at her words. "That being said, Hope Avery replaced a witch. The Council wouldn't have trusted her with such an important position if they didn't think her capable of serving the community's needs. I think we would do well to take her opinions seriously." Her smile was as serene as a moonlit pond.

"After all, we all depend on her for our potions and spells, don't we?"

A lot of nervous glances were sent my way. I tried not to look smug.

"All I mean to say," I said smoothly, "is that there are young local members who would like the chance to operate their own businesses, so why give something like the Corner Rose to an outsider chain? If they want to open in Olmeda, they can open downtown. Plenty of hotels and visitors there."

Murmurs of assent rose as everyone began talking among themselves.

Veva gave me a faint smile and sat back down.

I nodded my thanks and did the same.

Sonia clapped her hands one more time. "Everyone has made good points. If an offer is made, we shall bring it to a vote."

Dru's expression turned mutinous, but without the capital to convince the bank to sell her the Corner Rose, she couldn't simply jump in and dare the room to choose a chain over her.

Sonia dealt with a few squabbles after that, then set us free.

"That went better than I expected," I said as we walked toward Ian's SUV. Between Bosko and Veva's support, I thought we had a good chance at denying Preston if he put in an offer for the shop.

My phone vibrated in my pocket with an incoming text. From Dru. Who was walking by my side.

I checked it surreptitiously, in case it was some kind of secret SOS. It was a list of names. Definitely not a cry for help.

"You sent me a list of names?" I asked. "Why?"

"I wrote down everyone who argued for selling the Corner Rose to the bastard," Dru said. "So we can investigate them."

I studied her face. She wore quite the malevolent expression, complete with scary smirk.

"You mean blackmail, don't you? You want to see if there is anything we can blackmail them with."

The smirk intensified.

"Don't you think you're taking this a bit too far?" I asked earnestly. "We don't need to resort to dirty tricks. We have a strong argument. That's enough."

Dru shrugged. "It doesn't hurt to be prepared."

"Ian," I said, turning to him, "tell her she's overdoing it."

The paranoid bounty hunter shrugged. "It doesn't hurt to be prepared."

Well, that one was on me.

Instead of turning toward the mom-and-pop restaurant for our usual after-PBOA dinner date, we walked on to the parking garage, and I sighed wistfully at the street as we left it behind. I'd come to really enjoy our little PBOA tradition, but with Dru here, there was no chance for a quiet dinner. She'd spend it making plans on how to "convince" people to back us up. Ian had likely sensed that too.

We were piling into the SUV when Ian's loud phone alarm went off.

"What is it?" I asked, startled.

He scowled at his phone for a few moments. "Someone's trying to break into the house."

19

"Oh, no," I exclaimed. "Call the police?"

"Get in," Ian ordered.

Dru and I hurried to get into the car and strap our seatbelts on. Ian started the SUV and made it to the garage gate in record time.

He tossed me his phone. "Check what he's doing."

"Police?" I ventured again.

"No."

Nothing to do about that. His house, his decision. I checked his phone as he accelerated into the street—a security camera feed filled the screen, night vision tinting everything into shades of gray. A male figure dressed in black, including gloves and a balaclava, was tooling around the back door.

"He's not afraid of the dogs," I said.

"Because they're at your shop," Ian answered darkly. He took a corner at high speed and I braced for impact. "What's he doing now?"

"I think he's about to break a window."

Ian cursed, and our speed increased.

"Do you think it's your ex-partner's fake son?"

"Yes."

"Who?" asked Dru from the back seat.

I didn't dare turn to talk to her. If death arrived in the form of another SUV, I wanted to see it firsthand. "A mystery man came around trying to pass as Ian's ex-partner's son."

"Why?"

"He wanted his files."

"Why?"

"Might be related to the spellbook thing. We don't know."

"Let me see."

Ian nodded in curt approval. His jaw was locked tight and his eyes promised retribution. I hoped the burglar gave up and left because you did not want to mess with a bounty hunter who owned a cemetery.

Dru reached for the phone and studied it intently. "Could be him."

"Who? Preston?"

She returned the phone. "Yes."

"I don't think it's him. This man's too thin." The man changed angles, and I got a good look at his eyes and the bridge of his nose. "Not him." I showed the proof to Dru.

"He must have a partner," Dru said.

I wanted to point out she was starting to overdo it with her obsession in blaming her ex, but...

Two newcomers in town at the same time with a shared interest in the same part of an Old Olmeda block. Why wouldn't they work together? Mystery Man would get his spellbook, Dru's ex-boyfriend would get to distract me from stopping him.

Win-win, my favorite kind of situation.

On the screen, the man broke a pane in the back door and snuck a hand in. "He's trying to unlock the back door. Oh, no. He did it. He's inside now."

The tension in the SUV ratcheted up by about a thousand. Not because Ian was scared that the man would steal something precious, I imagined, but because he had dared touch his house. Probably a territorial thing. Very macho. Very shifter.

With a last screech of wheels, Ian came to a stop a whisper from the cemetery's front gate. By the time I jumped out of the SUV, Ian had grabbed his stun gun and was already unlocking the side door.

I pocketed his phone as we rushed toward the house.

"Stay," Ian barked as his movements became utterly sleek and silent.

Dru and I stopped in our tracks while he stalked up to the house and silently opened the front door.

"You check the back," I said. "I'll guard the cemetery side."

Dru took off toward the detached garage and the back door, and I made my way around the other side of the house. There were no doors on this side, but plenty of windows. I doubted the robber would make it this way since he already had the back door open, but we needed to cover all our bases.

Of the both of us, Dru had the highest chance of stopping the man if he evaded Ian and made a run for it. Her demon side made her agile and fast, hardened her skin to some extent, and gave her razor-sharp claws.

My witch side gave me a lot of good intentions and nothing much else, as witnessed by my fights with Vicky and the demon who tried to mug me and Key. And I didn't even have Fluffy to back me up this time.

I could really use Fluffy right now.

"Being alone is a choice, not a curse," I murmured, feeling the pinpricks of my magic expand down my arms. "Only you can find the greatness hidden within."

Trotting along the house, I tried to peer through the

windows. The night was dark, the moon hidden behind heavy clouds, and I could barely see where I was going.

One of the windows slammed open on the other end of the house, and I jumped a foot into the air.

A dark shadow jumped out and began running down the slope. The robber. Another one leaped nimbly over the windowsill and began giving chase—Ian.

Aware that Ian was gaining ground on him, the robber swerved toward the cemetery side. Between the lack of ambient light, the trees peppering the graveyard, and the few statues and small mausoleums among the graves, he had a good chance at getting lost and would never be found.

I jogged down, trying to make as little noise as possible, and reached the first row of graves. It was an old cemetery, and many of the headstones stood at odd angles. I bent into a semi-crouch and kept advancing, keeping my eyes and ears open.

A shadow darted between two trees ahead. I halted. Hurried squelching noises going to my right reached my ears. Ian or the robber? I moved that way until a twig snapping made me turn around and check behind me. Nothing but looming shadows.

Boy, could I *really* use Fluffy right now.

No more sounds rose in the air, so I zigzagged among the graves until I reached a small mausoleum, crossing my fingers I wasn't stepping on anyone's ancestor.

"Sorry," I whispered. "Sorry!"

The mausoleum offered me some protection, so I dared a peek around its corner. It stood by one of the wider paths, marked by the lack of tilting headstones. Farther back, someone crossed from behind a tree to behind a statue. Again, Ian or the robber?

It had to be the robber.

Farther back, another shadow advanced forward. I recognized the cadence of his movements—sleek and predatory. Ian. He was herding the robber my way.

Think, Hope. Think.

Suddenly, I knew what to do.

Calling on my magic, I bent low and darted across the path, tracing a line through the muddy grass to form the quickest, dirtiest, least elegant ward to ever come into existence.

I dropped to my knees behind a gravestone on the other side, never losing contact with the ground, and waited.

And waited.

Should I send Ian a text? But the light coming from the phone might give away my location. Not to mention Ian's phone was currently in my other back pocket.

Something squelched nearby. I tensed. Was that a step? Yes! And another. They sounded cautious, tentative. Like the steps of someone trying to sneak by a large wolf intent on eating them alive.

A shadow crossed my line of vision.

I planted my hand on the grass.

Halt.

My ward flashed into being, siphoning my magic like a greedy ten-year-old with a bowl of Halloween candies.

The man's feet stuck to the ground as he passed by the ward, and he went down with a loud yelp.

"Ian!" I shouted, and forced my noodle legs to push forward.

By some miracle of nature, they obeyed, and gave me enough of a burst to tackle the man down as he was trying to get back on his feet.

"Get off me!" He tried to shake me off, but I held on.

Until he planted an elbow in my ribs.

"Oomph."

I lost my hold, and he used the opportunity to push me aside and break out in a full-on run.

Not three seconds later, Ian leaped over me to give chase.

I wanted to get up and go after them. I really did. But all I could do was lie there on my back, staring at the dark sky and breathing hard.

I seriously needed to restock on freezing potions.

A few minutes later, Dru appeared in my field of vision.

She looked down at me, hands on her hips. "Got the shit beat out of you, did you?"

"Almost."

"I guess you tried."

"It's all in the attitude," I agreed. I held out a hand, and she helped me get to my feet. Then right back down onto my butt. "Oops." I gestured weakly toward the path. "You go see if Ian needs help. I'll guard the house."

Dru said nothing but set off in an easy lope that made me wonder if she was a habitual runner.

Eventually, I managed to get back to my feet and make my way to the house. Ian and Dru were nowhere to be seen, so I went in through the back door, switched on the lights, and cleaned up the broken glass. Then I sat at the big kitchen table, leaned my head on my arms, and waited for the cavalry to return.

———

Ian nudged me awake some time later. I sat up straight with a jolt, my pulse pounding in my throat as I searched my surroundings.

Ian's kitchen. Ian standing by my side.

"Mystery Man?" I croaked.

"Got away," he said. After another squeeze of my shoulder,

he opened a cupboard and took a couple of cans of pasta out. "Coffee?"

"Soda, if you have."

I rubbed my eyes and watched him start the coffeemaker, then open the cans and pour them into a pot, which he set to heat on the stove.

A small whine brought my attention down. Fluffy hovered by my chair, peering up anxiously.

"Fluffy!" I brought her up onto my lap and gave her a big hug. A scratch of nails against hardwood announced Rufus's entrance from the living room. "I'm sorry. I fell asleep. I meant to stand guard in case someone else came by."

"Thank you."

Fluffy squirmed, and I allowed her down. She went to her bowl and lapped some water.

"How did you get the dogs here?" I asked. Last I'd seen them, they had been given free rein in my backyard.

"We picked them up before I dropped Dru home."

I scanned the kitchen, the dark world outside the windows, and the beam of light from the kitchen's ceiling fixtures extending into the shadowed living room. "No strays?"

Ian set a can of my favorite brand of diet soda and a bowl filled with canned pasta in front of me.

"What? No handmade cooking? No strays to watch over me and no handmade cooking. Oh, how far my star has fallen!" I said theatrically, then leaned in as he sat by my side. "It was the magic, right? My poor ward wasn't up to your standards."

He snorted. "I assumed you'd rather eat now than wait an hour for me to make food."

"Excellent point." I dug into the pasta with relish. It was good.

Then again, after using my magic, everything always tasted good.

"You could've kept the dogs at the house and driven me back," I said. Unless he didn't plan on leaving them with me again...or himself. It made sense, since the robber had hit his house rather than my shop.

The food in my mouth suddenly tasted like mud.

"You're staying here tonight."

And just like that, flavor exploded on my tongue again. "I am?"

"I'm not sleeping on the floor two nights in a row. I retired as a full-time bounty hunter for a reason."

"I'm getting a couch, I swear."

"No need."

Now, what did that mean? I studied him from under my lashes as I ate my pasta, but as usual, his face was unreadable. He simply ate his food like it was the most natural thing in the world.

"Next time I sleep over," he added between mouthfuls, noticing my keen interest, "I'll take the bed."

"So you'll leave me on the floor?" I shook my head in mock disappointment. "How ungentlemanly of you."

He gave me a surprisingly arrogant look. "That'll be up to you."

I choked on my pasta and drained my soda, trying to recover. That had been direct enough.

Being completely unprepared to tackle *that* discussion, I asked, "How did the robber get away? You were two seconds behind."

"He used a freezing potion when I got over the fence. I lost him at Guiles and Romary."

Thursday nights weren't the busiest time around the clubs, but there was usually a good contingent of locals and tourists hanging around. It was possible to get lost in the crowd.

"Rufus?"

"Nothing to get his smell from."

"I'm surprised you couldn't catch up, even with the freezing potion." I had seen Ian move—he was *fast*. He should've been able to gain on the man even after being frozen for a few seconds.

"He's probably a shifter or a demon."

Witches and mages relied on their elemental powers rather than their physicality, and berserkers were all about bursts of strength, not endurance.

"Did he get to any of the files?"

"No, I locked them back up."

I ate the last of my pasta and licked the spoon. "We should take a look at them again."

Ian tensed. "Why?"

"The man came here instead of the shop."

"He might've gone to the shop first, but found the dogs."

"He still came here, though." I scowled. "He knew we'd be at the PBOA. Maybe he also knew you had brought Fluffy and Rufus to the shop."

Fluffy yipped.

"He knows more about us than we know about him," Ian agreed.

"Which is why we need to take a look at the files again." I pointed at him with my spoon. "Maybe you're right, and it's a coincidence that someone posing as your ex-partner's son came asking for the files at the same time someone asked for the spellbook. After all, the person interested in the spellbook knows where it should be. We took the robber's phone, so all he knows is that his hire failed at getting the spellbook. He doesn't know I don't actually have it."

"Yes."

"Or maybe it does have something to do with the spellbook. They offered a lot of money in the call, and if they know your ex-partner was involved in that bounty, they might suspect there's more information about it in his files. Or information about other equally expensive items. Breaking into a bounty hunter's house is a huge risk, especially one with your reputation. I'm thinking there is something in those files worth the risk. We should take a second look."

Ian sipped his coffee, his expression closed down. When he put the mug down, his jaw clenched, and he gave me a stiff nod of agreement, which took me by surprise.

I already knew about his ex-partner turning out to be a hitman, so why was he still so tense?

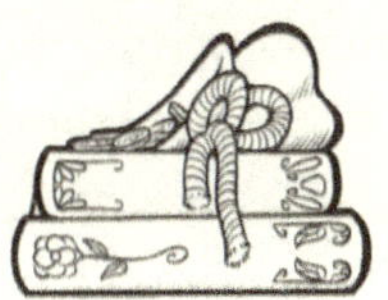

20

IAN INSISTED we wash my muddy clothes, so I dressed in one of his T-shirts and sweats, which were giant on me. They smelled of him too, and it took a monumental effort not to sniff them the whole time I sat on the living-room couch while he brought up the box of files.

He dumped the box on the floor between us and sat on the other corner of the couch. He picked up the first file and opened it on his lap, checking the contents with an intent expression.

We were doing this like ripping off a Band-Aid, then. No need for small talk or splashing some water on your chest, just straight jumping into the pool.

I picked up the second file rather than a random one, assuming they were in some sort of order and that he'd like to keep it that way, and opened it.

An old man's mugshot was clipped to the inside of the cover in the same way my grandma's photo had been. He didn't look kind like Grandma, though. He looked mean and dangerous and like he stole candy from small children. The folder contained photos of a couple of houses, an old car, and several pages of information, including a receipt of payment. The amount made me gasp, and I looked at Ian.

He was sitting straight like an arrow, a muscle on his jaw working as he scanned his own folder.

Swallowing hard, I returned my attention to the folder. Knowing Ian's ex-partner had been a hitman was one thing, but seeing the proof was another. And there was no way anyone paid this much money for something other than an assassination.

My first instinct was to drop the folder on the coffee table like it was scalding, badly brewed tea, but I forced myself to skim the rest of the papers. We were searching for a connection and a motive beyond Grandma's spellbook, and if Ian's ex-partner had killed a family member—a parent or grandparent—of Mystery Man, revenge might be a powerful motivator. It would be for me.

There were no mentions of the man's family in the pages, or anything other than his job, where he lived, and a map of a town with different spots circled in red. Dumping grounds? Would Grandma's file have looked like this if Ian's ex-partner had taken the hit to the end?

That brought up an interesting question.

I left the folder on the table and picked up the next. A woman in her forties this time, polished and ready to take on the world with a smug look in her eyes that suggested she might've already done it. There was information about her daily goings, her job, the paranormal club she frequented, a map, and the receipt for payment for a similar eye-watering amount of money.

"Grandma's file doesn't have a receipt," I said, checking another file.

"No."

"Does that mean the job got cut short?"

"Probably."

I shuddered, not daring to think about what might've happened if it hadn't. "How come?"

Ian didn't answer, leaving me to work it out on my own. Maybe the person who hired Duncan had changed his mind and canceled the hit, or had run out of funds, as Ian had suggested before.

The next file came with a photo of a piece of jewelry instead of a person. So Duncan *had* acted as a thief as well as a hitman. That was good to know. I wasn't sure of why, but maybe part of me still held hope that Ian's ex-partner hadn't been *all* bad, for Ian's sake if anything else.

But the next folder was another obvious murder-for-hire. An alpha this time, caught in both his human and wolf shapes. This one had cost nearly double the others, and I wondered if this was why the twins had gone at Hutton on their own rather than waste the money on a professional hitman. If they'd been less stingy, Hutton might dead now and Olmeda's pack territory sold for a nice profit and divided up to build modern condos.

I glanced at Ian again. He hadn't moved a muscle. Hadn't moved from the first file he'd taken.

Reaching over, I touched his forearm. It felt hard and unyielding under my fingertips, tension thrumming beneath his skin.

"There's no shame in having an ex-partner like this. Or in him being your mentor. It wasn't your fault. You didn't know."

"I'm not ashamed."

"You're something."

He narrowed his eyes. "I'm not."

I gestured at his face. "You're extra-extra stony."

His scowl deepened. "What do you mean?"

"Relax. Nobody is going to blame you for these."

He slapped the folder on his lap closed and reached for another one. "I know."

Uncertainty gripped me. Should I press further or let him deal with his feelings on his own? Ian was wearing *Do Not Trespass* signs all over his person, but I wasn't sure if I was included in the general population or if I'd earned a special pass yet. I thought I had, but maybe he needed to work on some things on his own before welcoming any more of my advice.

I'd give him five minutes, then try again.

But as I checked the files for hints at what might've drawn Mystery Man beyond Grandma's file, the enormity of the situation really started to sink in.

Ian's ex-partner had been a hitman for a long time. He had killed several people. For a lot of money. And still, he hadn't stopped taking jobs. He had been a career hitman, not a one-and-done. He had only stopped when he had died.

Died...at someone's hands? One of his targets? Whoever had hired him afraid he might spill the beans? Or...

An icy fist encased my insides as I turned toward Ian.

The number of folders in his lap had changed, his position, the hardness in his face hadn't.

Oh, good Mother Earth. The rumors were right. Ian did get his ex-partner killed.

Because he had killed him himself.

"You stopped him. Your ex-partner," I said, my voice soft and free of judgment.

He stilled but said nothing.

"You discovered what he was doing on the side," I continued, voicing my theory. "You discovered and put a stop to it."

Ian kept his gaze trained on the folder in his lap. His jaw sawed back and forth, and still he said nothing. He didn't need to.

I reached over again. "Ian..."

He didn't move at my touch, and part of me was glad of it. He was so tense he might break like a twig if he tried to.

"I'm sorry you had to do that."

"It was my job."

"A self-bounty, huh?" I asked, trying to lighten up the mood.

A deep silence followed my words, making me wish I'd lightened myself into a hole rather than having said anything. Ian's expression became so hard, the look in his eyes so distant, that my heart broke into a million shards.

Moving across the sofa, I transferred the files in his lap to the table. Holding his face with my hands, I forced him to look at me.

"I'm not judging you. You did what you had to do. He couldn't be allowed to continue."

Paranormal justice was harsh and swift.

The tension in Ian finally broke. With a big exhale, he blinked and ran a hand through his hair.

"Yes."

I couldn't begin to imagine having to kill my own mentor. A memory of Bagley complaining about my magical ineptitude from a tarot set on the bookshelf burst into my mind.

On second thought, yes. I could imagine very well.

It didn't mean I had to do it with my own hands.

"Why didn't you report him to the bounty hunters, let others do the deed?" I caressed his face with my thumb, and he turned his cheek into the palm of my hand.

"My partner, my responsibility."

"He wasn't your partner for that long," I pointed out. From what I remembered, Ian had lost his partner in his early or mid-twenties.

"Long enough."

And there lay the crux of the matter. The man had

continued his hitman career under Ian's nose. Once Ian had discovered what had been going on, his guilt at not realizing earlier must've eaten him alive. He must've blamed himself for whatever deaths had happened while he was around.

Ian might be a bounty hunter, but there was nothing wrong with his moral code.

But Ian wasn't a man of many words, and making him admit all this would not get us anywhere. He wasn't stupid—part of him must know it wasn't his fault.

So, I simply hugged him tight, telling him without words that I understood, and he'd find no pity or blame coming from me.

His arms came around me, pressing me close until I was sitting on his lap.

"Is that why you're helping me?" I asked after a long time. "Why you help the strays? To clear your conscience?" To become the kind of mentor he had deserved but hadn't gotten.

"No," he said, sounding more like himself. Then his voice became the tiniest bit like mine. "Because it's the right thing to do."

The callback to my words when I'd tried to convince him to help Hutton just about melted my insides.

21

FRIDAY DAWNED cloudy but not rainy, which was excellent weather for a tea shop. I had hazy memories of falling asleep in Ian's lap, but when I'd woken up, I'd been in his guest room. In his guest room and running awfully late, so I hadn't had the time to be nosy about his accommodations as I rushed out of the house.

Ian had killed his ex-partner to stop his killing-for-hire.

It was so simple, and yet so complicated. But the strays had already arrived by the time I'd woken up, and in my hurry to avoid being seen and getting home, I hadn't been able to talk to him.

Not that he'd want to rehash the whole thing again.

I shouldn't have taken so many pains to hurry because Dru had already opened the shop, looking like yesterday's disappointment at the PBOA and not catching the thief hadn't closed a door but opened a window into the land of steely determination.

"Let's take another look at your grandma's spellbook," she said the moment I stepped through the door.

I halted, startled. "What? Why?"

"I want to make sure we didn't miss anything."

"I've read it a thousand times. There's nothing to miss."

"*You* have read it a thousand times," she said triumphantly, as if it explained everything.

I got the gist, though, and she might have a point. How many times had I read the shop's introduction on our website without noticing I hadn't mentioned the word "tea" a single time until Doyle had pointed it out?

After washing my face and changing clothes, I grabbed Grandma's spellbook and brought it down. With any luck, Bagley was still in the ether, as I didn't relish her spying on us, but I also didn't want to leave the shop unattended.

The man who had robbed us at gunpoint might be gone, but my paranoia wasn't ready to stand down.

You know how it goes—find a robber unconscious on your floor, know there's a dozen waiting inside your walls.

Dru took the spellbook from my hands and studied the front and back before placing it carefully on the counter. Opening the cover, she ran her fingers around the inside binding.

"Checking for hidden notes?" I guessed.

Dru made a shushing noise, and I assumed I wasn't supposed to spoil her treasure hunting fun. When her investigation revealed nothing but fabric glued to a piece of hard carton, she repeated the action on the back cover.

"This has to be the key." Dru went back to the start of the book and carefully read the list of names written on the first page.

The key to something, at least. "I think the man who tried to break into Ian's is the same one who hired our robber."

Dru glanced up. "Why would it be the same?"

Hard to explain without revealing the truth about Ian's

hitman ex-partner and his files and the file on Grandma. "Too much coincidence."

"I doubt it. If that guy wanted the spellbook, he'd have come here, not the cemetery."

"Maybe he did, but the dogs stopped him."

"Then he'd try another day."

It was killing me not to spill the beans about Grandma's file, but that was one secret most definitely not mine to share.

"Whoever hired that man to rob us—"

"The bastard," Dru muttered.

"Whoever it was must think alchemy is real."

"Or wants to sell it to someone who thinks it's real."

The shop's landline began ringing, and I picked up the receiver automatically. "The Tea Cauldron."

"It didn't work," a female voice whispered harshly from the other side.

I tried to place it but came up lost. "Excuse me?"

"The love potion. It didn't work!"

Oh, good Mother. Holly the teen. "Are you sure?"

"Yes, I'm sure! She drank the coffee and nothing happened."

Considering the contents of the fake love potion, I feared for their target's taste buds more than her chances of falling under a spell. "Does your friend have any love potion left?"

"I think so. Why? Did she not use enough? I used half of what you gave me and it worked. Did you mess up? Are you trying to scam us?"

I glanced at the shop, searching for inspiration. My gaze fell on the cabinet of horrors—Bagley's old dark magic supplies cabinet. "Tell her to use it to bake cookies."

"Cookies?"

"Yes. Use whatever is left to make cookies, then give them to whoever it is." If cookies had worked for the evil hag to charm a whole town, it'd surely work for a single teenage girl to charm her crush.

"But we don't know how to bake cookies."

"Check a video online. Good luck!"

I hung up and returned to Dru. She had already gone through most of the written pages and was staring at the last entry, by yours truly.

"You added a grilled ham and cheese sandwich recipe to your grandmother's spellbook," she said without inflection.

My chest expanded with pride, and my smile widened to match. "It's a family recipe."

"It's butter, bread, ham, and cheese."

I pointed to a small spell written at the end. "Plus a secret ingredient."

"'While the sandwich cooks, be sure to center your intentions on sharing the goodness in your life that allowed you this moment of happiness.'" Dru began quoting. "'If unsure, repeat aloud, *I share my love with the universe so that it may touch the recipient's heart.*'" She made gagging noises. "I'm *never* eating your sandwiches again."

"Aww, but deep inside, you know you love them."

"So deep, we're talking septic tanks." Dru flicked through the rest of the empty pages. "What about something written in invisible ink?"

"I tried that when I first got the book."

My smile slowly disappeared as I watched the expanse of white flip back and forth under Dru's fingers.

I'd had Grandma's spellbook for six years, and all I'd added were a few affirmations and two spells to it.

My quest to make it the best spellbook in the world wasn't going as planned. The prospects of achieving my goal within my lifetime were...grim, to say the least. Two spells in six years. If I lived to be ninety, it'd put me at 20 spells, give or take.

But then, I reassured myself, family spellbooks were a group effort. Heirlooms only became so after several generations. My contribution might not seem like a lot now, but there was no quantifying keeping Grandma's memory and teachings alive, and passing them to whoever came next—my heirs, my children, or even someone like Key.

"It has to be Preston." Dru closed the spellbook and pushed it toward me.

"You're obsessed."

"Shut up."

"Think about it for a moment. What if it isn't him? What if he has nothing to do with this and you're barking up the wrong tree?"

"I'm not wrong."

"But if you are?"

"Then I'll figure out what he's up to some other way. Now, shush." She brought out her phone and scrolled through her contacts before making a call.

Suddenly, she tensed, her features rearranging into a hard mask complete with an extremely fake smile. "Mom? Hi, sorry to bother you. I know you're busy." Her voice had turned so sweet, I was tempted to take a video for blackmail purposes later. "Yes. Yes, of course. Yes, actually..." She drew a circle on the counter. "That's why I was calling. Yes, I've seen him." Now she looked more pained than anything else. "That's right, Mom. No, we haven't talked, but..." She sent a silent prayer to the ceiling. "Do you know where he's staying? Yes, I know you've tried to talk sense into me, Mom. Yes, he's a catch. He's still..." A tick developed in her left eye. "He's single, right? I don't want to step on anyone's toes. Yes, I know I'd know if I'd gone to the summer picnic. Mom, please. *Mom!* Did you really have to go *there*?"

Judging from Dru's expression, I'd love to know what *there* was—she looked like her head was about to explode.

"It's fine if you don't want to tell me, Mom," Dru said in a haughty voice. "I just thought that since you've been pushing me so hard to get back together, you'd help me. If you'd rather I go back to George, then I'll... I see. Yes, thank you."

She hung up and closed her eyes. Her chest expanded visibly as she took a few deep breaths.

"But we already know where he's staying," I ventured.

"He's not staying there."

"He's not?"

"I checked. He was there for a couple of days, then checked out. What's with that look?" she snapped.

I made a show of drying tears from my eyes. "Look at you, all grown up. Going around spying and trying to break into people's places all on your own."

"Hope, I swear to God if you don't wipe that expression from your face, I'll punch it in."

With an effort, I brought my grin back under control. "I assume you tried other hotels?"

"Yes," she gritted out. "Half of them wouldn't even confirm if he was staying."

Probably because expensive places like these were used to strangers trying to nose around famous people. "Perhaps for the best. There is a fine line between spying and stalking. Wouldn't want to get Officer Brooks involved."

Dru huffed. "She'd understand."

The way she said that made me wonder how many of Brooks's exes she and Dru had spied on together. Preston really knew how to push all of Dru's buttons simply by existing, someone who was usually the calmest and most collected person I had ever known. That was its own kind of power. Too bad Preston had chosen to use it for evil.

Sure, he might not be evil *right now* no matter how much Dru wanted to believe he was up to no good, but taking Dru's job then dumping her then coming after her dream shop, intentionally or not, wasn't good, cosmically speaking.

The shop's door opened and a young man entered with a laptop under his arm. I pointed at the Wi-Fi password taped to the shelf and asked for his order. By the time I had served him at the table by the window and was back behind the counter, Dru had returned to her phone, the devil's own smile stretching her lips.

"What are you doing?" I whispered.

"My mother gave me the bastard's number."

"You're trying to see where he is?" That didn't sound possible unless she hacked into his account.

She chuckled. A distinctly evil sound. "Nah. I'm signing him up for spam."

And that's when I knew I never, ever wanted to be on Dru's bad side, even if it cost me my soul.

The thought had just come to mind when Dru suddenly spoke. "Hope, did you ever answer that text about the potion delivery?"

"I didn't. I completely forgot about that."

"Let's set a trap."

I leaned in. "You think it's related to whatever is happening? To Preston? Stupid question. Don't answer that." But even if she was wrong and the anonymous texter had nothing to do with it, it was yet another coincidence. And it wasn't like we had any other leads.

In fact, the idea was pure genius. If it was related to Dru's ex-boyfriend, that'd clear the way for us to kick him out of Olmeda. If it was someone else, it'd allow us to track another dark magic user. And there was the slight possibility that Mystery Man had run out of glamour potions and had ordered one from outside town. After all, he hadn't used one last night. Why hadn't I thought of this before?

I brought up the text conversation on my phone.

Heard you were looking for deliveries.

What kind of deliveries?

The special kind. Willing to lose this one for the correct price.

I began typing, but Dru's hand shot out to stop me. "Don't mess it up."

"Hey, I can do this much."

She didn't appear convinced, but allowed me to continue.

Still available?

We had to cool our heels for about twenty minutes before we got an answer, during which it was my turn to stop Dru from growling at Hannah for daring to enter the shop.

The price just doubled.

I'd take that as a yes.

Original price, I wrote back. It never paid to be too eager or accept too easily.

Double.

Original plus 50%.

Agreed.

Excellent. *Time and location for the drop?*

I said I'd lose the delivery. I don't kiss and tell.

Ah, but for me he might reveal his secrets because... *And lose out on a beautiful relationship?*

Extra information costs another 50%.

Friendships, apparently, came with a price tag. *25%.*

40%.

Deal.

He named a price that made me choke on my saliva, then gave me an email address for the payment.

A third now, the rest when the extra information pans out, I wrote.

Flip that and we're in business.

Half-half.

I got a thumbs up emoji.

"We have a deal," I whispered to Dru. Then spent an hour setting up an online account unrelated to me or the shop to send the money from.

"I really hope I'm not getting scammed," I said dourly as my money disappeared into the internet.

"Charge it to the fire dude next time he comes around."

Excellent point. Hopefully by then I'd have access to Bagley's secret account too.

Half an hour after that, I got a time and address. I grinned and showed it to Dru.

"We're on."

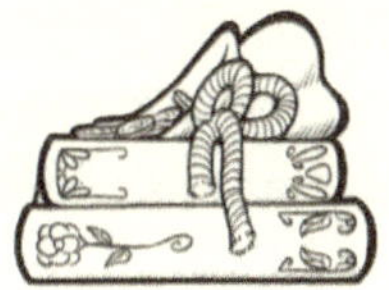

22

SETTING up a trap proved to be the easiest thing in the world.

My anonymous dark magic delivery person gave me the address of a twenty-four-seven private PO box service, a box number, and time for the drop. After some deliberation with Ian and Dru, we'd agreed to leave the dark magic potion where it was instead of switching it—anonymous was an "I don't look, I only deliver" kind of businessperson, so we didn't know the contents—and catch the dark magic user in the act.

Now we just had to hope I hadn't been conned.

Could I still use it as a business deduction if I got nothing in return?

Might as well call Crane and ask, since he was already charging me half a kidney. Talk about getting conned.

Ian, Dru, and I were squished in a small room marked "staff only," spying on the rows of lockers through the cracked door. Ian had wanted Dru to remain outside with Shane and Alex, in the car watching the building, but I'd argued that if Preston happened to be the guilty party and showed up, she might take control of the car and run him over.

The building was a bit off the beaten path, but it being

Friday night, the streets had enough people not to make it suspicious, and the room with the lockers saw brisk business. Tourists getting last-minute shopping deliveries, locals getting their mail and packages, and a couple of shady-looking people, which told me either there was more than one dark magic delivery person in Olmeda, or this was a common ground for illegal transactions, magical or not.

We had been waiting for about three hours, and I'd long given up my post by the door to sit on the carpeted floor, when Ian stiffened.

As he'd done every time he heard someone enter the room.

"Incoming," Dru whispered.

As she'd done every time anyone came into view.

At first, Shane and Alex had given us a heads-up anytime someone suspicious entered the building, but they'd stopped a while back and would only notify us if one of our prime suspects approached.

I wished they had Key with them, since she wanted to be a bounty hunter and, according to Ian, sitting in cars watching buildings was the bulk of the job, but we'd agreed the situation might get out of hand and the fewer people at risk, the better.

"Who is that?" Dru asked. Not for the first time. She tensed and beckoned to me excitedly.

I got to my feet, my legs complaining at the sudden change of position, and tried to slide between their bodies.

Ian shifted slightly, giving me an opening. I peeked through the slice of open door. An old woman stood by the row of lockers, white hair dyed pink and a slight curving to her spine.

As we watched, she inputted the combination on the electronic lock of our target box, and the door popped open. After looking furtively to her left and right, she reached inside with the speed of a viper and retrieved the vial.

Ian gently pushed us aside and opened the door. In two

steps, he was towering over the old woman, who gave a frightful little yelp and cradled the potion closer to her chest.

"Oh, my Lord, young man. Don't scare me like that."

Now that she was facing Ian, we had a good view of her features. They were familiar. I had seen this woman before. A customer of the shop?

No, not a customer. The old biddy who'd ranted at me, ran off without paying for her tea, and left me my first one-starred review!

"Hey!" Abandoning our hiding spot, I strode up to them.

The old woman jumped at my exclamation. Her scowl was immediate. "What are you doing here?" she spat, hugging the potion protectively.

"You know this woman?" Ian asked.

"Yes," the old woman said in outraged tones. "This is the quack from the witch shop."

"The..." I put my hands on my hips, my scowl giving hers a run for its money. "You left me a one-star review *and* ran off without paying."

She dismissed the charges with a wave of her hand. "Bah! You are no good, that's what you are. Well deserved. Theodora would've had my special more than ready."

Judging by the fact that she knew Bagley by her given name and we'd just caught her getting a dark magic delivery, I could take a good guess at what her *special* entailed. "Bagley is gone now, and we just caught you buying illegal magic."

"Illegal?" She sniffed soundly. "How *dare* you?"

"Oh, cut it off. We know that's dark magic." I pointed at the potion vial, now clearly visible.

"You can't prove that."

"We don't need to prove anything. He"—I pointed at Ian—"is a bounty hunter."

The woman gasped. "Bounty... Hunter?" She took a good

look at Ian and instead of paling or fainting with recognition, the glowering returned. "See here, Cavalier. I was a grown woman by the time your mother was a toddler. Don't try your tricks on me." She still held the potion like a lifesaver in her gnarled hand.

Ian kept his expression neutral. "Your name?"

"Agnes Dorsey," she said with great dignity.

I snapped my finger with recognition. "You own the bed and breakfast."

"So what?"

With a fast check that we were alone in the room, I asked, "You cater to paranormals, right?"

"None of your business, young lady."

I nudged Ian. "Show her the security camera photo."

Ian brought out his phone, swipped through the pictures, and showed Mystery Man's picture to the old biddy.

"What about him?" she demanded.

"Is he a guest?"

"Never seen him in my life."

But the fast flicker of her eyes betrayed her.

"We're done here," I said firmly, barely restraining myself from fist pumping in triumph. "Hand over the potion."

Now that we had a new lead on Mystery Man, I was itching to run to her bed and breakfast and dig around, but I had to be a responsible good witch and rid Olmeda of as much dark magic as possible.

She stepped backward, curving protectively around the vial. "No! It's mine. I paid for it."

"It's dark magic."

"It doesn't hurt anyone!"

"Tell you what," I said. "Tell me what the potion is, and I'll make you a better one."

"It's my tonic."

I extended my hand. "Hand it over."

She glared at us, then gave me the potion. I examined the liquid against the fluorescent ceiling light. The small bottle was tinted dark blue, so it was hard to determine the colors of the potion itself. Next, I twisted the cap open and took a good sniff. Lavender, valerian, maybe lemon balm. All herbs meant to help with sleep.

I put the cap back on and pocketed the bottle.

"You give that back *right now*," the old woman demanded.

"Come to the shop in two days. I'll give you something better." I pointed a finger at her and added in a menacing tone, "And don't even *think* of ordering another dark marketplace potion. We know where you live now."

I turned on my heel and strode out of the room. Ian and Dru caught up to me on the stairs. Dru wore a thunderous expression that told me she wanted to kick more than a couple of rocks.

"Cheer up," I told her, as we walked toward Ian's SUV. "We might find him at the B&B."

"Not likely." Her mouth formed a terse line, the disappointment obvious.

Ian called the strays to let them know we'd caught the buyer but to stick around for another hour, in case, then we got inside his SUV. Forty minutes later, thanks to Old Olmeda's Friday night traffic and revelry, we arrived at the bed and breakfast.

It was a quaint three-story old house painted in pastel blues and whites, with a lovely front garden surrounded by a low iron fence. "Dorsey House Bed & Breakfast" was written on a plaque on the wall, clearly illuminated by the front door's light.

Ian didn't pause; he took the steps up to the porch and opened the front door as if he'd known it wouldn't be locked. Maybe he had. While it was late, most of the guests would be expected to party for a long time on a Friday night, so no point in locking it, I supposed.

To the right of the foyer opened a sitting room with a couple of armchairs facing a small fireplace and a welcome counter on the other end, denoted by the leaflets neatly organized on a small shelf by the wall.

I studied them while Ian moved behind the counter and opened the old-style guestbook. There were so many things to do in Olmeda as a tourist. I picked up a couple of brochures and put them in my back pocket.

Veva wasn't the only shop I could cross-promote with, and I wasn't against collaborating with human businesses—the possibilities were infinite.

Ian abandoned the guestbook, grabbed an old-fashioned key from behind the counter, and made for the stairs. Ignoring Dru's look of disgust at my newly acquired knowledge of local tourist attractions, I followed Ian up to the second floor. He stopped by the room at the far end of the landing-slash-hallway and unlocked it.

The room was small but well appointed, with a bed covered by a quilt, a chest of drawers, a bathroom, and a TV.

It was also very clean, and very empty of personal belongings.

I stepped past Ian and peeked inside the tiny bathroom. Also empty.

"We're too late," I said, disappointed. "He's gone."

"Yes." Ian gave the room a thorough visual inspection. "Checked out last night."

"How do you know this was his room?" Dru asked.

Ian went to the bed and began checking under the mattress. "It was registered under Johnathan Smithe."

"Points for originality. Not," she muttered. She approached the chest of drawers and pulled open the top one. Empty.

I stared at the beige carpet, my spirits sinking. "He came here right after he tried to break into your house and decided to cut his losses."

"Yes."

"He knew you'd find him eventually."

"Yes."

"Now we're never going to find him."

Ian didn't reply, but I heard his "yes" all the same.

23

Saturday dawned rainy and depressingly gloomy. The world was tinted in hues of gray, not in the least helped by the black Halloween decorations taped to the windows.

Time to invest in some brighter orange garlands.

But even adding that to my to-do list felt like a chore.

So many chances, so many opportunities, so many plans. And I'd still found out nothing. Had fixed nothing.

Whoever wanted Grandma's imaginary alchemy spellbook, Mystery Man or not, was still out there, and they might try again. Grandma's reputation and legacy were still actively being tainted, I hadn't found Bagley's money, and Dru and I still hadn't uncovered a better reason to stop Preston from taking over the Corner Rose beyond *shop local* and *because he's an ass.*

It made one want to take a nap and not wake up for a week.

The bell tinkled as a new customer entered the shop, and I forced a smile. It was an older couple, and I served them some cocoa and a muffin each. I'd made a run for fresh muffins before opening, and having to stand twenty minutes in line at Fairy Circle Cakes hadn't improved my mood, no matter how much I reminded myself that good things come to those who wait.

Investigating had gotten me nowhere, so might as well try waiting.

Not the best affirmation out there, but I was grasping at straws.

After the couple left, the same young man as yesterday entered the shop and settled on the window table. He ordered a coffee and a muffin and opened his laptop.

The presence of what could be a new repeat customer should've filled me with pride, but all I could manage was a small twinge of something. More like a bug bite rather than genuine sentiment.

Oh, Mother.

I snuck into the small downstairs bathroom and stared intently at my reflection. At the sad eyes, the drooping mouth, the cloud of gloom hovering above my head.

"Good things come to those who wait."

Nothing. No burst of hope or even the smallest twinkling of anticipation.

"When investigation fails, wait for inspiration."

Nada.

This was not good.

The door's bell tinkled again, and I was forced to abandon my quest to improve my spirits to attend the newcomers—a young couple carrying several bags full of purchases.

They sat at the counter and chatted animatedly. At one point they asked me for recommendations for creepy places, and I dutifully told them about John B. Fieldman Park, the Three Sisters, the Modern Cabinet of Curiosities, and added Veva's shop—not exactly creepy, but they looked the kind who would love a tarot reading to get in the mood.

Once they left, I gave Veva a call. Maybe planning things for the shop would improve my mood.

No such luck.

By the time Dru dropped in for her evening shift, my mood was darker than the gray skies.

What was wrong with me?

Sure, I'd experienced bouts of despondency in the past—who hasn't?—but I usually bounced out of them after some introspection and a good round of meditation and affirmations.

Maybe that was the problem. I didn't have the time to stop for a good half hour and give it a better try than five seconds staring at the bathroom mirror.

Or maybe it was because my situation had changed. New city. New shop. New surroundings.

I needed to adapt.

I slammed a hand on the counter. "We're going out."

Dru and Key, who'd come to hang around, jumped at my sudden declaration.

It was late evening on a Saturday. Almost time to close.

"Out?" Dru asked.

"Out," I reaffirmed.

A change of scenery would do everyone wonders.

"Out where?" Key asked.

"Guiles and Romary."

They looked at me like I'd gone as green as the streak in my hair.

"You drink?" Dru asked, unconvinced.

"When the occasion demands it."

Dru grabbed her purse from behind the counter. "You're paying."

"Fine." A few extra expenses would be worth it if I could shake off this horrible, gloomy mood.

We closed the shop and walked over to the bars in Guiles and Romary. So strange, to be walking around for fun rather than in the pursuit of information. Strange, but nice.

Back home, I hadn't had that many real-life friends, and

none to go barhopping with. My sister and I had occasionally during the weekends, but it wasn't the same.

I pointed at Rena's. "Let's go there. It was nice."

The music was already at full blast, and the crowd spilled into the street. We presented our IDs and went inside the big space. We grabbed a table as another group of partygoers chose that moment to leave, and ordered our drinks—a Hurricane for me, a sangria for Dru, and a virgin Piña Colada for Key.

She pouted as I ordered for her but didn't complain. Dru asked to see her fake ID and whistled, looking more impressed than I'd ever seen her with any of my spells or potions.

I took a long swallow of my drink, the alcohol burning down my throat. It was overly sweet and tasty and did wonders to warm my insides. A few more sips, and the world would definitely start looking just peachy.

I was deciding on the pros and cons between slowing down or emptying the glass and asking for another when a man got onto the small karaoke stage on the corner and began singing a popular rock song.

Cheers and whistles rose from the audience, and the man sang harder.

He was having the time of his life. As if, for a few minutes, he had not a care in the world.

Was that why Ian liked to do karaoke? To forget everything for a short while?

"I'm doing it," I told Dru and Key, standing suddenly and taking another long sip of my drink. It seemed to chant *Do it! Do it!* as it made its way into my belly.

"Doing what?" Key asked, slightly alarmed.

I pointed at the karaoke stage. "Singing."

If Ian could do it to release his stress, why couldn't I?

———

I woke up with a strange taste in my mouth and a pounding in my head that made me wish I could keep on sleeping until Christmas. Prying my eyes open, I found myself back in Ian's guest room. I was still wearing yesterday's clothes and someone had removed my sneakers and draped the comforter over my body.

A huffing sound came from the edge of the bed, and two white paws anchored themselves on the bedding. A second later, Fluffy's lovely, eager black eyes came into view.

"G'mornin' flufee." I grimaced. Ugh, I sounded gross. Tasted gross. Felt gross.

Fluffy lolled her tongue and jumped onto the bed.

I pushed her fluffy face away when she came to greet me.

"You don't want to lick this," I told her. "Gross."

Fluffy was undeterred, however, so I gave up, allowed her to sniffle, then give a tentative lick, and attempted to sit up.

The movement turned the hammers inside my head into pointy little daggers with nothing better to do than turn my brain into a sieve.

You're a witch, Hope. You can fix this.

Witches weren't exactly healers, though. If I were home, I'd make myself a potion. Alas, no potion-making equipment available.

I dragged myself off the bed and into the small attached bathroom. Taking a shower was enticing, but I didn't feel comfortable enough yet in Ian's house to do it without the excuse of being covered in mud, so I simply washed my face with frigid cold water.

It helped somewhat. I also noticed a brand-new toothbrush had been placed on the counter. That, I had no problem making use of.

Feeling slightly more human, I ventured down to the first

floor and followed the sounds of voices into the kitchen to find a crowd.

Ian was leaning against the counter, a mug in his hands. Key was sitting at the table, laughing, while Alex and Shane stood around talking animatedly. Alex was, at least. Shane had crossed his arms and simply glared.

Key was the first one to notice me, her expression brightening. "You're awake!"

They all turned to look at me, amusement plain on their faces.

"Hey, boss," Alex greeted in a cheerful, loud, resonating voice that speared right through my abused head.

I pondered lifting a hand in greeting, but decided it was too much effort, so I simply shuffled the rest of the way to the table and sat heavily on the closest chair.

"Heard you had some fun last night," Alex continued, the cheerfulness dialed up to eleven.

Hazy memories of the night flashed through my mind. Karaoke. Drinks. Karaoke. Hutton?

Why had Hutton been there?

Ian planted a mug filled with coffee in front of me, and I didn't even care it was black and I'd rather have a soda. I wrapped my hands around it and awakened my magic. Just a tiny bit.

Clear mind, clear *head*.

Coffee might not be moon water, but a good witch had to make do with what was available.

My magic infused the drink as sluggishly as the rest of me. Not a lot, not enough to weaken me, but hopefully enough to help with the pounding headache.

It worked a little. A couple of sips, and I was feeling marginally better and like I could face the day. Or if not that, at least the next hour or so.

"Was Hutton at Rena's?" I asked.

They all looked at each other, then Alex and Shane burst out laughing. My attention snapped to Ian. He was clearly hiding a smile under the guise of sipping his coffee—the crinkling at the edge of his eyes betrayed him. Even Key had covered her mouth with a hand.

"What?" I demanded, then winced. My magic had helped clear my mind, not numb the pain.

Without a word, Ian opened a drawer, then handed me a couple of painkillers. I swallowed them eagerly.

"Everyone was there, boss," Alex said.

"Everyone?" I tried to remember. Dru and Key for sure, and that fleeting memory of Hutton. Wait, a couple of other faces were familiar. From the PBOA meetings? Bosko's daughter? The stables guy?

"Word got out," Shane said.

"Word of what?"

Alex brought out his phone and came around the table to show it to me. Strident singing filled the kitchen as he played a video. *My* strident singing.

I grabbed his phone and stared at the screen. There I was, on Rena's karaoke stage, belting out "All By Myself" like I'd just gotten dumped by the love of my life and this was now my personal hymn.

"Oh, Mother." I groaned, dropping the phone and burying my face in my arms. I barely remembered singing that song. That had been after my second—third?—drink.

Then the fact that the video was on Alex's phone finally registered.

I snapped straight, immediately regretting it. "Did *you* take that video?"

"Nah. Dru sent it."

"*Dru?*" I glanced around the kitchen. Shane was still grinning. Ian had his expression back under control, but his eyes gleamed with amusement.

When my gaze fell on Key, she hurried to assure me that "I deleted it immediately."

But something in the way she shifted told me she might not exactly be telling the truth.

"Who else did she send it to?" I lifted a hand. "No, don't tell me. *Everyone.*"

I was going to kill her.

"Not everyone," Key said.

"Yeah, it kind of went viral by itself," Alex agreed. "Not her fault."

That thing better not reach the Council. Or Sonia.

Who was I kidding? It was definitely reaching Sonia.

"I'm so done for."

Alex patted my shoulder. "Nah. You're good. Everyone had a good time."

I looked at Ian, searching for confirmation.

He shrugged. "There was a pleasant atmosphere."

"You were there too?"

The twitch of his lips was confirmation enough. Of course he had been there.

"Why didn't you stop me?"

"You seemed to be having a great time."

"Next time, stop me."

"You do this often? Go on drunken karaoke binges?" he asked, way too smoothly.

I dropped my forehead back on the table. "Nope."

"Aww, shucks," Alex said.

Ian sat kitty-corner to me and took another long drink of his coffee. "Celebrating something? Did you get good news?"

I gestured vaguely toward Alex's phone. My awful, woeful

singing still blasted out of the hellish thing. "Does that sound like good news?"

"Your affirmations didn't help, I take it?"

"They conducted a brave attack but couldn't take the hill," I agreed, returning to my own coffee.

"Why?" Alex asked. "What's wrong?"

"Everything."

Shane rolled his one good eye. "Dude, the trap failed and the spellbook suspect got away."

Alex's face lit up with understanding. "Oh, right."

I set down my coffee, and felt the now-familiar droop of my mouth take shape. "It's not just that."

"Can we help?" Shane asked.

"No. You've done enough."

He and Key exchanged a fast look that told me either she'd fill him in later or she was reminding him she'd already partially explained about my current woes.

I rubbed my eyes, suddenly tired, and not because of my headache or the small exertion of magic. "We have no leads on Mystery Man, no idea why he would think Grandma had a spellbook dealing with dark magic. What if he hires another thief?" What if the rumors about the spellbook spread? What if Grandma became known as a dark witch? What if someone came around asking for her supposed alchemy secrets and outed me as another supposed dark witch when I couldn't provide them?

My mood dipped with each word, each added thought, until I wanted to cry. Maybe that was what I needed—one good crying session to get it all out. Then my natural optimism would settle back in.

Fluffy came over and planted a paw on my leg, letting out a small whine. I reached down and sank my fingers into her soft coat, searching for that connection, that upbeat goodness…to no avail.

A nagging part of me told me that one crying session might not be enough. That this gray, gloomy weather was here to stay.

"I've been thinking about the Halloween cemetery tours," Ian said.

My head snapped up. The strays froze. My discordant singing cut abruptly, and you could've heard a pin drop in the silence that ensued.

"You have?" I ventured, a tiny spark of excitement building up in my chest.

He shrugged. "It might not be a bad idea, after all."

"Boss, are you sure?" Alex's amused expression was slowly transforming into that of a child discovering his parents were full of it and Santa was real after all.

Ian stood, his expression stern. "One night. Nobody comes anywhere near the house or the Cavalier graves." He narrowed his eyes. "And *you* organize everything. I want nothing to do with it. Understood?"

Alex whooped and did one of those manly high-fives-slash-shoulder-bumps with Shane. Key grinned widely, no doubt already planning how to redeem herself tour-wise. Fluffy barked happily, caught up in the sudden excitement. And me?

I looked at Ian with as much wonder as Alex had shown seconds ago.

"Really?" I asked, just to make sure.

Ian turned his back on us to wash his mug in the sink. "Yes."

Oh, my goodness. There was *so* much to be done! I opened my to-do list on my phone and began typing down items as they popped into my mind. Lights. Tour planning. Routes. Clear up the paths. Research headstone names. Check licenses were up to date. Sonia. Fog machine? Allot a day for cleaning afterward. Allot a week after to fly home.

That last item gave me pause. I had written it without conscious thought, but it felt good. It felt right.

When Halloween was over, I'd leave Dru in charge of the shop for a few days and fly home. Not the one I had shared with my parents, but the small town I had shared with Grandma.

I'd prove Grandma had nothing to do with dark magic one way or another.

Determination filled me in a way that made me want to pat myself in the back and say, *Welcome back, Hope.* Ah, how had I missed this me, even if she'd only been gone for a day.

Belatedly, I became aware of Shane and Alex bickering.

"You can't be Gareth," Shane was saying. "Your wolf is light brown."

"It'll look dark at night," Alex countered. "Besides, Gareth had two eyes."

"That you know of."

"Decide outside," Ian commanded.

Still immersed in their argument, Shane and Alex went out the back door. After giving us a shy smile, Key followed. I hoped she had the presence of mind to remind the two young men that they could take shifts playing the hound.

Once the back door had closed behind them, I stood and went to Ian. He eyed me warily, as if he wasn't sure what to expect. As if he wasn't sure his gamble had worked.

This man was going to crack my heart wide open one day, for all the good reasons.

I threw my arms around his waist and hugged him tightly, burying my head in his chest. "Thank you."

He stood still for a heartbeat, then pulled me closer and rested his cheek against my head. "You owe me one."

"*Another* one."

"You're keeping count. Good."

"Saves you the trouble to remind me later. Least I can do."

My fingers dug into the soft fabric of his sweater, and I was about to get on my tiptoes and see if I could start *repaying* some of the growing amount of debt I owed, if you catch my meaning, when my phone began ringing.

Ian's arms fell away, and I stepped back, pouting. I met his gaze as I brought out my phone and was suddenly breathless at the heat I found in his eyes. This debt repaying business would definitely continue shortly thereafter.

"Yes?" I said into my phone.

"I might have something of interest to you," said a robot-like voice. Not the same type as the call about the spellbook, but similar in style.

All thoughts of kisses fled my mind. "Who is this?"

At my side, Ian straightened, alert, catching on my sudden tension.

"I have the information about the spellbook, and I'm willing to bury it," the voice said. "For the correct price."

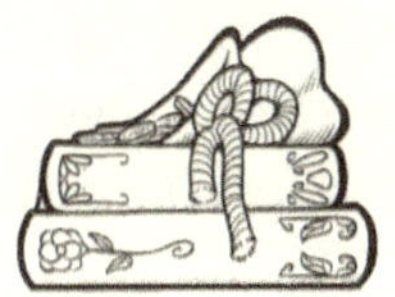

24

"What information?" I asked.

"You know what information," the electronically-altered voice said. Be ready to make a transfer to the account I'll be forwarding you. You have twelve hours to decide."

"And if I don't pay?"

"Then the information will go into the market."

Where anyone could buy it.

"How do I know you won't sell it even if I pay?"

"You have my word."

"I don't know who you are."

"I am Olmeda's broker."

"Did Johnathan Smithe give you this information?"

Silence met my question, and I checked the screen. The call had ended. As I stared at my phone, it vibrated with an incoming text. It listed an account and a money amount that made me inhale sharply. I'd never thought you could actually buy someone's reputation, but Grandma's apparently had a price tag on it.

"Who was that?" Ian asked.

"Olmeda's broker. Do you know who they are?"

Ian rubbed his chin. "I know there are a couple of them."

"What's a broker exactly?"

"What it sounds like. They broker deals between para-normals."

"Illegal?" Clearly, or they'd have given me a proper name. "Never mind. Do you know who they are?" I asked again.

"No."

"How's that possible? You knew Bagley was a dark witch. You must've done your research into the dark magical side of Olmeda."

"There's only so much people will tell a bounty hunter."

"And you didn't care as long as it didn't affect you," I finished for him, the reminder sour in my mouth. For all that Ian was willing to help me and be a good mentor to the strays, I had almost forgotten his see no evil, hear no evil stance where illegal paranormal matters were concerned. I had forgotten his unwillingness to meddle unless a bounty was involved.

Maybe because he had already meddled once with his ex-partner, and that one act of judgment and punishment had been more than enough to last a lifetime. The experience had likely taught him not to get involved in other people's business.

I couldn't fault him for that, but it didn't make it any easier to swallow. It didn't abate the frustration of knowing Ian could walk through life, happy to ignore the wrongs in the world.

"Are you sure you've never heard a hint of who it might be?" I asked.

"What did they want?"

"They said they have the information about Grandma's spellbook and I have twelve hours to pay up or they're selling it on the dark market." A sudden thought made me catch my breath. "Do you think it's not a broker but Mystery Man trying to get some money out of this, since they couldn't get the spell-book itself?"

Ian gave the idea some thought. "Doubt it. I think it's more likely the man sold the information to the broker to get some of the money they invested back and wash their hands of the whole affair."

"Money they invested?"

"Thieves for hire aren't cheap."

"And the potions they used were powerful," I murmured. Not cheap at all. I began pacing, trying to organize my thoughts. "So, Mystery Man, a.k.a. Johnathan Smithe"—because there was no doubt in my mind they were the same person—"learned about the spellbook bounty and your ex-partner's role in it. First, he tries to see if he can get his files from you, assuming if your ex-partner got this job he might've gotten similar lucrative magical item bounties."

"Yes."

"At the same time, he tries to buy the spellbook. When that fails, he tries to steal it. When that also fails, maybe he tries to come for the spellbook himself and the dogs stop him, so he goes for the files and fails too. That would explain why he left your house for so late, risking us returning from the PBOA meeting early. He's also smart enough to assume you'd track him down no matter what, now that he went and broke into your house, so he skips town before you can catch him."

"Can't always count on the bad guys to be idiots," Ian said, sounding like most of the criminals he'd apprehended during his bounty hunter career fell on that side of the equation.

"And now he's left all the information with this broker person, who knows they can get a pretty penny out of me. *How* does the broker know they can get me to pay for the spellbook?"

"You didn't sell it, meaning you want to keep it and the information inside all to yourself. Even if that wasn't the case, they lose nothing by trying you first."

It made sense. Which meant the broker didn't necessarily

know I'd do anything to keep Grandma's memory and legacy untainted, so they might have no direct connection to me I could pursue. How irritating.

I rounded on Ian. "I still can't believe you didn't bother to figure out who they are. Are you *sure* you don't know?" I studied him closely as I waited for his reply.

"There's usually more than one active at any time."

I poked his chest. "You didn't answer my question."

"I made some inquiries but..."

"But?"

"These kinds of things are normal in a city as big as Olmeda. Digging any deeper might've burned my contacts. There was no need to press before now."

"And will you press now?"

He gave me a considering look. A considering look! As if he was pondering if Grandma and I were worth him burning some bridges!

"Forget it." I spun on my heel and made for the back door. "I'll find them myself."

"Hope, wait."

I yanked the door open. "Nope."

"I'll ask around, but it's Sunday. I'm not sure what I can discover in half a day."

"Don't break your back on my account," I said in my haughtiest voice. "Oh, and maybe I don't want to do Halloween here anymore." I slammed the door behind me.

It was petty, but he and his callousness where the dark paranormal world was concerned deserved it.

———

My mood hadn't improved by the time I got to the shop and found it still closed because Dru had taken the day off. It was already midmorning on a lovely, chilly October day, which meant I was losing possible customers.

I showered and opened the shop as fast as possible, then retreated behind the counter to keep simmering in my outrage. Today, I was determined to ignore the fact that, again, I knew who Ian was and had accepted *all* of him when agreeing to date him. The nice gestures, and his natural propensity for keeping to the sidelines and doing nothing about anything, and argh!

"You seem stressed, dear," Bagley said from one of the T-shirts stacked on the shelf behind the counter.

I had gotten really good at pinpointing the origin of her voice, and I wasn't sure what that said about me or my current life.

"I'm not stressed."

"Perhaps make some of that chamomile with honey you like so much?" Her voice was kind and grandmotherly, her words the kind of thing *my* grandmother might've said.

It made me want to throw things.

At Ian's head.

"It's nothing." But I busied myself preparing some tea, anyway. The evil devil spawn was right—it would help me cool down.

My phone pinged with a message. It was from Keith, congratulating me on my karaoke performance. Wonderful. I sent it and him to the same mental space as the other five people who had already messaged me about the video.

"Anything I can help with?" the evil old hag asked.

"Can, yes. Will you? Hah!"

"My, my. We're in a temper."

The landline began ringing. I answered automatically.

"The Tea Cauldron." More like the frozen cauldron, from the way my voice came out.

It's not the customers' fault that life has thrown you a brick, then tied you to it and is currently trying to drown you, I reminded myself.

"I've been calling aaall morning," said a familiar, petulant voice. Holly, the love potion girl. If she demanded her money back, I was hanging up.

"I just opened," I gritted out. "What do you need?"

"Oh, nothing."

Rainbows, Hope. Think of rainbows. And Fluffy. Fluffy running across a rainbow. Happy, calming thoughts! "How can I help you, then?"

"The potion worked!" She was all excitement now. "She baked the cookies, and it worked."

"Wonderful," I said dryly.

"We're not paying you until we get married, though," Holly hurried to remind me.

"Excellent." And I meant it. One more satisfied customer. One less thing to worry about. "Remember. Don't tell anyone, or I'll cancel the magic."

A gasp came through the line. "You were serious about that?"

"Yes." I used my most severe tone. "So don't mess around, or you'll find out."

"I won't tell, I promise. Thank you!"

The chances of her not telling another of her friends were slim, but hopefully the threat would stick. It was all about balance—if personal life bad, then business life good.

I had looked up a lot of formulas when making my income spreadsheets.

"Another satisfied customer?" Bagley asked.

She still sounded chirpy, and I wondered what had put her in such a good mood. I eyed the shop, but nothing appeared out of sorts. No signs of a break in or dark magic spell. My wards were intact, although that didn't mean much. I sniffed the air. No strange smells.

"Perhaps a shower is in order if body odor is in question?" the witch suggested.

"I just showered." I took out my phone and browsed to my text conversation with Brimstone and Destruction.

Do you know Olmeda's broker? I wrote, then pressed send.

"A broker?" Bagley asked, all fake concern, reminding me she could see *everything*. "Why, you don't need those kinds of people, my dear. If you want, I can tell you how I ran my business without involving any other intermediaries. It's very easy, really, and saves a lot of money."

"As easy as murder and body dispatching."

"Very easy if you know what you're doing," she agreed with obvious approval.

My phone shook with the mage's answer.

Which one?

Great. Ian was right.

All of them.

Brimstone and Destruction took his sweet time answering. When he finally did, I was busy with two customers on the tables and Hannah had come to hang around at the counter, so I didn't have a chance to check until much later when I was alone in the shop again.

Never dealt with them, sorry. Nice video, BTW.

I ignored the last part and answered with: *Do you know who they might be? I need their services.*

Try this one. I hear he's the biggest.

He attached a link that took me to an anonymous page in the dark marketplace.

"Ah," Bagley said in a reminiscent tone. "I see Desmond still likes to dabble."

My head snapped up so fast it was a minor miracle it didn't

fly right off my neck. "Desmond?" As in Desmond Crane. My accountant?

"Oh, don't worry about it, dear. You forgot to clean the right corner of the window table."

I grabbed the cloth and went to wipe the table, more to give myself a way to hide my shock and maelstrom of thoughts than because I thought the surface was actually dirty.

Had Bagley just told me who one of the brokers was?

The thought left me thunderstruck.

Why?

Bagley never did something that didn't benefit her somehow. *Never.* I liked to believe the best in people, but I wasn't so naïve as to think Bagley would have a random change of heart about helping for the sake of it.

Or had she?

No. No way. She must want Crane to suffer in some way and was being sneaky about it by pretending to be accidentally helpful. Judging by Crane's reputation among the other shop owners, she might've given me freebie information simply to get back at him.

Very suspicious. I should definitely be wary and check this gift horse's mouth.

But I wasn't going to, because life was short and my savings account not big enough to pay for Grandma's spellbooks' information.

Abandoning all pretense, I threw the cloth on the counter and locked the front door.

"You're never going to grow your business if you keep closing in the middle of the day," Bagley said as I went into the back.

The moment I was past the bead curtain, I called Ian.

Just because we were mad at him, it didn't mean we couldn't gloat.

"I know who one of the brokers is," I said the moment he accepted the call.

"Oh?"

He sounded cautious, and not at all impressed. It only made me madder. The least he could do was sound amazed that I'd unearthed the information before he had.

"If you don't want to know, I'm hanging up." The discomforting thought that I was acting like a churlish ten-year-old crept into my head. I cleared my throat. "Forget that. I'll tell you if you help me put the fear of everything holy in him so he forks over Grandma's information and doesn't sell it to someone else."

"You want my help?" he asked, still cautious.

"Yup."

"But you're still mad at me."

"I can multitask."

"And you don't want me to take him to bounty hunter jail?"

I wondered if the fact that he was asking meant he was willing to take the broker to the bounty hunters, even though an edge in his voice told me he didn't think it was a good idea.

After all, a broker simply dealt between people. If he arrested Crane, the other brokers in the city would simply take up the slack. And if the bounty hunters took away the next one, another one would fill the spot. And in the meantime, sellers would move to the dark marketplace or who knew where.

"No," I said with conviction. "You don't need to."

"Are you sure?"

"Yes. It's better if we know who he is but let him go. We can keep an eye on him, and it might come in handy later."

"All right."

I dissected his tone, but didn't find a single hint of patronizing notes. Good.

No, bad. Very bad! This was why I couldn't stay mad at him. He was always so...*reasonable.* Even in his callousness, he was reasonable and matter-of-fact. He didn't discount my opinion by default, or think me stupid if I didn't agree with him. He accepted my ideas at face value.

If I'd told him to haul Crane's ass to bounty hunter jail, he'd have simply told me why it was a bad idea, and waited for me to agree or not. And if I hadn't agreed, he wouldn't have blown a gasket or turned his nose up at me. He'd have either done it or not. No drama, not thinking less of others. His actions, his decision.

Then I remembered how he had taken my decision away before. Like, say, taking Bagley out of the shop in fear she might influence me.

No, wait. Last time he'd asked.

So, he could be trained.

Well, this was most irritating and unfair.

"Name?" Ian asked, unaware of my desperate attempts at staying mad.

"Pick me up and we'll drive there. Your SUV is a lot scarier than Bee-Bee."

"I don't know about that," he said, as if the thought of me gallivanting around town on my second-hand Vespa terrorized him.

"You want to help or not?" I snapped. I would not stand for this disrespect of Bee-Bee.

"I'll be there in twenty."

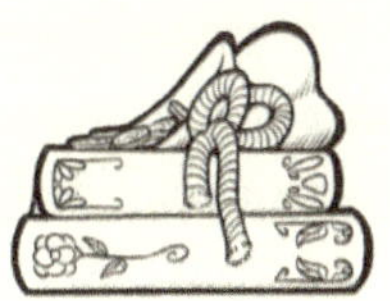

25

TRUE TO HIS WORD, Ian parked in front of the shop less than half an hour later. I was already waiting outside, sad that I had to close but reassuring myself this was more important—Grandma's reputation was at stake, after all, not to mention I'd like people to never attack me over a non-existent spellbook again—and jumped into his car almost before he'd completely stopped.

His fingers drummed on the steering wheel, but he didn't glance my way. Maybe he was scared of what he'd find.

"Where to?"

"Desmond Crane's house."

Ian arched his brows, and I basked in the surprise to be found on his face.

"How did you find out?" he asked.

This was where things might get tricky. If I admitted Bagley had told me, he'd be instantly suspicious and lecture me about accepting information from her. On the other hand, he deserved to know if he was going into the situation with me.

"Bagley let it slip."

His brows dipped into a frown. "That woman never does anything by accident."

"Maybe I'm finally winning her over to the good side?"

"Unlikely." He picked up his phone from the console and busied himself sweeping the screen. "What exactly did she say?"

"I asked, uh, one of my customers if he knew about an illegal magic broker." Ian knew I was supplying fake dark magic to a few people, but he didn't know exactly who yet, and I didn't want to reveal Brimstone and Destruction's identity, even if he might be going around burning up houses for profit. It might get me into trouble if Ian sniffed around, not to mention he was Key's uncle. "My customer gave me one dark marketplace link to try." I told him how Bagley had piped in with a comment about Crane while I was browsing the listing.

"It's likely she's lying and setting Crane up," Ian said.

"I know. But what if she's not? We need to check it out."

"Yes."

"I checked online, and he closes on Sundays, so he's probably home."

Ian found whatever he'd been searching for and inputted an address into the GPS.

"Is that Crane's house?" At Ian's nod, my attention switched to his phone. "Do you keep a database with the home addresses for every paranormal in town?"

"No."

Yep, he totally did. He might not be willing to dig deep into people's businesses, but he wasn't so far gone that he wouldn't keep track of their locations in case the need arose.

Without another word, he pulled into the lazy Sunday traffic and we crossed Old Olmeda toward an upscale neighborhood at the outer edge of the city proper. The houses here were smaller versions of the grand mansions found in the heart of

Old Olmeda, surrounded by actual lawns and containing cute, tiny garages. No parking in the elements in this neighborhood.

Ian parked by a corner lot, and I studied the white and red brick house with its gables and lovely windows. A skeleton waved from the edge of the roof and a few pink tombstones rose from the mowed grass. "Is this it?"

"No."

He was glancing toward another red brick house down the road.

"Ah," I said in understanding. "We're trying to be inconspicuous."

"We need a plan."

"Then we should've formed it on the drive over," I pointed out, clearly putting the blame on him.

He flashed me a smile. "Takes two to tango."

"I have a plan. You're the one who doesn't."

"Oh? Elaborate."

"We go in." I gestured vaguely toward the windshield. "And you do your scary bounty hunter glower thing while I tell him if he ever spreads rumors about Grandma's spellbook, you'll come back to haul him into Hutton's pit of bad guys. Maybe growl a little too," I added after a moment of consideration.

"Hutton's pit of bad guys?"

"You know. Where he buries all these people he keeps making disappear." Vicky, the twins, etc, etc.

"Crane might have something on Hutton," Ian said. "Better come up with something else."

"Because of Hutton's potion?"

"Yes."

Hutton's use of dark magic to gain and retain alpha powers was supposed to be a closely guarded secret, but in this day and age, anything could easily leak.

I sighed dramatically. "I guess we'll just have to remind him you own a cemetery and nobody's going to notice one more grave."

Ian started the car. "That's the spirit."

We parked in front of Crane's house and jumped out of the SUV. The lawn was manicured to perfect HOA standards with not a flower in sight. The house had no front porch, and a small awning covered the recessed front door.

I pressed on the doorbell, and a loud ringing echoed from within the house. After a minute, I pressed again.

I was about to suggest we check around the house and see if any windows were open when the door jerked open.

"What do you want?" Crane said. He was dressed in "weekend chic"—slacks and a polo shirt. Warm air wafted out into the chilly day.

"Hello, Mr. Crane," I said, stepping forward. "We're here to talk business."

Crane moved back out of habit, and I sneaked inside the foyer. It was all light hardwood floors and white paint on the walls, giving it an airy, summery atmosphere.

"If you want to talk business, make an appointment with April. Now, get out of here before I call the police."

I thumbed toward Ian, who, I was gratified to see, wore his scary scowl. "He's the police." Kind of.

Crane narrowed his eyes. "What is this about?"

"Your secret life as a paranormal broker."

A sudden gust of wind slammed into me, and I was thrown backward into Ian. We stumbled a few steps back, and then the front door flew toward my face.

I yelped as the door closed right in front of my nose. "Air mage."

"Yes."

Pushing up the sleeves of my jacket, I got ready for some

action. "You better get ready to shift. He might not go down easily."

"No," Ian said, and I wasn't sure if he meant the shifting part or if he was agreeing about the incoming fight.

It didn't matter. He had my back.

I pounded on the door with my fist. "Mr. Crane, open up! We're not going away."

"I'm grabbing my shotgun," he yelled from the other side.

With his air magic, he didn't even need to aim properly to hit us.

"Let's not be hasty. We just want to talk."

"Get lost!"

Asking wasn't going to get us anywhere, so it was time to change tactics.

"We know you're a broker," I said in a lower voice but still loud enough to carry through the door.

"I don't know what you're talking about."

His response was immediate and carried so much certainty I almost believed him. Almost.

"Come now, Mr. Crane, we both know it's true. I only want to come to a deal about one of your, uh, services."

"Miss Avery, consider our business agreement terminated. Find yourself another accountant."

"Okay, but I'm more interested in your other business. We mean you no harm. We just want to talk." And intimidate. And possibly blackmail.

That last part gave me an idea.

"Bagley left a note about you," I said.

Silence reigned. Ian abandoned my side and slipped around the corner of the house. I watched him go with mixed feelings. Why was he checking the rest of the house now?

"Ms. Bagley? The old owner of the witch shop?" Crane asked, catching my attention.

"You know perfectly well who I'm talking about."

"What about it?"

"You're in her...*dark* book."

"I don't know what that is."

The apparent confusion in his voice was making me second guess myself again. Had Bagley given me his name knowing full well he wasn't involved to get me into trouble?

Ian and I had agreed on the possibility, but Bagley wouldn't simply drop random people's names. She knew as well as I did that if the wrong person learned about the shop's dark magic side, the Council would sweep in and destroy the building, and then she'd really be screwed with no place to haunt, no chance to regain a body.

No, I was right to press Crane. He was involved in the dark side of Olmeda somehow.

"You know perfectly well what I'm talking about," I said. "I have the proof, and I will use the information unless you let us in for a talk."

Silence fell again, stretching. Had he gone for the shotgun?

I knocked on the door again. "Mr. Crane? Don't make me start counting down."

No response. I eyed the handle of the door, wondering if he was still using his air magic to keep the door closed and if I should use the hem of my jacket before touching it, so I didn't leave fingerprints. Before I could decide, a loud yelp and a series of muffled noises came from the back of the house.

Trotting, I made my way around the corner and to the back to find Crane stuck halfway across a window into the back deck with Ian blocking his way, arms crossed and his best blank, stony expression on his face.

"Ah," I said, approaching, "you *do* know about Bagley's dark book."

"I'm escaping you two lunatics! What are you doing?" he suddenly demanded, focusing on me.

I took a photo of the scene with my phone. "For the record."

He made a grab for my phone, which was ridiculous because I was nowhere near him, but then I remembered his air magic and I gripped the device firmly.

"Delete that right now!" he demanded.

"We can do this two ways, Mr. Crane—go back inside like civilized paranormals, or talk while you hang out of your window like a chicken trying to flee the coop."

His face reddened. With a last glare, he went back inside the house with considerable grace, considering he'd looked like stuck poultry.

Air magic could do wonders. It made me a little envious.

"Well?" he snapped. "Get in or get off my property."

I pointed at the back door. "What about..."

But Ian was already slipping through the window. Maybe the door was alarmed in more ways than one. I followed and slipped inside a sunny kitchen. There was even a small step resting right under the sill, which told me this was Crane's usual way of reaching his deck.

Bizarre.

Crane rounded on us, still flushed and emanating waves of anger.

"What do you want to know?"

"Did you call me earlier about selling the spellbook?"

His stance changed in the blink of an eye. The outraged, angry man disappeared, and a familiar cunning, sharp-gazed man with dollar signs in his eyes took his place.

Bingo.

"No," he said. "But I know who might have."

"You're lying. It was you."

He dragged a chair from the small kitchen table on the side and sat on it, crossing his arms and perfectly at ease with leaving us the higher ground. As a man on the shorter side, he must be used to being towered over and didn't let it affect his superior attitude.

"Let's talk business," he said.

"Let's talk making the information disappear," I countered.

"You know the price."

"I have another offer."

"I'm not a haggler." To underscore his point, he gave me a dismissive look-over, letting me know I wasn't worth his time.

I noticed he didn't do that to Ian, though.

"I don't haggle either," I said. "I will pay nothing, and you'll never try to sell the information to anyone, ever."

"That's not going to work for me."

"Then you shouldn't have chosen to blackmail someone with close contacts to the bounty hunters. Who gave you the information, anyway?"

Crane's gaze flicked to Ian. A fast, measuring glance that told me he was trying to determine how much he could push before Ian acted on my threat. "I don't reveal my sources."

"We know it was Johnathan Smithe." Crane didn't appear to recognize the name. Our mystery man had probably used another name, or, most likely, some random anonymous user name in the dark marketplace. I changed tactics. "How do you know the information about the spellbook is true?"

"I don't."

"You would've sold uncorroborated information?" What a silly question. Dark market brokers wouldn't exactly concern themselves with matters of ethics. "Of course you would. But wouldn't it destroy you reputation if you sold lies?"

"I'm not an auction house. I conduct deals between individuals. Up to the buyer to figure out if the goods are worth their investment or not."

I smiled. A sly curve of my lips that would've made Dru proud. "So you know how to contact the seller after the transaction is finished to give him his cut?"

Crane tilted his head and said nothing.

"Tell you what," I continued. "You tell us how to contact him, and we'll forget what you do for the dark marketplace in your spare time."

His attention didn't deviate from me. "My offer stands. Pay within the next..." He made a show of checking his expensive wristwatch. "Within the next six hours, or I offer the information to the rest of my clients."

Ian's alpha's presence overwhelmed the room, making my senses prickle with unease and my heartbeats pick up their pace. There was a hunter in this kitchen, and the need to scurry into one of the cabinets and hide was turning into an unscratchable itch.

A bead of sweat formed on Crane's temple and a muscle jumped in his jaw. Still, he didn't look at Ian or otherwise allow any fear or concern to show. The man had nerves of steel.

Time to press.

"Tell us how to contact him, or you're going to bounty hunter jail."

"We both know you're not going to do that," he gritted out.

To steal one of Ian's trademark expressions, "Oh?"

"If I go to jail, I'm taking you with me. You think I don't know about your dark magic ventures?"

The alpha vibes disappeared abruptly, and I snapped straight.

"Fine." I turned to Ian. "Your cemetery or Hutton's pit?"

"What?" Crane asked, sounding genuinely confused.

I gave him the same dismissive look-over he had gifted me earlier. "Wondering where to better dispose of your body."

His eyes widened. "You want to kill me?"

"You won't tell us how to contact your source, you won't bury the information, and you threatened to snitch on me to the bounty hunters. Easier to just dispose of your body."

His mouth tightened. "You won't do that."

A current of air fluttered my hair—a warning of what was to come if I insisted on threatening him with deadly harm. Ian tensed behind me, ready for action. Crane didn't move a muscle.

And suddenly, I knew why he was an accountant mob boss, a dark marketplace information broker, and why he was sitting in our presence. And it had nothing to do with attitude.

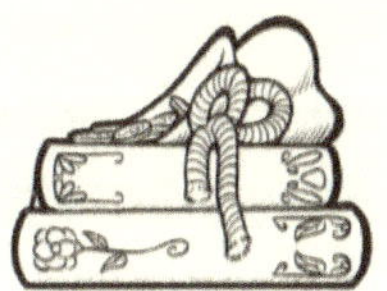

26

GRINNING, I crossed my arms. "You can't do a damn thing to stop us, can you? Your magic is all for show. You used most of it earlier to shove us out of the front door and when slipping back into the kitchen."

He glowered menacingly. "You don't know what you're talking about." The current of air intensified and my hair flew into my face.

"Stop that," I said, pushing back my hair. "It's annoying. We're not going anywhere."

The wind stopped abruptly.

"What do you *want*?" he demanded with a bit of a growl.

"I told you—how to contact the seller and for you to forget you ever had the information about the spellbook."

"I can't tell you how to contact the seller."

"I doubt that very much."

"I bought the information outright."

My eyebrows flew up. "You did?"

"The seller was in a hurry." Crane shrugged a shoulder. "It was an excellent deal."

Ian and I exchanged glances. As we had assumed, Johnathan

Smithe had wanted to recoup some of his investment before skipping town while leaving no way to trace him.

"What made you think I wouldn't figure out who you are?" I asked.

He bristled at that. "Did Bagley really leave a note about me?"

"Yes." Of sorts.

"That conniving old hag," he muttered. "I should've known."

"Seems fair to me that she knew your business if you knew hers." Running a fake dark magic business was proving to be quite a balancing act in secrecy. Couldn't blame the old woman for keeping blackmail material, just in case.

"Goddamn witch."

I pointed at him. "That better be about Bagley."

Crane said nothing.

Hmph. "Are you going to take our offer? You never reveal the information about the spellbook, and we forget you're a dark marketplace broker?"

"Why would I agree to that? The information wasn't free."

I waved toward the beautiful kitchen with its top-of-the-line appliances. "I think you can take the hit."

"I have a reputation to consider."

"Nobody needs to know beyond us."

"It's the principle of the thing!"

"What principle? You were trying to blackmail me."

At that, he shot out of the chair. "Listen here, missy. I didn't blackmail anyone. I offered you an early deal on the information."

He had me there. "In any case, I think it's still a good price to pay for remaining alive."

His eyes gained a sharp gleam I didn't trust. "The information is worth that much to you?"

"Remaining alive," I repeated, enunciating clearly. "Besides, the spellbook doesn't exist."

"So?"

"So if you try to sell the information to someone else and they learn of this, you'll be in trouble."

"The trouble goes to the seller, not the broker."

"Can't be good for your reputation if rumors start spreading that you're willfully selling fake information. I don't believe for a moment only the seller will get blamed. You will too. People will start to wonder about the quality of your sellers."

He made a face. "Very well. I will keep the information about your spellbook to myself."

"Great! Now, what about Bagley's accounts?"

His expression went blank. Too blank, too fast. "What about her accounts?"

"You were her accountant; you knew about her dark magic business. Where are her secret accounts?"

"I only deal with taxes."

And you don't pay taxes on ill-gotten earnings. Still, it made sense he'd know about them. He was probably as nosy as Bagley.

"Sure," I said dryly. "Where are her secret accounts? How can I access them?"

He must've read the resolution on my face, or maybe he was tired of us standing in his kitchen and wanted us out so he could get started on lunch, but he capitulated fast. "I found one, but it was empty."

"What do you mean?" My stomach growled, and a flush crept up my cheeks. "Empty? How's that possible?"

"How would I know?" he grumbled, looking as dissatisfied as my stomach. "Either Bagley moved the money somewhere else, or someone got to it before me. She must've shared them with someone else."

I shook my head. "Not Bagley." Although Vicky could've learned about it. The thought gave me pause. If that was true, then I might as well kiss that money goodbye.

"All I know is that when I got to it, it had already been emptied. Now, if we're done, get out." He pointed imperially toward the open window.

"One more thing," I said. "About my taxes..."

"Yes, I will do them," he snapped. "Out!"

"At a discount?"

"If you want a discount, find someone else." Glee filled his voice. "And good luck with that."

I chose not to argue and snuck out through the window. Ian followed, and the window slammed down as soon as his fingers cleared the sill.

"What an annoying man," I muttered as we walked back to his car.

Ian said nothing as we got inside, and we put on our seatbelts.

I waited for him to drive away, but he paused to make a call.

"Chris. That thing you were looking into for me? You can drop it. Yes. You still owe me one."

He hung up and dropped the phone in the cup holder, then started the SUV and pulled into the street.

"What was that about?" I asked, curious.

"A nearly wasted favor, thanks to Bagley."

Delight filled me, all reminders of being mad at him long gone. "You *did* ask your contacts for me."

He shrugged, focused on the driving. "Is the shop doing so badly that you need Bagley's money?" he asked, effectively destroying my burgeoning mood.

"I wanted to use it for the Corner Rose. Besides, people

keep paying somewhere I can't find. Fake dark magic potions still need supplies, and there's the magical expenditure, not to mention a mental health cost."

"Why don't you give them a new account to pay into?"

The question stunned me.

Why hadn't I simply opened a new account and given it to Brimstone and Destruction and Hutton?

I watched the houses go by.

"I guess... I guess it felt somehow wrong to take money for selling dark magic."

"But it's not real dark magic," Ian pointed out.

"But they think it is." I stared at my hands. "It's...tainted."

"You told me you wanted to convert Bagley's clients into good magic users." Ian's voice was gentle, coaxing.

"I do. But..." How to explain this strange feeling in my heart? That while they were paying into Bagley's accounts, I could remain separated from her sick business like some sort of substitute witch. I had stepped in out of necessity, but was not *part* of it.

"What would you do with the money you get for the fake dark magic potions?" he asked.

"Help Dru." An image of Fluffy and Rufus flashed through my mind. "Donate to animal shelters."

"You'd put it to good use." When I remained silent, he said, "You're a smart woman, Hope."

He didn't add anything else, and I wished he did because at that moment I wasn't feeling particularly smart.

"Thank you," I whispered after a few minutes of silence.

"For what?"

"Having my back." Always having my back, even when I was mad at him.

His right hand moved to touch my thigh for a moment.

"It's what I do."

Yes, but he only did it for a select few. Following a sudden instinct, and making use of a straight patch of road with no traffic, I carefully hugged his right arm and leaned my head against his shoulder for a few heartbeats, letting him know I appreciated him, and I'd be kissing him senseless if he weren't busy driving.

Unfortunately, knowing I could count on him didn't fix much.

We might've buried the bounty on Grandma's spellbook, but nothing felt resolved.

Mystery Man was still out there, suffering no repercussions. The chance that he might sell or act on the information down the road hovered like an anvil above my head, and I still had no idea why anyone could've thought Grandma had owned a spellbook about alchemy.

"Why wait twenty years to get the spellbook or try to get your ex-partner's files?" I asked in a murmur.

"I have a theory about that," Ian said.

I sat up, alert. "You do?"

"The file on your grandma. It doesn't have a receipt, meaning Duncan never got paid for the job."

A spark of hope lit within me. "Maybe he discovered she didn't have it because she was a good witch."

"He'd have still gotten paid for that." He sent me a fast glance, as if trying to gauge my mood. "My theory is that whoever hired him disappeared."

"No chance of payment, no point in continuing the job," I finished for him, disappointed. It fit, though. Hitmen were nothing if not realistic. No point in spending hours on the job out of the goodness of their nonexistent hearts. "So the client went broke and couldn't pay, and your ex-partner stopped working."

"Or the client died or went to jail."

A bit too fatalistic for my tastes, but sure. "And then what? The information lay around until someone else found it?"

"Exactly."

I gave that some consideration. "So the info about the spellbook and Grandma was in a box or a computer until an heir got their hands on it, or someone bought it at a sale, or something."

"Yes."

"And that person—Mystery Man—must've gained access to the original client's files and your ex-partner's updates and simply followed Grandma's line to me. Since I have the witch shop, it was easy to assume I'd also have any of her witchy materials. And since you happened to live in the same city, you might've had something on me as well."

"Yes."

"How awful. I wonder what other erroneous information the original client had."

"Are you still sure it was erroneous?"

"I am." My chest filled with pride and renewed determination. "Grandma would never own a dark magic spellbook. If it ever crossed her hands, she'd have destroyed it."

Unfortunately, there was no way to prove it.

———

The feeling of leaving a thousand threads unresolved persisted long after Ian dropped me at the Tea Cauldron and drove on to check on his strays and Key.

I opened the shop and prayed for some clients to keep my brain occupied, but when they came, the burst of activity only lasted for a few minutes. Once drinks were served, there was nothing for my brain to do but meander and dwell and do useless things like stare at imaginary ponds of melancholia and wonder how deep they went.

Not even the fact that the Tea Cauldron's social media had doubled in followers overnight helped improve my mood. I followed everyone back dutifully, but oh, what was the point? They'd soon lose interest when no more drunken videos followed.

The last customer of the latest wave left, and the shop stood empty. I slapped my cheeks lightly.

"You will never find a path forward if you stop searching for it. Open yourself to the possibilities."

"Indeed," Bagley agreed. "Open yourself up, child, and listen to what I have to teach you."

Good Mother Earth, the evil hag had the perfect timing. I'd be envious if I wasn't so irritated. "I will *never* listen to your teachings."

"Dark magic is not all I have to teach."

That gave me pause. "You'd teach me good magic?"

"Maybe. Depends on the incentive."

Of course it did.

Removing myself to the back, I texted Brimstone and Destruction with the account I'd opened to pay for the delivery location. It might not have been Bagley's intention, but the reminder of her existence had served as a wake-up call. An opening of a new path, if you will, in the form of a new payment account.

This was why affirmations worked.

Ian was right—I had been silly about the whole payment thing. There had been a mental barrier there I didn't even know existed until he'd pointed it out.

No more.

As I stared triumphantly at the ceiling, basking in my newfound freedom of mental blocks, my phone rang. Unknown number.

Given the last few days, I should've been wary of any

unidentified incoming calls, but I was riding high on my first step toward reclaiming my sunny days, so I gave it a chance.

"Hope Avery," I answered with a soul-deep brightness.

"Hello. This is Thomas Porter from Bluebeach's Council returning your call."

Grandma's Council. I gripped my phone tightly. "Yes, hi. What can you tell me?"

"You put in a request for Hazel Oakes' information. Is this correct?"

"Yes, that's correct."

The bell tinkled, and I peeked through the bead curtain. Hannah stood by the door, taking off her jacket and hanging it on the hanger. I caught her eye and pointed at the phone. She gestured for me to stay on my call and sat at the counter, happy to wait.

I have her a thumbs up and let the bead strings drop.

"I'm afraid there's been some mishandling of files," the man on the other side of the call was saying.

The words brought me up short. "Mishandling?"

"It appears that when we reorganized the archive some two decades ago, some of the files ended up filed under the wrong names. We only recently became aware of this mistake through our campaign to digitize our old records."

Suddenly, I found it hard to breathe. "What does that mean, exactly?"

"To be blunt, all of Hazel Oakes information registered with the Council—address, registered family members, and so on, was filed under another member's name."

"I... I see."

"Unfortunately," Thomas continued, "everything is rather muddled up, and while we know it happened, we haven't been able to figure out under which name your grandmother's files ended up. The project takes a lot of resources so it's been slow going. I hope you understand."

"Yes. Yes, I understand. And the mix up happened twenty years ago?" I asked to make sure.

"Twenty-four years ago, to be exact."

"That's... How unfortunate."

"Indeed. I have put a priority on finding your grandmother's information, but I wanted to notify you of the issue. It might take a while to get to it."

"It's no problem. I can wait."

I could wait for the rest of my life because it no longer mattered.

Ian's ex-partner, or whoever had hired him, must've accessed the Council archives, then taken the wrong address and information—Grandma's—and not the dark witch's. They must have assumed she was using a new identity and name—not uncommon in the paranormal world—and that's why the names didn't match. I didn't remember seeing any other names on Ian's ex-partner's files, but I'd have to double check.

Grandma hadn't been evil, and now I had the proof.

A colossal wave of relief swamped me, leaving me lightheaded.

Thank you, Mother.

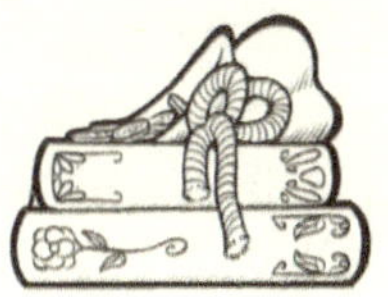

I ENDED the call with the Council witch and went inside the shop, my spirits as buoyant as if they'd been made of foam. But less environmentally damaging. Highly buoyant wood. Yes. That.

"What do you want today?" I asked Hannah, all smiles. "On the house!"

"You're in a good mood," she said with a laugh. "Got good news?"

"The absolute best."

Hannah stayed around for a round of tea and a muffin, and by the time she left, I had two couples occupying the tables.

I used a lull between orders to fire Ian a fast text.

Found proof Grandma was the wrong target. Will tell you later.

OK.

To anyone else, that might've seemed dry and unenthusiastic. But it being Ian, the fact that he had bothered to text back a word rather than a thumbs up emoji spoke plenty.

The door opened again, and Dru's ex-boyfriend walked in, today dressed in casual pants and a blazer, all bright dentistry.

"Good afternoon," he said, sitting at the counter.

My stomach growled at the reminder of the fact I'd missed lunch time. I grabbed a banana muffin from the display and took a good bite, not caring a bit about the crumbles raining down on my long-sleeved T-shirt.

"What can I make you? Coffee? Daily special?"

His smile didn't abate at my less-than-welcoming tone. Or the crumbles.

"A coffee, please. No milk. Sugar."

I filled a mug and set it on a coaster in front of him, along with a bottle of sweetener.

"Thank you." He prepared the drink and took a small sip. "Delicious."

"Only the best coffee at the Tea Cauldron." Arching a brow, I dared him to contradict me.

"Yes, I can see that," he murmured with some amusement, studying me.

One of the couples stood to pay for their drinks, and I hurried to wipe the muffin remains off my front. After they left, I returned to Preston.

"Why are you here?" I asked. "You know I'm friends with Dru. She deserves the Corner Rose, you do not. I'm not going to—"

The front door slammed open, sending the bell into a jarring series of stressed tinkles.

"You!" Dru stalked up to Preston. "What are you doing here?"

"Dru," I whispered. "Clients."

Dru gave the couple on the second table a glacial smile. "Sorry."

"Back," I snapped, pointing at the bead curtain.

Dru grabbed Preston's arm and dragged him off the stool and into the back.

"Family fight," I told the couple apologetically. Dru and Preston's heated voices rose in volume. I turned the voltage of my smile up to eleven. "You know how it is."

The couple exchanged glances. One muttered, "We better go." They rose in a hurry and made haste to pay.

I shoved the bead curtain aside. Dru and Preston were in each other's faces, their expressions twisted in anger, fingers poking each other's shoulders. Loud, distressed gurgling echoed through the pipes.

Oh, Mother, I hoped they wouldn't start making out in the hallway.

"Seriously?" I said, louder than their argument. "Don't do that in the shop."

Dru whirled toward me. "You can't trust anything this bastard says."

"Did you tell her *your* version of events?" Preston demanded.

"It's the only version!" she replied.

"You are messing with my job!"

Dru took a step back, crossing her arms and giving him a frosty stare. "No kidding. Like you messed with mine?"

"I didn't mess with that."

"You stole it from under me."

"They were never going to give it to you."

"Of course they were!"

I put two fingers in my mouth and let out a loud whistle. As I expected from my long experience in the coffee shop industry, they jumped and immediately spun toward me.

"What?" they asked in unison.

I made a T with my hands. "Time out." Addressing Preston, I asked, "Why did you come here?"

He straightened and tugged his shirt collar back into place.

With a last glare at Dru, he turned his charm back on before facing me.

"I came to let you know you can stop your campaign against me."

Dru gasped. Not a maidenly shocked gasp, but the kind of sharp inhale that preceded an all-out brawl.

Preston lifted a hand in a *wait* gesture.

As if that'd stop Dru.

"Someone else outbid us."

Dru's mouth clamped closed.

"Who?" I asked.

"An art gallery."

My eyebrows shot up. That came as a surprise. "Whose art gallery?"

"I don't know yet." His lips pursed. "But I'll find out."

A slow cackling filled the air. It came from Dru.

"An art store on steroids? Perfect." She laughed again, her eyes full of evil glee. "Now, get out."

Preston gave us another wide smile. "I'll be seeing you. We're still opening in Olmeda."

Dru scrunched her nose at his back as he went through the bead curtain and out of the shop.

Without paying for his coffee.

The nerve.

I studied Dru's somewhat gleeful expression. Like she had won, even though she had lost. "You're not upset the Corner Rose sold?"

She made a face. "As long as he didn't get it, I'm good."

"But you wan—" I shut my mouth abruptly. What good did it make to remind her of how much she'd wanted the Corner Rose?

"It sucks," she admitted with a grimace, "but there are other shops." Determination filled her voice. "I'll get another loca-tion, and I'll show them."

"Hell, yeah, you will!" And I'd be here to back her up the entire way. I offered her my hand, high up.

She rolled her eyes but high-fived me, anyway.

"Forget about the bastard. I got something for you." She pulled out a folded paper from her purse. "It's why I came."

"Really? I thought your bastard-detecting radar had gone off the moment he stepped into the shop." I *had* been wondering how she'd made it to the shop so fast. Demons had increased speed, but she wouldn't dare show off that much during daylight.

"A happy coincidence." She thrust the paper into my hands. "Take a look."

I unfolded the sheet and was met with a printout of some-one's driver's license.

Mystery Man's.

There he was, staring at the camera like he was facing jail-time, his full name and address clearly printed on the side.

"How...?"

Dru preened, then shrugged, as if it wasn't such a big deal. "I went back to the bed and breakfast."

"Dorsey's? Why?"

"I wanted to see if the bastard was staying there."

"He wasn't?"

Dru shook her head. "Nope. But that nasty old lady owner was totally the kind of person to nose through her guests' belongings."

A slow grin widened my mouth. "She took a photo of Smithe's driver's license."

"Yep. She said she copied it in case his payment bounced. Said he looked 'iffy' and 'up to no good.'"

And thus a man who had thought two steps ahead at every

turn and dodged us like the best of them had been taken down by a rude, old biddy.

A lesson to be remembered.

I threw my arms around Dru and hugged her tightly, barely restraining my urge to jump up and down at the same time. "This is amazing! Thank you so much."

She patted me awkwardly and pried my limbs off her person. "You can thank me by giving me a raise."

"Done." I'd eat instant noodles all year if that's what it took.

I refolded the sheet and put it in my back pocket, then touched her arm. "Are you sure you're okay?"

Her mouth pulled to one side. "No," she confessed. "It absolutely sucks. But I'll figure out something else."

"Yes," I assured her. "We will."

———

I left Dru in charge of the shop and met Ian at his place. The side door of the cemetery was unlocked, so I pushed Bee-Bee right in and parked her by the gate.

Ian was waiting by his front door. As I approached, shrill, sporadic whining noises and conversations drifted from the garage-turned-workshop, and I assumed the strays were busy preparing materials for the housing projects.

"Let's go inside," Ian said, stepping into the house.

I followed, returning Fluffy's enthusiastic greeting and Rufus's more sedate bump of my hip.

Ian closed the door and the outside noises lowered in intensity. Without saying anything, I walked up to him and wound my arms around his waist.

He lost no time in hugging me back.

"What's this for?"

"You're nice. It's warm. I missed you," I said into his chest, inhaling the scent of his soap, fabric softener, and a not unpleasant waft of manly sweat.

The rumble of his laughter reverberated against my cheek. "You just saw me earlier."

"Don't complain."

"Good point." With a last squeeze, he pulled away and searched my eyes. "What happened?"

I took out the folded sheet and handed it over, along with a face-splitting grin. "Dru got this from the old biddy."

Ian's brows shot up. "Bagley?"

"No, the other one. B&B lady."

He folded the paper and a faint smile curved his mouth. "I should've thought of it."

"It's good to be part of a team," I agreed. "Can you do anything about it?"

"Yes." He refolded the paper and put it into his back pocket.

"What?" I demanded when nothing else was forthcoming.

He smiled again, as if my curiosity amused him, which it probably did. He probably did it on purpose just to rile me up, the fiend.

"I will send the information to some contacts. They'll find him and make sure he has no other old bounties in his pocket." He studied me closely again. "But that's not all?"

"Nope." I preened like Dru had earlier. "I figured out why they thought Grandma had the spellbook." With a squeal, I threw myself into his arms again and gave him a sound peck in the lips. "She's not evil!"

"Of course she's not."

For someone who'd asked me more than once if she was, he sounded awfully sure of himself. It made me laugh. "They mixed up records at the local Council building twenty-four years ago. Her information ended up in another witch's file."

Ian's boyish grin was a thing of beauty and molten heat. "You're happy then?"

"Ecstatic!"

"Does that mean I don't have to open the cemetery for Halloween?"

"Nope. You're still on the hook."

"Aw, shucks."

I pulled back, studying his expression as my good mood cooled fast. "Unless you really don't want to do it? I know you only agreed to cheer me up. If you seriously don't want to do it, you don't have to."

The slight curve of his mouth remained, making this the longest I'd see him smile since I'd met him. "The kids are happy about it. Who knows? It might do everyone good. But..." The smile dropped in favor of a glare. "I'm *not* getting involved. Don't even think to ask."

"I wouldn't dream of."

I tugged his head down and gave him a proper kiss.

Then he gave me another proper kiss, so hot and deep it awoke my magic and sent it tingling through my veins along with slightly unnerving thoughts that felt like *keeper* and *forever*.

But they didn't scare me so much anymore. Not today, not now, not here, in his arms, with him murmuring endearments against my lips and the rest of the world lying very, very far away.

The week might've started on a sour path, but things were most definitely looking up. Grandma's reputation was safe, Mystery Man would get his reckoning, Dru's ex-boyfriend had been thwarted, and while we were still missing some things— Dru's actual dream and Bagley's money—who knew what we could achieve in the coming months?

For now, though, I'd use this opportunity to make my first Halloween in Olmeda one to be remembered.

And, oh, how it was. Completely spectacular, and for none of the reasons I expected, starting with the dead body in my shop.

Yes, that's right. A *new* dead body.

———

Thank you for reading! Don't miss Hope's spectacular Halloween adventures in Real Fake Hauntings.

For a full list, please visit:

www.isa-medina.com

Good Bad Magic

Good Bad Witch

Right Wrong Shifter

Fresh Old Bounties

Real Fake Hauntings

(ongoing)

Magical Artifacts Hunter

Stealing Fae Heirlooms

(Sequel to Magical Artifacts Institute)

Realms Unleashed: Red Angel

Mortal Secrets

Angelic Deals

Demonic Mayhem

Chaotic Souls

Magical Artifacts Institute:

Finding Fae Artifacts

Playing Fae Games

Breaking Fae Spells

Fixing Fae Problems

Extra Story:
Choosing Fae Gifts

———

Stand-alone Novelette:

Whispers of Ink

ABOUT THE AUTHOR

Isa Medina loves writing and reading Fantasy and Urban Fantasy books, playing MMORPGs, and scouring the Internet for pet pictures and beautiful art.

Her love for adventure Fantasy books was ingrained early in her childhood after getting her grubby little hands on the first Dragonlance trilogy, and it only grudgingly shared the spotlight when she discovered the wonderful worlds of Gothic novels and Romance in her early teens.

If it has Fae, ghosts, vampires, demons, mythical creatures, or magic in it, she's all in.

Find out more at www.isa-medina.com.